The Fight for Life series, book one

# COLLISION

## KATE STERRITT

Editing and cover design by Murphy Rae at Indie Solutions
www.murphyrae.net/
Formatting by Integrity Formatting

# DEDICATION

*To Adriana Leiker.*
*I forged on because of you.*

*Be yourself;*
*everyone else is already taken.*

~ Oscar Wilde

# CHAPTER 1

## Juliette

HIGH-OCTANE FUEL AND HOT rubber fumes lingered in the cold morning air as I waited for the moment. Idling in neutral, I blipped the accelerator hard to hear the engine's roar—music played by the god of petrol heads. My hands gripped the black leather steering wheel, not with fear but anticipation. Through the windscreen, the strip ahead beckoned with its smooth perfection, and the rush was so close I could taste it.

I glanced to my right and locked eyes with my rival, Scott Henderson. He shook his head, and despite the helmet covering his face, I could tell he was laughing by his full-body shake. I'd seen Scott before at the track and he was an awesome driver, but he was a peacock and a trophy hound. He'd lurked at the back of the line to pair off with me, no doubt assuming a mere female would present him with an easy victory. Peacocks are pretty, but show-offs didn't intimidate me. He drove a BMW M-Roadster, and its power-to-weight ratio should see him cross the line ahead of my Mini Cooper, even if it was the John Cooper Works model.

Returning my gaze to the tarmac ahead, I concentrated on the multi-coloured starting lights—the 'Christmas Tree.' On each side of the Tree are seven lights: two small amber lights at the top, followed in descending order by three larger LED lights, a green bulb, and finally a red bulb. We moved forward until the pre-stage light illuminated, indicating our front tyres had crossed the first marker. We were approximately seven inches from the starting line.

Edging forward, the stage bulb lit up, which meant we were positioned exactly on the starting line and were ready to launch. My whole body quivered with a surge of adrenaline as I focused solely on the lights on my side of the Tree. I revelled in the feeling of it pumping through my veins.

With my senses blissfully overloaded, the moment of truth had arrived, and a serene feeling that everything was exactly as it should be engulfed me. I depressed the clutch, engaged first gear and dialled up three and a half thousand revs.

The amber lights flashed simultaneously, followed four-tenths of a second later by the green light. My brain registered one thing.

GO!

I released the clutch and smoothly buried the accelerator into the firewall. The world became a fast-forward blur, and I momentarily sensed a cloud of tyre smoke on my right.

Seven thousand revs. Red line. Second gear. Slam!

Red line. Third gear. Slam!

Red line. Fourth gear. Maximum torque.

Approaching red line. Maximum speed.

Finish line. Maximum rush.

"Better luck next time, Scottie." I couldn't resist flicking my long blonde hair over my shoulder and grinning as his mates consoled him with pathetic theories of electronic malfunction and inferior grip on his side of the track.

"That was hilarious." My good friend, Jim, a gargantuan wall of a man was buckled over laughing. When he straightened up, he gave me an enthusiastic high five.

"You might as well have chopped his balls off, Jules," Jim's stepbrother, Shorty, added in his strangely high-pitched voice.

"Thanks, guys. The schmuck underestimated me and paid the price."

I enjoyed the win, but I lived for the magic moments—calculated risks where I could dance precariously on the subjective line between skill and recklessness. I was an adrenaline junkie and would take risks normal people actively sought to avoid. I revelled in the inevitability of my own demise. Some might call that selfish, cowardly and inconsiderate, but I could live with that. It was my secret, and it helped me accept the fact that almost every other part of my life was out of my control.

"Hey, Jules," Jim said when he'd recovered from another laughing fit. "Are you free this Friday night?"

"What have you got in mind?" I raised my eyebrows and cocked my head.

"Any interest in coming to fight night with Shorty and me?"

A while ago, they'd mentioned the illegal fight clubs they attended, and I'd been more than a little intrigued. I just didn't think they'd ever invite me, so I'd started dropping hints about my boxing classes. They were at least ten years my senior and treated me like their little sister.

I'd met Jim and Shorty at Winton Raceway when I first got my Mini and wanted to take her on a track. Jim had approached me and offered to give me some pointers. A few pointers had turned into many driving lessons, and when I'd offered to pay, they flat out refused. *"We just like seeing the look on their faces when you kick their arses,"* they'd said.

"Are you serious? Of course I'm interested."

"Thought you might be," Jim replied, chuckling again. "It's a pretty rough scene though, Jules."

"I can handle that," I said, gesturing around me. I was well-accustomed to male-dominated environments.

"Different league, Jules. We'll look out for you though."

"I can defend myself, too, you know."

They both nodded their heads and smiled. "We don't doubt it," Jim said. "I'll get you on the list, then."

# CHAPTER 2

## Juliette

WHEN I FINISHED HIGH SCHOOL seven years ago, I'd wanted to see the world. I'd never had a job as my spare time was spent in hell, otherwise known as deportment classes, modelling school and makeup lessons. I'd asked my parents to lend me the money for an airline ticket, and their reaction gave me my first real indication of how tightly I was bound to my life in Melbourne.

"You can't leave me after all I've done for you." My mother had sobbed. "Please don't leave me." She'd cried for a week and had to eventually be sedated when she threatened to kill herself.

"Please, Juliette," my father had begged. "Not yet. Get a degree first."

I was never going to be a hotshot lawyer like my father, but I'd agreed to put a tick in the degree box, somewhat placating him. When I graduated from uni four years later—my father had talked me into an Honours year—I should've packed my bags and gone travelling. I wasn't career driven, and my desire to break free and explore the world had only increased.

"Let's talk about it at your graduation dinner tonight," my father had said when I'd tentatively informed him of my travel plans. I should've known how that was going to go down.

"How could you be so selfish?" she'd wailed, her eyes wild, flashing with pain and betrayal. "You won't survive out in the world. You need me."

"Get some work experience under your belt first," my father had suggested. "I don't think cocktail parties and dress shopping can go on your resume."

Completely manipulated by them once again, I had put my travel plans on hold and got an administrative role at Donoghues, a small stockbroking firm yet to be swallowed up by the big banks. I'd also agreed to a first date with Richard Sacks, the man my mother had been trying to set me up with.

"Thirteen years of private school education," my father had joked when I told him about my new job. I knew he hadn't meant to hurt my feelings, but a lifetime of little jabs cut deep, even to the strongest of souls.

I'd known I couldn't win, but I'd keep trying because I wasn't a quitter, I loved them and they loved me.

Three years later and I'd found myself in a comfortable routine assisting the most successful broker in the firm, Heath Mathers, who needed extra support for his demanding client base, and I was still dating Richard—my mother's idea of Prince Charming and ideal son-in-law prospect. Perhaps I was a weak pushover, easily manipulated and lacking a backbone, but I had my reasons and in my mind, they were legitimate. I'd found a way to exist that was acceptable, and I wasn't interested in being judged for it.

"We have three new listings this week, Juliette," Heath announced, dumping the prospectuses on my desk as soon as I sat down. "I'll have the list of clients taking stock to you by this afternoon."

"Morning, Heath," I replied, smiling.

"It will be if Tom Higgins calls me back to confirm his allocation." He then retreated to his office. Heath was the only broker who had his own office. He brought in more revenue than any other and was treated accordingly. My desk was just outside his office. Sometimes I was envious of the other assistants who sat at the long desks on the trading floor amidst the buzz and activity, but usually I was happy with the privacy and solitude.

With cult classic Wall Street movies rushing through my mind, I'd been initially disappointed to find stockbroking was no longer like that. There was no trading floor, no one shouting numbers and scribbling on notepads. It was just line after line of desks, computer screens and predominantly men in suits, permanently attached to their phones.

Heath was tough, focused, and I had a great deal of respect for him. Despite having almost zero interest myself, he floored me with his vast knowledge of the stock market, and he also sounded like he genuinely gave a shit about his clients. He probably did to a certain extent, but his charm was also manipulation and sometimes it made my skin crawl.

Once my computer was powered up, I checked my emails. There were several reminders from my mother about her Fontaine charity soiree in the Yarra Valley on Saturday night. I knew Richard would be far more thrilled about it than I could ever be.

Lost in my pile of paperwork, the morning passed quickly, and I was startled by my gorgeous friend Sia standing at my desk. I enjoyed my job, but the greatest thing to come from it was my first real friend. I hadn't realised how lacking I was in the friend department until

Sia made it glaringly obvious.

"Ready to go?" she asked, looking over my shoulder into Heath's office.

I glanced at the time on my computer and was surprised it was lunchtime already.

"Sure. Give me a few minutes to finish this form. I'll meet you at the lifts if you like?"

"No, that's okay. I'll wait here." Her goofy smile made me laugh.

Sia worked for a couple of the junior brokers and sat at the other end of the office. We'd become friends at a work function soon after I joined the firm three years ago and had lunch together as often as we could.

Heath came out of his office just as I was grabbing my handbag. "Lunchtime already?" he asked, looking at his watch.

"I won't be out long," I replied as I reached for my handbag under my desk. "Sia and I are just going to grab some sushi downstairs."

"I like your tie," Sia said through her long eyelashes.

Confused, I glanced from Sia to Heath.

"Thank you." Heath looked a little flustered.

"Call me if you need me." I don't know why I bothered saying it. I knew he wouldn't hesitate to call me day or night if he needed something.

"Bye, Heath," Sia said, pushing her long, dark brown hair behind her ear.

Standing at the lifts, I couldn't contain the laughter.

"What?" she asked, her arms crossed over her chest.

"What was that back there? Were you flirting with Heath?"

"Maybe," she replied, trying not to smile. "Or maybe I was just being friendly."

"You're a very friendly flirt."

"Well, he's hot."

"You don't think he's a little old?"

"Age is completely irrelevant. You must be so loved up with Richard you don't notice the fine specimen right in front of you."

"That must be it." I hooked my arm through hers, and we made our way to our favourite lunch place.

When we were settled at a table with our sushi boxes, Sia dropped her bombshell on me. "I just booked my flight to London."

I'd stuffed a whole California roll in my mouth, and I nearly choked on it.

"What? When? Why?" I asked, devastated by the thought of her leaving.

"Don't get your knickers in a twist. It's just a long holiday. I'm going at the beginning of July—right in the middle of their summertime—for six weeks."

Relieved, I let out the breath I'd been holding. "Okay. Phew. You've talked about moving there before. What are you going to do on this long holiday?" I was confronted by how far my stomach had dropped at the thought of her leaving and by the shackles still around my neck.

"Wander from place to place, really. I don't want a set itinerary. Maybe I'll have a few sordid affairs with some ridiculously hot Italian men." She raised her eyebrows suggestively, and we both laughed. "If you weren't with Richard, I'd ask you to come with me." She put her chopsticks down and looked me in the eye. "You're so lucky to have him. I've never once heard you complain about him. He's hot and successful, and I bet he worships the ground you walk on. I want that, too, but I want to do some travelling and have some more life experiences before I find my Mr Right."

I didn't want Sia to know how wrong she was about

my relationship with Richard. I barely wanted to acknowledge it myself and managed to avoid thinking too much about it most of the time.

"Fair enough." I stared at my sushi and mentally chastised myself for the tears welling in my eyes.

"So, I think now is the perfect time to have a fling with your boss." She raised her eyebrows and tapped her pointer finger on the table.

I laughed, hoping she was joking.

"Seriously, Juliette." She leaned forward and whispered so our fellow diners at the next table couldn't hear. "I think he'd be a dark horse in the bedroom."

I pretended to gag, not wanting to think about my boss in that way. "I think he works twenty-four seven. He's a workaholic, Sia."

"Richard's a workaholic, too. I've only ever met him once briefly. He works almost every weekend, doesn't he?"

I nodded, trying not to smile. "Yes, he does." *Thank God.*

"There you go."

Our conversation drifted to safer places—clothes, movies, her sister's upcoming wedding and the cute guy who'd just started in the mailroom. I looked at my watch regretfully, knowing I still had a mountain of paperwork waiting for me.

"Come on. I have to get back to work."

We stood up and found a bin for our sushi boxes.

"I'll walk you back to your desk." She winked and elbowed me in the side.

Much to Sia's disappointment, Heath was on the phone when we got back, but she made several excuses to visit my desk throughout the afternoon, as always.

# CHAPTER 3

## Juliette

IT WAS THURSDAY EVENING, AND that meant it was time for my weekly boxing session with Zac.

During my first year at uni, I had been walking back to my car after an evening class when I was grabbed and pushed up against a brick wall. In my mind, I'd had the man writhing on the ground, clutching his crotch and contemplating his threatened chances of fatherhood. I'd wanted desperately to hear him cursing me with every profanity his tiny brain contained. I hadn't been as afraid as I probably should've been, despite my inability to defend myself. From somewhere deep inside my reptilian brain, my mind had conjured up the many different ways I could incapacitate and maim anyone who tried their luck with me.

In reality, a security guard had saved me, and my attacker was arrested. I'd gotten lucky. Last I heard, he was still serving jail time for multiple sex offences. I'd joined the gym the next day so if it ever happened again, I'd be better prepared. That was six years ago.

What had started out as learning self-defence had

quickly exploded into a full-on love affair with fighting. My mother and Richard would be completely horrified and humiliated, but what they didn't know wouldn't hurt them.

Zac stood over me as I did my stretches. "Hey, Jules. You alright?" he asked in his cute English accent. His background before becoming a boxer was a combination of European kickboxing and Asian Muay Thai. He was now a passionate trainer, and he wanted me to compete. From time to time, he'd teach me a little of the other styles—a blend of kicks, knees, punches, elbows and grappling were all incorporated to vary my training. He was an exceptional instructor because of his ability to help me understand the techniques rather than just go through the motions.

"I'm okay. Thanks, Zac." I jumped up and did a final stretch with my arms over my head. "I'm ready."

"Let's do this."

For the next hour, Zac pushed my body to the absolute limit, and then he pushed some more. By the end, I was dripping with sweat and high on endorphins. For the first half-hour, we worked on technique and endurance. The second half, we sparred. I'd never come close to beating Zac, but he was an ex-amateur boxing champion, so it wasn't likely that would ever happen. He could've gone pro, but he sustained a terrible head injury trying to spar with the much bigger heavyweights without a head guard at a training session. He would often tell me his arrogance nearly cost him his life. He was very fortunate, but doctors advised him any further heavy impacts could give him permanent brain damage.

"You're a star, Jules," Zac praised, looking down to me collapsed on the mat. "You'll get me next time."

It was the same thing he said at the end of every session, and it made me smile every time. He was a good guy. I'd introduced him to Sia's sister, Juniper, a year ago. They got engaged soon after and were getting married in June.

"Hey, Jules. I got a call from the promoter of a gym out in Lilydale last night."

I looked up at him and wiped my arm across my forehead. "Oh yeah? What did he have to say?"

"He's looking for female boxers for an amateur night he's got planned in a couple of months' time." A goofy grin spread across his face. "I might've mentioned you."

I bit my bottom lip, unsure what to think. I'd always said no when this had come up before, but Lilydale was well outside Melbourne, so I was unlikely to run into anyone I knew.

A shiver ran down my spine and excitement bloomed in my belly. "Okay. Sign me up."

"Really? That's awesome, Jules. You won't regret it. I promise."

❧

Despite insisting I was more than capable of getting home by myself and he should meet me there, Richard met me outside the gym every Thursday evening. He really was chivalrous, and I tried to appreciate that about him. He thought I did aerobics classes at the gym, so I wasn't going to point out what I actually did with Zac. He and my mother got along famously, and it would no doubt come up in conversation. 'Fighting is not an appropriate activity for a lady,' she would say with disdain. If they knew I was training for a boxing match, they'd have a conniption.

Halfway across the Yarra Footbridge, Richard stopped.

"Hey. Look at these, babe." He was pointing to a large quantity of padlocks clipped to the bridge railings.

"They're love locks," I informed him.

He lifted a couple of them and read out the names.

"I noticed them a few months ago and did some research." I remembered how romantic I'd thought it was, even if I couldn't personally relate to the concept of unbreakable love. "Apparently, it began in Rome around the turn of the century, inspired by characters in a cult Italian novel. I can't remember the name of it. Anyway, couples in love would inscribe their names on the padlock, clip it to the Ponte Milvio, then throw the keys in the Tiber."

"Well, it can't be good for the bridge. They'll rust and damage it," Richard said, dropping the padlocks and letting them swing. "I'm surprised the authorities don't remove them."

I knew that would be Richard's reaction, but it still made me feel desperately disappointed for reasons I tried to push away.

Peering over the railings, I watched the dark water flow freely beneath me. The pale silt swirled around, hypnotising me with its chaotic patterns. I closed my eyes and imagined myself leaping over the edge and plummeting into the water below. I was fully submerged, and instead of swimming back to the top, I would allow my body to sink slowly towards the muddy riverbed, my lungs screaming for the air they craved. The rush made me smile—a secret smile just for me.

"I'm starving," Richard mumbled. "Let's go."

"*I Want You,*" I declared suddenly.

"Really? Didn't we already do that this week?"

"No, I didn't mean that." I rolled my eyes. "I just remembered the name of the book that inspired the love locks in Rome. It's *I Want You* by the Italian author Federico Moccia."

"Oh. Right." He started walking away, leaving me

standing there.

When I caught up, Richard didn't reach for my hand. When my mother had been trying to set us up, he had been quite romantic, charming, handsome and persistent. According to her, he had all the right breeding and social etiquette, not to mention the fact that he kissed her butt at any available opportunity. I wanted to feel something more for him.

When I'd told my mother I would go on a date with him, she looked happier than she had in a really long time. I liked seeing her happy, and it didn't seem like a giant sacrifice to stay with him for her sake. I did my very best to be the perfect girlfriend, but my happy façade was cracking over time, and one of these days, I was sure they were going to notice.

"I'm really looking forward to your mum's cocktail party on Saturday night."

"I know you are." It was all I could muster.

# CHAPTER 4

## Juliette

"WAKE UP, DICK." I PULLED the covers back and gave him a not-so-gentle shove. "You have to go."

"Don't call me Dick." He sat up and rubbed his eyes, yawning. "You know I hate it when you call me that."

"Oh right, sorry." I'd stayed up too late reading a fascinating book about street fighting techniques and hadn't had any coffee yet. I *really* wasn't sorry.

Richard rolled his eyes, yawned again and then dragged himself off towards the en suite.

"No time for a shower." I threw his clothes at him. "Heath messaged me overnight and wants me in early to set up for a meeting."

"Are you serious, Juliette? This is crazy. It would be far more convenient if—"

"I'm deadly serious," I replied, cutting him off. "I'll see you tomorrow, okay? Can you pick me up on the way to Mum's thingy?"

"Not sure Isabel would appreciate you calling her event a *thingy,* but yes, I'll pick you up around four. It'll take over an hour to get there, and she wants us to arrive early to help welcome guests."

Even though he'd just woken up and was being booted out the door, it was obvious how excited he was about another Isabel Fontaine affair. I wasn't dreading it—my mother's charity work was admirable—but I didn't look forward to society engagements the way Richard and my mother did.

When I'd ushered Richard out the door and watched the lift doors close on him looking unimpressed and holding his shoes, I pulled my oversized t-shirt off and over my head and padded to the bathroom for a quick shower. As the hot water slowly woke me up, I mentally chastised myself for not telling Richard I was nowhere near ready to move into his townhouse a few streets away from my parents. Whilst he was dropping hints about co-habiting, I was busy formulating my next excuse to put it off. We hadn't had sex the night before. He was tired, and I was happy to read. I knew our relationship was lacking, but my mother was fragile, and it made her happy.

I wasn't a complete martyr. I had two guilty pleasures I managed to keep a secret from everyone I knew: fight training with Zac and car racing. Tonight, thanks to Jim and Shorty's invitation after the race last Sunday, I was hoping to add a third.

I rarely saw Richard on Friday nights as he socialised with his own colleagues and I was ashamed about how happy that made me. We only really saw each other on weekends when we were attending a social function together. Any shameful feelings, however, were going to be forgotten when I planned to leave my colleagues at the bar sometime before midnight under the guise of heading home.

Instead, I'd get in a cab with adrenaline surging and

go underground for what I hoped would be a blissful few hours. During those hours, I wasn't going to be twenty-five-year-old Juliette Salinger, daughter of social elite Isabel Fontaine and legal royalty John Salinger. I wasn't going to be anyone's puppet, hanging from strings I couldn't seem to untie. I was just going to be Jules, and I thirsted for the blood spilling in front of me. Not like a vampire or anything paranormal. I'd studied plenty of fights on TV, and I simply craved the energy I gleaned from watching the pummelling impacts, the uppercuts, the right hooks and the sublime confrontation of man against man. In my mind, I pre-empted every move the fighters made and cringed when they deviated. It would invariably end in them being knocked out, unconscious or comatose. Illegal fight nights were a whole new level, and I had a feeling I was going to be counting the hours, the minutes and the seconds between each one.

Work passed quickly. Most brokers and assistants left soon after market close on a Friday, so Heath and I were alone in a quiet office when I stood up from my desk and decided to do something I'd never done before.

"Heath."

He looked up and raised his eyebrows, giving me the signal it was okay to interrupt him. "Is it okay if I head out now?"

"Of course. Have a good weekend." He smiled and then went back to his work, looking back up a few moments later, obviously confused that I was still there.

"I was wondering if you have any interest in a drink with us after work," I asked hesitantly.

"Oh." He sat back in his large black leather chair and swivelled gently as if that would help him contemplate an answer.

"We meet each Friday night at the Z Bar. Sometimes we grab some dinner, too."

"Hardware Lane. I know it."

"No pressure. Just thought I'd ask." I paused before risking my next statement without eye contact. "I know Sia would love you to be there." Cringing, I looked up and saw a slight redness to his cheeks and the hint of a smile. "Well, that's where we'll be if you decide to join us." I turned and walked towards my desk.

"Thanks, Juliette."

I turned back and smiled.

"I'll try to make it."

The Z Bar was buzzing with the collective release of city workers letting off some steam at the end of the working week. It was the same each Friday. From five to around seven, it was civilised. Seven to nine would see the older and possibly wiser leave to go out for dinner or home to their families. From nine onwards, it started getting a bit loose. I often wondered how many one-night stands, couplings and potential marriages could be attributed to alcohol.

"He might not come, Sia." She had been glancing at the door since we arrived two hours ago. "He's got a lot on his plate at work with this new listing." I kicked myself for telling her I'd asked him to come.

"He's coming." Her confidence was admirable, and I couldn't help feeling excited for her. "He's all powerful and sexy at work, but underneath all that, I think he's just a bit shy and needed a push."

"Well, why didn't you say that months ago?"

"Months ago I wasn't planning on being out of the country for six weeks."

"You're a little crazy. You know that, right?"

"You say crazy. I say awesome."

I was still shaking my head when I felt a tap on my

shoulder.

"Can I get you ladies a drink?" Heath asked. He had removed his tie and jacket, and I was surprised at the transformation.

I was genuinely shocked to see him there and annoyed at myself for not asking him sooner.

"Corona with lime, thank you," Sia requested.

I glanced from her to Heath and back to Sia. They were mesmerised by each other, and I felt very much like the third wheel.

I interrupted their silent gazing. "I'll have the same."

Heath disappeared to the bar.

"Told you so," Sia said with a smug grin.

"You did. You're very smart."

We were both laughing when Heath returned with our drinks. I spent the next few hours being social. As the time ticked on, I checked my phone more regularly, waiting for the message that would apparently be sent from a different number and at a different time every month. It finally arrived at a quarter after ten, and I immediately commenced my exit strategy.

# CHAPTER 5

*Juliette*

"ARE YOU SURE THAT ADDRESS is correct, miss?"

The question was probably fair enough, but I wasn't paying him to question my destination. I was paying him to take me there.

"It's correct." I sat back and looked out the window of the cab as we moved away from the curb.

As we drove farther and farther from the city centre, I started to breathe. When we arrived at the parking lot of a closed shopping mall, I paid the driver and got out. It was dark and fairly cold, but I was soon warmed by the bodies of around five hundred other people who'd obviously received the rendezvous message. I retrieved the black loose-knit beanie from my bag and pulled it down over my head.

Within minutes, the organisers took our ticket money and then motioned to one of the buses waiting to take us to another secret location. There, I anticipated spending the next few hours being me, being happy and being free.

I took a quick look around the bus. It was mostly men with plenty of ink and piercings—pretty much my polar opposite in every way, barring their desire to be there. I wasn't an extrovert by nature, and to blend in as much as I could, I'd worn my fitted black suit with a black sleeveless silk shirt to work. I had changed from heels to flat shoes in the cab, removed my jewellery and switched my suit jacket for a hoodie. Men noticed me, and I wasn't arrogant enough to pretend otherwise. I certainly didn't want to dress in a way that would get me any extra attention.

Jim called out, gesturing to an empty seat across the aisle from him and Shorty. "Hey, Jules. Over here."

"Thanks," I replied, gratefully slipping into the seat near my racing buddies.

Despite being one of very few women, I felt no physical threat from the men.

The bus reached its destination in around fifteen minutes—a deserted warehouse in an industrial estate. I was completely disoriented. We all assembled in front of the buses, awaiting further instruction. I noticed far more women in the crowd than I'd been expecting. From what I could tell, most were wearing very skimpy outfits and were draping themselves all over the men.

Within five minutes, we were told by the organisers to enter the warehouse through the side door. The chivalrous 'ladies first' rule definitely didn't apply to this situation, and I took no prisoners getting in as quickly as possible. I wanted to be front and centre. The excitement was palpable as I left my usual persona behind and entered the outlandishly exciting world of illegal cage fighting.

I'd done some research during the week in anticipation. From what I understood from the few articles available on the net, the main reason for cage fighting to be illegal here was its perception as a blood sport. Despite the fact that the Professional Boxing and

Combat Sports Board is made up of ex-fighters and industry members, they are bound by the current legislation and how the media represents the sport. New South Wales recently took over from Victoria as having the strictest rules due to a recent death in the sport. Knee-jerk reactions were unsurprisingly common, so promoters had no alternative but to say 'up yours' to the government and go underground.

A functional moral compass knew the fighters' safety should be paramount, but I also knew it would drastically change the scene. Every fibre of my being rebelled against it. According to my search results, the fights were brutal and atavistic. The mere idea of it sent raw energy pulsing through me.

Jim and I took our places against the cage. I could barely stand still I was so excited.

"I'm gonna go say g'day to Bob," Shorty squeaked over his shoulder as he disappeared into the crowd.

"Right, Jules," Jim said. "This is a Cage Muay Thai Elimination series. It's one of the most brutal and exciting sports in the world."

"Okay. So, what should I expect?"

"There'll be eight fighters who will pair off in the first four fights, halving the number who continue. The next two fights will be the winners of the first four, giving us our final two. The ultimate winner has to win three fights. There's strategy and a lot of psychology involved. The fighters want to do enough to win, but not too much. If they get too many injuries, they might not be able to participate in the next round."

"Are there any rules for what they can and can't do to each other?"

"Cage Muay Thai has almost everything—the kicks, the punches, grappling. They can smash their opponents with their elbows, and even head butts are permitted.

The wrestling and Jujitsu elements you'll see in the more famous mixed martial arts comps have been removed."

"I can see why they'd do that. It must be harder to see what the fighters are doing when they're on the ground."

"That's it. Exactly. Cage Muay Thai is a much better spectator sport, in my opinion, but I'm sure wrestlers and Jujitsu enthusiasts would disagree."

"What about dirty tactics? We're at an illegal fight. Surely it's all pretty loose."

Jim laughed. "Bloody hell, Jules. Are you for real?"

"What?" I gave him my most innocent puppy-dog eyes.

He shook his head. "Yes, we're at illegal fights, but there are still rules. Cage Muay Thai doesn't have many, and of course they might not always be strictly followed, but you don't hit the groin, you don't punch in the back of the head, no contact after the bell or when a man's down. Usual stuff—and oh, kidney shots are out." Jim winced as if he were in pain. "Bloody hell. You can be pissing blood for a week after one of them."

"Have you seen much of this kind of thing?"

"Let's just say the last fighter seen punching his opponent in the back of the head after the bell has disappeared off the scene. The repercussions here can be far greater than getting disqualified."

I clenched my teeth. "Got it. Don't mess with the bad guys."

"Pretty much."

"Thanks for getting me on the list, Jim. I'm totally pumped for this."

"Feel bad I didn't ask you sooner. I wasn't really sure if it would be of any interest until you mentioned your own training."

"I'm just full of surprises." We were both laughing

when I felt the energy in the room change.

I scanned the warehouse for the first round of fighters. In the far left corner, I could see two groups of people in huddles. Bingo. The MC's voice filtered through the sound system, momentarily quieting the dance music to introduce the prize fighting meat for round one. My excitement hit fever pitch. Feeling the heat from so many bodies still jostling for the pole positions, I pulled the beanie off my head, allowing my hair to spill free.

The crowd erupted with a chaotic mixture of encouragement and abuse as the first pair of fighters made their way to their cage. The men who entered the cage were of similar build and height. One had a shaved head. The other had a mop of ginger hair tied back in a ponytail. They both looked like they were on prison release from maximum security. I barely registered their introductions because to me, they were faceless bodies. Their names were of zero consequence.

When the fight began, I studied their defensive stances, first engagements, their footwork and their use of dirty tactics in a bid to decide how best to overcome them. It had been one thing watching professional fights on the TV, but this was a different experience entirely. This was dirty, rough and primal. I was in heaven.

It didn't take a great deal of my headspace to envisage my comparatively tiny body defeating either of these two thugs, and in my mind, I had them flat on their backs with their eyes rolling in their heads within a few minutes. If you put me up against Zac in the cage, I would defeat him, too. My wonderful trainer would never fight dirty, but the same couldn't be said for me. I would do what was necessary to fuel my adrenaline addiction. A snap kick to the family jewels was the quickest way to end a fight, but I would always keep my eyes on theirs and be prepared to change tactic if necessary.

Romper Stomper and Ginger were evenly matched, so the crowd was getting a good show. I'd seen several opportunities for both of them to end it, but they'd overlooked them all and I was getting frustrated.

I yelled out to Ginger, "Spit in his eyes." For some reason, I'd decided he was marginally more skilled.

"Love your enthusiasm, Jules, but how's he gonna do that with a mouthguard in?" Jim asked, clearly trying not to laugh.

Slightly embarrassed, I grimaced. "Oh yeah. Got a bit carried away."

In a back alley brawl, throwing dirt in your attacker's eyes drastically increases your chances of walking away and them rueing the day they chose you as their victim. We weren't in a back alley though; we were at a paid fight.

Something else I'd learnt from my research was to go after their fingers and do some damage. Hands are an important part of a fighter's arsenal, so making it so he can't grab you or close his fist is an excellent strategy. My first-hand experience of these tactics was non-existent, so my brain was going into overdrive absorbing it in real life.

Ginger was eventually victorious on points, but it was a close match. Both men looked like they could benefit from a trip to the hospital, and I wondered if Ginger would be okay for his next fight later. Two new fighters, David and Peter, entered the cage, and I watched more of the same. David was declared the winner, again on points. I wanted to see a knockout. My thirst for blood was being quenched, but my hunger for new skills rumbled on unsatisfied.

When the MC announced a short break, Jim offered

to introduce me to one of the women he knew would be there.

We approached a group of three women I hadn't seen outside. It was actually a bit of a relief to have some female company. Unlike the women I'd seen outside in next to nothing, these ladies were dressed more like me and looked completely at ease in this environment.

"Michelle," Jim interrupted their conversation. A very attractive woman, I guessed to be in her early forties, turned and smiled. "This is Jules, the girl I was telling you about who kicks all the guys' butts at the track."

Michelle threw her arms around me, laughing. "Jules. I've heard so much about you." Leaving her arm around my shoulder, she introduced me to her friends, Barb and Lynn.

"You okay here, Jules?" Jim asked.

"Absolutely," I replied. "Thank you."

Jim sauntered off, probably to find Shorty and his other mates. I knew he felt protective over me, so I was glad to give him a break.

"So, Jules," Barb started. "How are you enjoying it so far? Bit much?"

"Oh my God, no. I love it. I was actually hoping to see some hard-core decimation if I'm honest. You know?" I punched my right fist into my left palm. "Someone really taking control and smashing someone." My enthusiastic reply elicited more laughing from the group.

"You'll fit right in here, love," Lynn said, raising her eyebrows and glancing over towards the cage. "I think you'll really enjoy the next fight. I believe Leo is up next."

The three women noticeably swooned at the mention of Leo's name.

"Who's Leo?" I asked, naturally intrigued.

Barb smirked. "Other than being smoking hot, his name definitely suits him," she said seductively. "He's untouchable and undefeated—always takes the lion's share of prize money. I wouldn't mind if he wanted to take me, too, if you know what I mean." She winked, and they all laughed and nodded their heads in agreement.

"Not everyone enjoys his style though," Michelle said. "And obviously most men don't have the same appreciation for his appearance."

"Why wouldn't anyone appreciate his style?" I asked.

"It's over too quickly. No one stands a chance against him," she explained.

"Well, I can't wait. Sounds like he has awesome skill."

"Unlimited will always overcomes skill," Michelle stated in a sing-song deep voice. "That's what my husband says, anyway."

"Who's your husband?" I asked, smiling.

"The ginger ninja from the first fight." She flicked her hand up towards the cage.

"Oh, okay." I nodded my head, recalling his victory over Romper Stomper. "He deserved the win, I thought."

"Thanks." She smiled warmly. "Speaking of which, I really should go check on him, make sure he's okay. He took a few nasty blows."

"Do you ever get used to watching your husband up there?" I asked, wondering how I would feel if someone I loved were in the cage. The fact that I had no one to compare that to spoke volumes about my feelings for Richard.

"Yes and no." She cocked her head from side to side and contemplated her answer for a few seconds. "Adam needs this. He didn't have a great childhood, and he has a criminal record from some of the trouble he got into when he left school. He has the skills to go pro, but this is where he wants to be. This is where he feels at home."

"Has he ever gotten seriously injured?"

"He has." Her eyes cast downward, obviously struck with painful memories. "Fortunately there are several doctors who are keen supporters of the sport and are willing to be on standby. Without insurance, it's high-risk for them, so we're lucky to have their support. It helps knowing they're here."

"It was really nice to meet you, Michelle." We embraced, and then she pushed her way through the crowd and disappeared.

"Where's the bathroom?" I asked, turning back to Barb and Lynn.

"I'll come with you," Barb said. "I need to go, too."

After saying goodbye to Lynn, I followed Barb towards the other side of the warehouse, through a heavy white door and into a hallway where we found the facilities. After I relieved my suffering bladder, I glanced in the mirror as I washed my hands. Even I could acknowledge the fire burning in my eyes. I felt more energised than ever before and knew this night was going to be life-changing. It already had been.

When we returned to the warehouse, we quickly realised the next fight was about to begin, and the massive crowd was going to make it hard to resume my original cage-side position.

"I can't believe I nearly missed the start."

"Go get a closer look, Jules," Barb encouraged. "Push your way through to the front. Watch out for Leo's groupies though." She clenched her teeth. "Those women are fierce."

"Are you going to come with me?"

"The blonde guy up there in the cage with Leo is my husband," she replied, shrugging. "It'll be over soon, and I'll have to see if he needs me to take him to the hospital."

"Oh." I suddenly felt awkward being so excited to see

the man who she fully expected to crush her husband. "Sorry."

"Don't be," she said, shrugging her shoulders. "He knows the score. He'll be fine. Will you be okay?"

"I can see Jim up at the front. I'll elbow my way through to him."

We embraced quickly and both said, "See you next time."

Before I made it to Jim, the fighters entered the cage. The blonde I knew to be Barb's husband, so Leo had to be the one with his back to me—a back that made my whole body hum with electric desire. He had two tattoos that I could see. At the nape of his neck was a geometric design with nine spires shooting out from oval shapes. Below that, were two powerful and intimidating tigers. I'd never thought too much about tattoos, but at that moment, I was thinking of little else.

By the time I made it to Jim cage-side, they had tapped fists and were starting their dance around the cage.

"Oh hey, Jules." Jim ushered me in beside him, and I reefed my eyes away from Leo against their will. "You nearly missed Leo's fight. Just wait. This guy's a fucking lunatic."

"So I've heard." I hoped the heat I felt burning my cheeks wasn't too obvious. I hadn't yet gotten a proper look at him, but his presence was overwhelming. Even my inexperienced eyes could tell his opponent stood no chance whatsoever. Fear was clearly evident in his eyes and body language.

Leo moved like a predator around the cage, circling his terrified prey. Barb's husband, a relatively small guy, was already in defensive mode and was probably just hoping it would be over soon. To his credit, he attacked first in a scrappy blur of punches and kicks, expending a huge amount of adrenaline-fuelled energy on his fruitless endeavour. Leo blocked every single one effortlessly before going in with a series of killer blows that were both unexpected and clearly strategic. I was awestruck, rendered mute by the incredible display of brute strength that seemed to come from somewhere deep within. He was a man possessed by something dark and primal, and for reasons I couldn't explain even to myself, I felt a magnetic pull towards him.

The crowd cheered and shouted in appreciation or frustration. It was impossible to tell the difference. I looked at Jim, dumbstruck.

"I told you." He shook his head and chuckled to himself. "Fucking lunatic."

The next fight was evenly matched, and a tall Asian guy with metal teeth named Jeff won on points. When another break was called, I refused to budge from my spot. There was no way I was going to risk missing a second for the rest of the night.

"So the next two fights will determine who's in the final."

"My money's on Cheryl's husband and Leo."

"Leo's a sure bet, and I think you're probably right about Cheryl's old man. You've got a good eye, Jules."

Sure enough, the next two fights we watched saw the ginger ninja and Leo claim a spot in the final. I was worried for Cheryl but thrilled for Leo. He had held little back in his two fights, but I had a feeling he would unleash the beast for the ultimate win.

When the time finally came, the fight that unfolded was like nothing I could've conjured up in my very vivid imagination. Leo, in Jim's words, was a fucking lunatic, and I was a puddle of desire, anguish and unfulfilled need. Ginger gave it his all, and Leo certainly didn't get the easy win he had in his two previous fights. There was, however, one clear dominating force, and Leo was declared the ultimate winner.

He showed little emotion while the referee raised his hand, and within moments, he exited the cage, barely acknowledging the referee, officials or the chanting crowds.

"Hey, Leo!" a voice from the crowd shouted.

My eyes were fixated on the retreating figure, and I was surprised to see that he stopped but didn't immediately turn around.

"Ya fight like ya mummy!"

The crowd had gone silent, which was odd given I'd have thought those types of goads were not unusual. When he did turn around, I immediately felt intimidated and small, overcome by the power of his icy stare. Shirtless, his tanned torso, just like his beautiful back, was a powerful mass of sculpted muscles, slick with sweat. His dark hair was short but still had a sexy, tousled look. He strode back across the cage until he was only a few feet from me. Striking blue eyes scanned the audience a few times before coming to rest on mine.

I felt shockwaves pulsing through my body and rocking my core. It was unlike anything I'd experienced, and it was a life-altering rush. His cold expression remained unchanged, and he said nothing. After what felt like minutes, but was more likely a few seconds, he turned and disappeared.

The noise level in the warehouse stayed low for a few minutes. Hushed whispers soon became excited cheers before the crowd started to dissipate. I just stood there motionless and unsure of what had just happened. Had he actually seen me? It felt like he was looking straight at me, but perhaps that's how everyone in the room felt with his overwhelming presence. Monthly fight nights had become my third guilty pleasure, and the thoughts running through my head felt like the ultimate sin.

I got back to my apartment around four in the morning, buzzing with excitement. Sleep came quickly. Images of a six-foot-something, muscular Adonis conquering his unworthy opponents flooded my brain, making my body relax with a smile.

# CHAPTER 6

## Juliette

I WOKE UP STILL SMILING. My grin was bigger than usual as I stretched my arms above my head and allowed myself to relive the night before in exquisite detail. My smile faded when I glanced at the clock. It was almost lunchtime, and Richard would be picking me up in about four hours. Poor, oblivious Richard. The contrast to Leo, who was still at the forefront of my mind, was too extreme to deal with, especially without coffee.

"Morning, George," I said cheerily. My coffee machine had a name. It seemed right to refer to him as George—a good, strong name befitting the greatness he offered. I was physically dependent on him and he never let me down.

I flicked the power button and he sang a little tune of beeps in reply. As he warmed up, I set about making myself a sandwich. Similar to a fight, it was all about the combinations. Sometimes you had to take a risk to achieve greatness. Sia understood my sandwich prowess and benefitted regularly from it, but Richard mocked my enthusiasm. He encouraged me to sample his gluten-free alternatives, and if he didn't serve a purpose, it would be an irreconcilable difference.

The character I'd been playing every day for as long as I could remember was well-suited to him. Sometimes I wished I weren't such a good actress. Unfortunately, that would mean he might notice the disingenuous smiles, gritted teeth, self-protective body language and shortness of breath as I struggled to breathe under the lies. Suffocation was a miserable way to die.

The aroma of hot water flowing through freshly ground beans and into my favourite coffee mug reminded me why I'd never give up this actual drug addiction. Richard's daily lecture on the detrimental effects of caffeine on the body elicited a tight smile and the occasional nod. He no doubt misinterpreted my smile as appreciation.

As if he knew I was having impure thoughts about him, my phone rang and his name flashed up. I squeezed my eyes shut tight as I answered with as cheery a greeting as I could muster.

"Morning, babe. How was your night?" His cheery tone matched mine exactly.

"Oh, you know. Same as usual," I lied. "How was yours?"

"Fantastic."

"Really? Why?"

"Your mother called."

How that could possibly be fantastic was well beyond my imagination.

"And what did Isabel have to say?"

"She wants me to give a speech at the event tonight on the investment opportunity of philanthropic funds. She asked me to come early to rehearse, so I drove up this morning."

Of course he'd left me behind to go running to my mother's lair. I was completely thrilled by the change of plan.

"Oh, right. So…" I took a sip of my coffee and inhaled the delicious fumes, hoping he couldn't hear the smile in my voice.

"I'm sorry, Juliette. Are you okay to drive yourself? If not, I'll drive back now and get you."

"Oh, no," I said, possibly a little too enthusiastically. "I'll drive up later. No problem."

"Drive carefully in that ridiculous little car of yours. It's more powerful than you might think. And make sure you're here no later than four so I can run through my speech with you."

I shook my head and rolled my eyes. I knew exactly how powerful my car was.

"Bye, Richard."

I'd read about a coffee house in a small town not far from where the event was being held. It wouldn't be too much of a detour—best coffee in the Yarra Valley, apparently. How could I resist verifying that claim?

With my sandwich and coffee, I sat out on my small balcony overlooking the river and the city skyscrapers. I had just enough room for a table with two chairs squeezed amongst the mini jungle of greenery I tended daily—a small oasis where I could let my mind float away. Within seconds, I was mentally recounting a documentary I'd watched fifteen times about dangerous jobs. My favourite were the avalanche ski patrollers who headed out in the first light of dawn each morning to assess the mountains for danger. They carried dynamite in their backpacks, and they knew every time they did their job, their life was on the line. From my cushy apartment, which Dad had bought me as a graduation gift, and job, where the most exciting thing to happen would be a stock suspended for unknown reasons, the sadness descended.

Knowing I couldn't procrastinate any longer, I headed back inside to get ready. One of the emails from my mother had informed me that the theme was 'Black and White.' My mother was famous for elaborate and over-the-top extravaganzas, so this theme showed great restraint. She'd already asked me to wear a conservative white dress to give Richard some visual hints. We'd been dating for three years, and my mother was determined to have me married off as soon as possible. The thought made me nauseous, but I would wear the damn white dress she bought me because that's what I always did. When I slipped the white lace over the fitted underlay, I felt like the fraud I was. I was already a prisoner in my own life, but marriage would be a life sentence.

Navigating my way out of the city in my red rocket was easy. I loved the Yarra Valley wine region and wondered if I'd be happier living out of the city, surrounded by animals and wide open spaces. My parents were xenophobic city dwellers. Whenever I'd tried to bring up my mother's childhood on the Mornington Peninsula, I was shut down with a ferocity I couldn't understand.

# CHAPTER 7

## LEO

THE FIGHTS WERE BARBARIC—MEN beating each other half to death—and the guilt should've weighed heavily on my soul. But it was a consensual arrangement. I needed an outlet, and fight night was it. The prize money wasn't great, but money wasn't my sole motivator. The sense of relief I felt from pummelling men into the ground was disturbing. My rage just poured out of my fists, and for a few hours, I didn't feel like a ticking time bomb with a fast-burning fuse. There was something addictive about putting myself in the firing line, to feel the pain and to see exactly what I could endure.

The stunning young blonde staring at me through the cage had snapped me out of doing something really stupid. She looked like a displaced angel caught in Hell. I couldn't take my damned eyes off her and was momentarily mesmerised. She held my stare with a steely resolve. I was intrigued and more than a little turned on. She was completely out of place, but there was a strength emanating from her that told me she could handle herself.

My phone's ringtone interrupted my thoughts.

"Leo. Hey. It's James."

"Hey, mate. What's up?"

"I'm working a function tonight, and the bartender has pulled out last minute. I told the boss lady I might know someone who could step in."

I paused. My body was screaming at me from the fights, but I could always do with the extra money.

"Where and what time?"

When he gave me the details, I didn't respond immediately.

"She pays almost double the normal rate," he continued.

Fuck it. I could handle it. Fight night had been good for me. "Okay. I'll be there. Thanks for the job, mate."

Dressed in black suit trousers and a white button-down shirt, I jumped in my old Jeep and headed out of the city. I wanted to make a detour to see one of my best friends, Beatrix, who also happened to make a mean cup of coffee.

Bea's Beans had recently been profiled in an online travel magazine as having the best coffee in the wine region, which I thought was a massive understatement. It was easily the best coffee I'd had anywhere. Tourists were making a point to stop in to sample her special blend, and her little business was booming.

"Leo!" Bea screeched from behind the coffee machine.

I pushed my Ray Bans on top of my head and smiled. "Hiya, Bea. How are you?"

"Better for seeing you. What brings you out this way?"

"I hear your coffee isn't too bad." I winked.

"Can you have it here or do you need it to go?"

"I've got a bit of time." I pointed to the blackboard menu above her head. "Better get me one of those toasted sandwiches, too."

"Coming right up, handsome."

I took a seat by the window, grateful the lunch rush was over. I had half an hour for some caffeine and carb loading. The Saturday paper was open on the table, and I flicked casually through the pages. A small article on Melbourne's illegal fight club scene caught my attention. I knew the scene might change sooner or later, but I wasn't looking for accolades or recognition. I was looking to expel the anger no amount of therapy would quash.

Bea came out from behind the counter with my coffee and sandwich. "What happened to you?" she asked, leaning in to inspect the few plaster strips I'd placed over cuts on my face and hands.

"Oh, that's nothing. I was out last night and got caught up in a fight. You should see the other guy." I laughed, hoping she'd drop the subject.

"Can you sit down for a bit?" I took my seat and gestured towards the empty place opposite me.

"Have you hired someone to help you out yet?"

"Angus has been hassling me to let Kayla take over a few shifts, but I don't want to give up my full control. I feel like it's a big part of who I am." She raised her eyebrows and cocked her head to the side, indicating the framed pictures on the wall. "You'd understand that."

I knew exactly what she was getting at.

"It's different, Bea."

"I know. I just wish…" She shook her head, knowing this was a pointless conversation we'd had too many times.

"Hey, is it okay if I crash at yours tonight?" I asked. "I was out late last night and don't really want to drive back to the city after work tonight."

"Of course. The side door to the spare room will be open. Let yourself in."

"Thanks, Bea."

A noisy family came bustling through the door, interrupting her train of thought. She leant down and kissed my cheek. "I'll see you in the morning," she said then went back behind the counter.

I had to get going anyway, so I took the last swig of coffee and gathered up my phone and keys.

"Bye, darlin,'" I called out as I walked towards the door. "Thanks again."

# CHAPTER 8

*Juliette*

ON MY WAY TO THE coffee house I'd seen online, I'd taken a wrong turn and had become mesmerised by the Gruyere countryside, beautiful old houses and lavender fields. One particular home stood out. I pulled over on the side of the road and stood on the grassy verge to get a closer look. It was so quiet and peaceful. An occasional bird cry was the only noise to break the silence. I took a deep breath, and my lungs thanked me for the cool, fresh air despite the scent of lavender that, unlike most, I found offensive.

The house was a heartbreakingly beautiful double-storey stone farmhouse that appeared abandoned. Ivy grew with reckless abandon over large sections of it, and some of the stonework was crumbling. It didn't look like the gardens had been tended in a really long time. Despite the state, I admired the drystone wall lining the property's front boundary, adding to my budding love affair with this house. With no signs of life, I pushed the iron gate open and shuddered at the screeching sound it made. Glancing around quickly to make sure no one was there, I walked through. I knew it was trespassing, but it really didn't look like anyone lived there, and the idea of getting caught gave me a small rush.

I stepped gingerly from stone to stone in my peep-toe heels my mother had bought me. She insisted I dress "appropriately" for her functions and didn't trust me to accomplish that goal myself. At twenty-five years old, my mother still treated me like an irresponsible child.

A brass plate was fixed to the wall next to the front door: "Gwendolyn." I walked around the side of the house and stepped carefully through the overgrown garden beds to one of the large sash windows towards the back. Clearing a patch on the dirty glass with my hand, I peered in. The smudged pane made for poor visibility, but I could see sheets over the furniture. The whole place just felt sad and lonely.

Sitting back in my car, I glanced over to the house one more time, curious as to why I felt so incredibly drawn to it.

~~~~~

Bea's Beans had an unassuming shopfront and was located only a few minutes' drive from the beautiful farmhouse on the edge of a small township.

"Long black, please," I ordered from the girl behind the counter.

"Take a seat. I'll bring it over to you."

"Sorry. I should've asked for it to go. I'm in a bit of a hurry. I got a bit sidetracked on my way to find you. You see, I read about this coffee online somewhere and had to check it out. Might have been a travel magazine. I'm not sure. Anyway, it's just so beautiful around here, and you also have the best coffee in the state, so you could say I'm in heaven." I had no idea why I was rambling.

"Hey. Slow down, darl. I'm not sure you actually need

caffeine." She laughed in a friendly tone that wasn't mockery.

I took a deep breath and thanked her.

"I'm Beatrix, coffee connoisseur," she said. "This is my place."

"Oh. Hi. I'm Jules." I rarely introduced myself as Jules. Always Juliette or Juliette Salinger. I just felt instantly comfortable with this girl. "I like to think I'm a coffee connoisseur, too."

"Well, Jules, if that's the case, you can call me Bea." Her smile was warm and genuine. "I sell my special blend beans if you wanted to take some home." She pointed to a table on the wall to the left of the counter. "I can grind them for you if you like."

"Thank you."

I walked over to the table to check out the various beans and coffee machine accessories she was selling. Above the antique wooden table was a corkboard jam-packed with hundreds of flyers advertising local events and services. There was an ad for the amateur fight night I would be competing in at Lilydale, which was close by. I still couldn't believe I was actually going to do it.

My eye was drawn to a collection of framed photos next to the corkboard. One of them I could have sworn was Gwendolyn—the stone farmhouse—in immaculate condition.

"Here's your coffee," Bea said from behind me.

Startled, I turned and took the coffee from her hands. She looked to be about my age and was ridiculously pretty with short blonde hair, green eyes and a heart-shaped face.

I smiled. "Thank you."

"So you're not from around here, then?" she asked.

"Oh, no. I live in the city."

Bea perched herself on a stool. "I couldn't live anywhere but here. I've been here all my life." Her face was pure contentment. "So what brings you out this way, then?"

"Your coffee, for one thing." I didn't want to talk about my mother's charity or the fact I was running late for Richard's speech rehearsal. I took a sip of my coffee and let out an involuntary moan of pleasure. "This may be the best coffee I've ever had. Puts George to shame, and that's saying something."

"George is your city barista?" she asked, smiling broadly.

"Nope, and don't laugh. He's my coffee machine. I call him George."

Bea threw her head back and laughed. When she stopped, she pointed to her coffee machine, grinning. "Meet Charlie."

I liked this girl, and I didn't have many friends I could be myself around. It was hard being friends with those who knew me only as the society princess.

"So why do you have a picture of that house in here?" My curiosity needed a little fuel.

"One of my best friends grew up there." She rubbed her forehead lightly as she spoke, and a flash of sadness washed across her face. "It's still his family home, but no one lives there anymore."

I had so many more questions, but before I could ask anything else, the door opened. A tour bus had stopped out front, and a line of customers filed in. I glanced at my watch and nearly dropped my coffee. I was late and would incur my mother's wrath. Richard would be annoyed with me, too, for upsetting her and not listening to his speech.

"Sorry, Jules," she said, stepping down from her stool. "I'd better get back to it. It was lovely to meet you."

"You too." I held up my empty coffee cup. "Best coffee ever."

"Thanks. Coming from someone who names their coffee machine, that means a lot."

I put my cup back on the counter, waved to her and headed for the exit.

I held the door open for a few stragglers from the bus. "Bye, Bea." I waved again when the exit was free.

I had to drive back past the stone farmhouse and couldn't resist pulling over again, even though I was now horribly late. This time, I was looking at it in a different light. I started envisaging it as a family home full of laughter and noise. I imagined the lawns mown and the flower beds flourishing with colour. I wondered what state the inside was in, and I wondered why no one lived there anymore.

I wanted to lose myself in that house in the countryside, miles from my life in the city. If my mother could read my thoughts at any given moment, she'd have a heart attack. She felt it was a matter of time before Richard and I got married and moved in together. It would kill her if I disrupted her fragile world in any way. My fierce determination to help maintain her illusion was taking its toll, but the alternative was unthinkable.

My phone's ringtone broke the silence. I knew who it would be before I looked at the screen.

"Hello, Mother." I closed my eyes and rested my chin on my chest with my shoulders slumped forward.

"Where on earth are you, Juliette? You should be here already. You're being very disrespectful. I'm disappointed in you."

I wondered if it had occurred to her to be worried about me. I could've been in an accident and lying injured in a hospital, or worse. Instead, her concern was keeping up appearances.

"I'm sorry. I got lost, but I'm on my way."

"I was relying on you, and you've let me down." She sniffed.

She was crying. Of course she was.

I sighed. "It's okay, Mum. Tonight is going to be a huge success. I'll be there really soon."

"Well, hurry up," she said, still sniffing. "Are you wearing the dress I bought you? I brought an option for you just in case." She went silent for a moment before she screamed, "Not over there!"

"What?" I asked, confused.

"The help can't follow my simple instructions either."

"Right. Well, I'll see you soon."

She hung up without saying goodbye, and I just stared at my phone as it disconnected.

I was exhausted. I didn't want to turn the car back on. I wanted to stay right there in the middle of nowhere, where I felt completely at home. The object of my fascination shimmered in the late afternoon sun, highlighting the yellows and browns of the crumbling sediment.

I had a feeling deep in my gut that I was meant to find that house, and that it somehow held the key to my freedom. I had no idea how long I sat there, but when my thoughts came back to the present, I was aware of the darkening skies. I turned the key and floored it.

# CHAPTER 9

## LEO

"SURE THING, MA'AM," I REPLIED through gritted teeth and a fake smile. Mrs Fontaine, the woman running the charity event, was a ball-breaker.

She had changed her mind about the exact placing of every table no less than five times. I had to keep reminding myself this woman paid her event staff almost twice the going rate. I was just grateful I didn't have to associate with the type of people who attended her functions in my everyday life.

"That'll do," she said finally.

The event was being held on the lawn behind the homestead of the most luxurious estate in the Yarra Valley. It was a cocktail party, and everything was black or white. *How original,* I'd thought. The setting, however, was unique. Situated at the top of the hill, the guests would be overlooking the rows of vines and the mountains beyond. It was wine country at its best.

The homestead was impressive—an old white weatherboard with plantation shutters and a full wrap-around veranda.

"Is there anything else you need?" I asked politely.

She gestured towards the veranda. "I'd like a wet bar set up over there. Make sure my guests' glasses are never empty. I'll leave it up to you to—"

A man appeared out of nowhere and interrupted, "Where the hell is Juliette?"

Instead of being irritated by his rudeness, Mrs Fontaine tried to appease him. "I'm so sorry, Richard darling. I'll give that inconsiderate daughter of mine another call. Come with me. We'll find somewhere private to run through your speech."

The rude son of a bitch had stood directly in front of me as if I didn't exist. I supposed in his world, I didn't.

"I'm sure I can find a way to help you relax," she continued.

His back was to me, but I could see her hand grip his arm and then rub it up and down. *Well, that seemed inappropriate,* I thought to myself. Shrugging, because I genuinely didn't give a shit, I walked away to get on with my job. I couldn't help feeling sorry for the girl they were discussing. She was about to incur her mother's wrath, and whoever this guy was to her, he was a complete wanker.

The string quartet began playing as the guests started arriving, and I walked around with a tray of filled champagne glasses. There were four staff members including James and me. We were there to serve the fifteen couples who'd no doubt paid a pretty penny to attend this exclusive shindig. They would all be staying in the luxury accommodation, so the champagne was flowing.

An attractive woman, probably in her forties, approached, eyeing me up and down like I was her next meal.

"What can I get for you, ma'am?"

"What are you offering?"

I replied in a serious tone, "French champagne, wine, spirits, mineral water. What are you drinking?"

She leant over the bar, invading my personal space. "I was hoping you were on the menu."

Was she serious? Surely her husband was witness to this awkward situation.

I laughed, trying to pretend I thought she was joking.

"Celia," Mrs Fontaine huffed, saving me. "Leave my staff alone, for goodness' sake."

"Just having a little bit of fun, Isabel." She looked me up and down again and ran her tongue over her top lip. "This one is scrumptious."

"Remind me of your name," Mrs Fontaine said, appearing stressed.

"It's Leo, ma'am."

"Okay. Leo. Can you please take the empty bottles to the recycling bins? I don't like seeing them in view of the guests. You'll find them around the side of the main house next to the parking area."

"Of course, Mrs Fontaine."

"Also, can you keep an eye out for my daughter while you're out there? She should have arrived by now in a red Mini."

I filled up a milk crate with empty bottles and made my way around the veranda through an open courtyard area. A large wooden gate led out to the parking area, filled with an array of luxury cars. The bins were in a fenced-off enclosure just to my right, so I set about emptying the crate.

As I dropped the last bottle into the bin, I heard a screeching of tyres on the crushed granite driveway. The car I'd been sent to look out for came careening down the drive and expertly swung into the only available spot between two Porsche Cayennes.

I could see her silhouette from where I stood. She switched the engine off but turned the internal light on and flipped the mirror down. She was obviously fixing her makeup before she entered the lion's den, or maybe the lioness' in this case. I hadn't heard any reference to a Mr Fontaine. I was just about to step forward and offer her an escort—it had become suddenly very dark in the last hour—when Richard the toolbox stormed over to her car and pulled the door open.

"What time do you call this, Juliette?" he asked, tapping his watch.

The light in the car went out, and a figure dressed in white was pulled from the car, a little too roughly for my liking. My instinct had me stepping out into view, ready to intervene.

"You were meant to be here two hours ago to listen to my speech," he continued as she locked the car.

She said nothing. Her shoulders were slumped forward, clearly resigned to this type of treatment. If they looked my way, they would see me, but he was oblivious and she was staring at the ground.

I took another step forward, and my shoe crunched on the gravel. They both snapped their heads up.

"What are you doing snooping around back here?" Richard asked, clearly unnerved. "Just can't get good help these days," he muttered when I failed to acknowledge him.

I ignored the fact that this guy was a fucking cliché with his head up his arse. I ignored the fact that in different circumstances, I would rearrange his smug face and I'd enjoy it. I ignored everything because I was locked in a shocked stare. *Juliette*—I allowed her name to float through my mind. It was her. She was even more painfully beautiful than I'd been able to appreciate the night before across the cage.

My mind reeled, trying to process her transformation from dark angel to fancy rich girl and passive doormat to this schmuck. White lace hugged her perfect body, and her long blonde hair hung in gentle waves over her left shoulder. Her wide eyes and the fact she was yet to release her breath let me know she recognised me, too. Fear passed across her features, and I felt compelled to help her.

"Sorry to startle you, miss. Your mother asked me to see if you'd arrived and needed an escort."

Her shoulders relaxed slightly, and she let out a small breath.

"Well, as you can see, my girlfriend doesn't need an escort from you," Richard stated. "You have guests to serve. Now run—"

"Richard!" Juliette cut him off but then gently placed her hand on his arm.

My body flinched seeing her touch him. I didn't know her, yet I felt a primal connection to this girl. There was something very wrong with this picture. I just didn't know what it was beyond the fact that Dick was punching well above his weight range.

"I know you're annoyed with me for being late," she continued. "And you're nervous about your speech, but there's no need to be so rude to this man." Her dark navy-blue eyes caught mine again.

"Don't patronise me, Juliette. Now, let's go. This isn't like you at all." He pointed in the direction of where the party was being held. "The guests are already here."

Without waiting for her, he strode off. She stared at his back but made no move to follow him.

"Sorry about that," Juliette whispered, staring at her

feet.

I felt irritated and, if I was honest, disappointed that she would apologise on his behalf, but then again, he was her boyfriend. What did that say about her? "It's none of my business, but please don't apologise for him."

She gently kicked the gravel with her shoes and shrugged her shoulders before she looked at me again. Her eyes were suddenly void of emotion, vacant and dull as if she'd pulled a mask down over her face.

"I'll walk you in," I suggested, breaking the silence.

"No need. I can take care of myself." Without looking at me again, she walked away, leaving me standing there dumbfounded. Dressed in white, she looked more like an angel, but my intuition told me she didn't belong here either. She was just caught in a different kind of hell.

Snapping out of it, I walked quickly to catch up but didn't speak when I fell in next to her. Before we rounded the back corner of the veranda, I glanced to my right. She didn't look at me. I could tell she was bracing herself.

"Good luck," I said. I wanted to say so much more but couldn't. I wanted to ask her what she'd been doing at fight night but couldn't. I wanted to ask her why she was with such a douche. But most of all, I wanted to protect her from whatever she was about to face. She was a breathtakingly beautiful walking contradiction, and I was wildly attracted to her.

She looked at me as if for the first time. It was disconcerting.

"Okay then." I raised my eyebrows and cocked my head, waiting for some sort of reaction. When none came, I walked away shaking my head. I had to get back to work anyway.

# CHAPTER 10

## Juliette

"YOU CAN DO THIS," I chanted to myself, blocking out the fact that my ultimate fighting fantasy, Leo, was walking away after looking at me like a crazy person. I'd felt his eyes burning into the side of my face, but when I glanced at him, a sudden rush of anger overwhelmed me. What the hell was he doing working for my mother? What kind of horrible twist of fate was that? I wanted him gone. I didn't want him to exist in this world.

Despite the party being outside, I felt walls closing in around me as I stepped onto the lawn. Richard was at my side immediately with a fake smile plastered across his face.

"Sorry again for being late," I offered. "I know how much all this means to you." My hand did a general sweep of the party, and my sarcastic tone would've been hard to miss for anyone other than Richard.

"It should mean a lot to you, too, Juliette. These are very important people in our lives, and we have to behave properly. Turning up late with dirt on your dress is not behaving properly."

I looked down at my dress and saw there were, in fact, a few specks of brown across my chest. It must have been from when I was looking in the windows at the farmhouse. I couldn't help but smile.

"Why is that funny? We have standards to uphold."

"You know I don't enjoy these stuck-up affairs, but I'm here for my mother, Richard." He turned into someone I didn't even like at these functions, and he was being worse than usual. He was really pissing me off.

My mother appeared next to Richard, glaring at my chest. "For goodness' sake. Are you a child? How on earth did you manage to sully your dress already?"

"It's barely noticeable, Mother. I'm sure no one else will notice. And if they do, they shouldn't be looking at my breasts." I laughed, but it quickly turned awkward. They both looked dumbfounded. I glanced over and caught Leo's eye. His smile took my breath away.

Richard followed my gaze. "I don't want to see you talking to the bartender. We don't fraternise with the staff."

"Oh, you don't have to worry about Leo, Richard. He's a professional," my mother assured him. "He is very handsome with all those big muscles and those piercing blue eyes..." She cut her sentence short, her cheeks enflamed.

"You don't have to worry about Leo?" I repeated, outraged by her lack of faith in me and disturbed by her obvious ogling. "Are you saying you have to worry about me?" Yes, I found Leo outrageously hot, intriguing and unlike any man I'd ever known, but that didn't change my situation. The few guilty pleasures I indulged in were harmless as long as they remained a secret. My relationship with my mother, whilst strained much of the time, was better than no relationship at all. I would never jeopardise that for some silly attraction and was deeply hurt that she thought I might.

My mother drove the knife in further. "You're weak, Juliette. Always have been. It's my fault for sending Leo to look for you." She turned to Richard. "My apologies."

My mind flashed, imagining my hands gripping her pearl necklace and tightening it around her neck to cut off her air supply. I would watch her eyes bugging out of her head as she struggled to get a single word out. I wondered how *weak* she'd find me then. A matricidal scenario was an unwelcome new twist to my dark thoughts.

"It's absolutely fine, Isabel. I put Leo in his place. He won't be bothering Juliette again."

The only way I could deal with Richard's arrogant lie was with an imagined knee jab to his crotch, whilst the pearl necklace noose tightened around my mother's neck.

"Good. Now make sure you greet the guests, Juliette." She waved her long, manicured fingers between Richard and me. "Everyone's been asking when you two will be tying the knot." She turned and disappeared, no doubt smiling triumphantly, believing she had worked in another hint.

I cringed but tried to suppress it. I glanced at Richard, who was nodding his head and smiling.

Before we had a chance to start the torturous mingling routine, Leo's gravelly voice made my whole body thrum. "Champagne?"

I closed my eyes, remembering his naked torso slick with sweat after his three fight wins, his presence commanding absolute attention from his riveted audience. Seeing him standing in the dark parking lot had given me the fright of my life. Not because I was afraid of his intimidating frame but because I didn't want my worlds colliding.

"Thank you." I took the glass and drained half of it without meeting his eyes.

"Dick?"

The gulp of champagne I had just taken spluttered out of my mouth and dribbled down my chin. Leo was holding his tray out for Richard. A chuckle I had battled to restrain bubbled out of my mouth as I tried to dry my chin with the back of my hand.

Richard was seething. "What did you just call me?"

"I see your glass is nearly empty. Would you like another?"

With Richard distracted for a few seconds, trying to work out if he'd heard correctly, I took the opportunity to study Leo's face more closely. He wasn't smiling, but the ice I'd seen in his blue eyes the night before had thawed, leaving a two-toned effect I wanted to drown in. They reminded me of the ocean's changing depths. High cheekbones and a strong jawline befitted a man who radiated strength, vitality and dominance. Bronzed skin suggested a life spent outdoors. I wished I weren't so interested in knowing more about him.

"No, I don't want another," Richard replied. "Please leave. I'm talking to my girlfriend here, and you're interrupting."

Leo shook his head, and his mouth turned up slightly at the corners. He was amused. As he walked away, I couldn't help wishing I could just be 'amused' by Richard, instead of battling committing my life to his more and more every day.

An hour of polite chit-chat ensued, and I was ready to shoot myself when I made my excuses to use the restroom. Richard caught my arm as I left.

"Don't be long," he warned. "I'm doing my speech in fifteen minutes, and you need to be there."

Gently tugging my arm away, I returned his tight

smile with a fake one of my own. "I wouldn't miss it."

I made my way inside and looked around for the restrooms. The inside of the homestead was stunning with high-vaulted ceilings. Eclectic lounges and wingback chairs were grouped together around coffee tables and ottomans. The upholstery patterns should have clashed but didn't for some reason. The mixture of modern and classical pieces should have been disastrous, but they blended perfectly. My eyes were drawn upwards and became mesmerised by the chandeliers hanging on long chains. They each held five large, white candles with crystal beading looping between them. They were magnificent.

"I was just admiring those earlier."

Leo.

Talking to him was dangerous, and I had to repel his strong magnetic pull.

"I'm looking for the restrooms."

He studied me for a few seconds before answering. "Just past the staircase. Second on your left." He gestured behind me, briefly touching my arm.

My left arm whipped over to my right, protectively covering the place he had just touched.

"Thank you." I turned and quickly followed his directions.

I turned the lock on the bathroom door and exhaled. I switched the lights off and closed my eyes, allowing absolute darkness to descend. I focused on my breathing and willed my thoughts to find some order. Darkness had always been my friend, and with the absence of light, it wrapped me in a blanket. Ironically, it made my world a little bit brighter.

Richard gave his speech. When he thanked his receptive audience, I hoped he wouldn't ask me any questions. I hadn't listened to a single word. I couldn't even remember what the topic was. I had just stared at him and wondered how different my life could have been. Tears pricked my eyes. My mother depended on me. These unwelcome thoughts brought a fresh wave of guilt I'd spent so many years navigating. When Richard stepped down from the podium, I glanced at my mother beaming with pride. She adored him, and when he wasn't being a pompous dickhead, I liked him enough to give her that.

I steeled myself. I owed it to my mother to be the woman she needed me to be, whatever the cost.

"You were amazing," I gushed. "Really interesting and informative." It wasn't necessarily a lie.

Far more relaxed post-speech, he leant forward and kissed me. "Thanks, babe."

A few hours later and the party started to wind up. My mother stood up and gave a heartfelt speech about the important work her foundation was doing and how much she appreciated the ongoing support of her guests. She dedicated herself to charity work, and it would be selfish of me to begrudge it. If it weren't for the distraction it gave her, she would have nothing else to focus on other than making me a society princess.

Guests were informed of their accommodation arrangements, and soon, they had all retired to their various villas.

"Well, I'm about ready to turn in. We're staying in the main homestead in a king suite. Shall we?" Richard asked, holding out his hand.

"I'll meet you in the room in a little while."

"Juliette," he said, looking skyward before his eyes met mine. "Is there something going on with you? I know we don't spend enough time together, but that will come down the track. I'm working hard now for our future, and all these people are a part of my success.

Plus, you know how much these events mean to your mother, and I would've thought you'd show a little more interest."

Ouch. The emotional blows were never far away from any conversation with both Richard and my mother.

Defeated and tired, I gave in as usual. "I'm sorry." I cupped his face with my right hand and placed my left hand on his waist. "Work's been really busy lately, and I've been a little distracted."

"You're a secretary, Juliette." He looked down at me with pity in his eyes. "You're not saving the world."

I knew I wasn't saving the world, but neither was he. I hated the way he put down my job at any opportunity.

"How about we go to our room now and worry about the future tomorrow?" I was such a coward.

He didn't say anything further, but he nodded his head and smiled briefly.

As we walked back up the steps and along the veranda to the homestead entrance, I felt eyes watching me. I glanced to my right, and my breath hitched when I saw Leo. He was helping pack up but had stopped when we walked by. I tried to smile, but it felt awkward and contrived. Lust was not in the stars for me, and the sooner I forgot about him the better. His icy stare was back, so I quickly turned away.

Up in our room, Richard took the first shower while I brushed my teeth and laid out my cotton pyjama set on the bed. It was a beautiful room, tastefully decorated primarily in white with muted grey accents. It was clean, fresh and minimalist. The fit-out was modern and sleek but managed to be warm and comfortable at the same time. I stripped my clothes off onto the bathroom floor and stepped past him into the hot water. He didn't give me a second glance, and right then I found that deeply depressing. The bigger issue was that I suddenly wanted to be slammed up against the tiles in a rush of passion, just not by him.

When I finished up in the shower, I got dressed and climbed in bed. Richard smiled at me and turned the bedside lamp off. I lay stiffly with my arms clamped to my sides.

"Do you want to?" Richard whispered.

"Do you?" I whispered back.

"It's been a long day. Do you mind if we just go to sleep?"

Part of me was relieved, but the rest of me felt rejected and lonely. The battle to stay present in this relationship was growing harder and harder. Sex had never been our strong suit, but a physical connection, however weak, made you feel like you weren't just part-time flatmates.

"Goodnight, Richard."

"Goodnight, Juliette."

When he started snoring lightly less than a minute later, I allowed my mind to fill up with images of a certain fighter come bartender. Every fibre of my being wanted to know him more intimately. Locked away in the safety of my tormented mind, in a moonlit room in the Yarra Valley surrounded by grapevines showing first signs of new life, it felt like I cheated on Richard for the first time. When I touched myself, I imagined it was Leo's hands on my body. When I brought myself to climax, I imagined it was Leo deep inside me. When a small groan escaped my lips, I imagined Leo's mouth muffling the sound with his passionate kiss. It was the most erotic experience I'd ever had, and when it was over, my shame and my loneliness found new depths.

I woke up in the morning completely alone. I had no idea where Richard was, and I didn't care. I just didn't care. I felt exhausted and depressed by my darkening thoughts. A long shower helped to wash away my fatigue, and I dressed and packed up quickly. I looked around the homestead half-heartedly for either my mother or Richard but gave up, quietly relieved. They were probably having breakfast together, discussing the success of the event and his riveting speech. I rolled my eyes in their honour.

# CHAPTER 11

## LEO

I WOKE UP THE NEXT morning in Bea and Angus's spare room, still thinking about Juliette. Why couldn't I get that crazy, complicated woman out of my fucking head?

When the function had wrapped up, she and Dick were the last to leave. She'd shivered when our eyes met. If she was cold, the arsehole hadn't given her his coat. Or perhaps I had an effect on her, too. Either way, she'd been about to go to bed with Dick, a man she appeared to barely tolerate. I didn't know her, and for all I knew, she was happy with him. He clearly had money and social standing, and perhaps she wanted the lifestyle that went hand in hand in these circles. Perhaps I'd read her all wrong. To me, she was like a wild animal pacing her cage, looking for a weak place to break free. With a thousand warring thoughts rushing through my mind, I'd given her nothing. No smile. No wave. Nothing. And then she was gone.

I needed to clear my mind and run, so I got dressed then slipped out the side door and took off. My legs carried me faster and faster, dulling my brain until the burning sensations were all I had to focus on. I headed uphill to the Anglican Church, built in the early 1900s. There was a narrow dirt track that ran along the church boundary and the cemetery behind. I didn't look sideways, instead focusing on the road ahead.

When I reached the old wooden bridge crossing the upper Yarra River, I slowed down to a walk. The sun was warm, but I hadn't run far enough to break a sweat. I couldn't wipe Juliette from my mind. Images of her in black flicked through my mind as quickly as ones of her in white lace. It wasn't just her changing appearance that had confused me. At fight night, she'd looked like she might take on the world, and last night she'd looked like she had the weight of the world on her slender shoulders. Shaking my head, I took off again, determined to replace confusion with exhaustion.

The path back to Bea's would take me past my old family home. As I got closer, I was shocked to see a red Mini parked on the grass verge. It was the exact type of car Juliette had driven. A cold dread settled over me when I noticed the front gate, hanging from one hinge, had been pushed open. I walked tentatively down the path and made a full perimeter of the house, glancing with increased anxiety around the overgrown garden.

"Hello," I called out when I got back to the front door. No answer. "Hello," I repeated, louder this time. Nothing.

Baxter, the neighbour's cat, slinked his way out of the house, alerting me to the slightly ajar front door. I stood at the opening and called out into the house. As I pushed gently, the door swung the rest of the way open, and I stood on the threshold of my childhood home. It all felt so wrong, and I was pretty sure at that point I would never be ready to face these demons. What was once the centre of my world was now a place I couldn't bear.

I reached down to pat Baxter, who had started to wind

himself around my legs, purring, then took a tentative step forward. *Surely no one would go inside uninvited.*

"Help." I thought that's what I heard coming from inside the house somewhere.

"Hello," I managed to call out when I had composed myself a little. "Where are you?"

"Help." The voice was a little louder and sounded increasingly distressed.

"Shit, shit, shit." I ran my hands through my hair and sucked in some air, forcing it into my lungs. "I'm coming," I shouted, trying to push away my own fears. "Where are you?"

A muffled female voice carried down from above. "In here."

"That's not helpful," I muttered to myself, taking the stairs two at a time. I tried not to look around too much for fear of some kind of panic attack. I would just find her, then get her the hell out of my house.

"Call out again," I instructed so I could follow her voice.

"I'm really sorry. I'm trespassing again. I mean... shit. I just wanted to see inside this beautiful house, and now I'm stuck in one of the bedrooms. A gust of wind must have blown the door closed and the door wouldn't open from the inside and—"

I opened the door and walked into my old bedroom. Her rambling stopped mid-sentence and, for the third time in as many days, my heart stopped, too. The sheer impossibility of the situation made me question my own sanity again. The fact she wasn't speaking made me wonder if she was a conjured-up illusion of my messed-up brain. Was my mind playing tricks on me?

"What are you doing? You shouldn't be in here."

"I wasn't going to steal anything" she said, gesturing around the sparsely-furnished room. "It's not like there's anything much to take." She visibly cringed at her own words. "I didn't think anyone lived here, and the door was open. I'm really sorry."

"I'll need you to get out," I said through gritted teeth. I could feel the panic level rising.

She nodded, shrugging her shoulders the way she had when Richard reprimanded her. It made me feel like shit.

"I'm sorry," she repeated. "I shouldn't have made a joke about stealing when I'm trespassing on your property. I'm just a bit shaken up about being locked in a room in someone else's house that I shouldn't have been in in the first place, and then you appear. Again. I mean, who the fuck are you? Are you following me or something? Are you a crazy stalker?" She shook her head and shuffled from one foot to the other. "Sorry about cursing. I don't usually curse. Well, not out loud, anyway."

Her apology that had turned into an attack then back into an apology threw me off guard, and the ridiculousness of her accusations blew the tension out of the room. "Seriously? You show up to my fight. Then you show up at the function I was working at. Then you show up at my house. And you think *I'm* the stalker?" I could hear my own voice softening.

"Okay. I guess you're not a stalker," she conceded with the hint of a smile.

"Thank you. That's big of you to admit." Our eyes locked and we stared at each other with such intensity, I couldn't look away.

"Right. Well, I'll get out of your hair, then." She shook her head, then started walking towards the door. When she passed, I grabbed her slender arm. A shock of electricity hit me, and I snapped my eyes back to hers, where I saw what I imagined she was seeing in mine—

dangerous lust.

"Wait," I spoke in barely more than a whisper. Realising I was still holding her arm, I dropped it and took a step back. I didn't want her to leave just yet. "I'm sorry I told you to get out."

"Why?" She looked confused. "You had every right."

"It's not you. I wanted to see you again." I paused, unsure how to explain it. "I don't live here anymore. I haven't been in here in five years." I wanted her out because no one that beautiful belonged somewhere haunted by so much ugliness. But I didn't want her to leave right away. "I could show you the garden." It sounded lame, but I was clutching at straws.

A smile lit up her entire face, brightening her beautiful eyes. "I love gardening. Apartment living doesn't call for it much, but yours is incredible."

I was in trouble. My desire to kiss her was overwhelming and completely ridiculous. Juliette was definitely spoken for, and that in itself was an absolute deal breaker. Despite that fact, there was something about her that gave me a deep sense of calm.

# CHAPTER 12

*Juliette*

HE TOUCHED ME. LEO TOUCHED me. The fighting god with the icy stare and the rock-hard body I wanted to run my hands down and do all kinds of naughty things to touched me. We both felt it. I would have bet my ticket to fight night on it. Was he the reason I'd felt so drawn to this house? Why did we keep running into each other? I didn't believe in coincidence. I believed in fate.

The crushing pressures imposed on me by my mother were pushed to the furthermost parts of my mind.

I wasn't lying about my love of the garden. It was overgrown and more like a jungle than a garden, but it had a tangible beauty, just like the house. Despite its neglect, I could still see that someone had gone to a lot of trouble establishing it. It just needed a lot of love. Seeing the garden also gave me an excuse to stay there longer—stay with *him* longer. I wanted to be there for as long as possible.

He gestured for me to exit the room ahead of him.

Standing at the top of the staircase, I examined my manicured nails and smooth hands. "I used to spend lots of time in my grandmother's garden when I was young. I loved getting my hands dirty." I paused. "I miss it."

I looked up to find Leo studying me. When he realised I was staring back, he smiled, and I placed my hand on the bannister to steady myself. This man made me weak at the knees. It wasn't just his hard-to-fathom good looks, bad-boy edge or ability to crush men with his bare hands. There was something deeply calming about being in his presence. He didn't say anything further. He just bit his bottom lip and ran his hands through his hair. He was so sexy; I found it incredibly distracting.

We walked down the stairs in silence, a delicious tension hanging in the air between us. At the bottom, instead of going straight ahead towards the front door, Leo led me around to the left and down the hallway. I tried to look everywhere at once—double-height ceilings, exposed stone walls I was compelled to touch, the occasional spider web and a definite lack of any touches making it a home. I was looking at the bare bones of a house, built when time, skill and care were taken to ensure a quality rarely seen in more contemporary homes.

As Leo led me further down the hallway, I stopped outside an open door. Leo stopped, too. I couldn't resist poking my head through the doorway and taking a tentative step in for a quick look. It was the room I'd peered into when I dirtied my dress—I recognised the furniture.

"It's a beautiful room," I whispered. Despite the dusty furniture and the grimy windows not allowing the natural light in, it was still a beautiful room. Much larger than in contemporary homes, the room was given a focal point by a cast-iron fireplace with a slate hearth. Despite the size of the room and the high, decorative ceilings, I had visions of a warm and cosy lounge room where I could relax with a good book on cold winter evenings.

"It was."

He was standing right behind me and the words sounded like breaths, kissing the air that separated us. I turned slowly, and what I saw in his eyes was pain. Deep, cutting, agonising pain. I could not only see the tension in his tight shoulders, but I could feel it rolling off him. There was something really off about this beautiful man in this beautiful house. I just didn't know what it was. What I did know was that I had to get us out of that room and out of that house to diffuse the tension, so I stepped past him back into the hallway.

"Take me to the jungle, Tarzan." *God, did I just say that?*

Leo's shoulders dropped slightly, and I heard a quiet chuckle as he shook his head. Then he turned to face me. After a few quiet seconds of what felt like him studying me again, he spoke. "Come on, then, Jane of the Jungle." The pain in his eyes had dissipated, and the joy that gave me was confronting.

"*Jules* of the Jungle," I corrected.

"Jules," he repeated, reverently, as he moved past me and started to walk slowly towards the back of the house.

I followed, admiring his broad shoulders and powerful physique. My eyes travelled south down his back and over his backside. I scolded myself for the dirty thoughts I had of my manicured fingernails digging in, pulling him deeper. Further south. His calves were a finely-tuned mass of muscle I longed to see put to work again at the next fight night. In my lust-driven perusal of his body, I almost bumped right into it.

He didn't turn around—he was just standing motionless in the doorway to what I realised was the kitchen. The tension I'd seen in the lounge room had returned tenfold. There seemed to be a mild tremor starting in his hands, now balled into fists. *What the hell was going on?* I wondered.

Gingerly, I took a step closer to him and lightly touched his shoulder, hoping to help a situation I couldn't comprehend. In what felt like an instinctual move of a seasoned fighter, he whipped around and grabbed my hand, his strength crushing me. I cried out in pain both from the shock of being so easily overpowered, as well as the sensation that he'd really done me some damage. When he dropped my hand, I fell to my knees, cradling my throbbing hand. I looked up into crazed, wide eyes. When they met mine, he seemed to snap out of his stupor.

"Oh my God, Jules. What have I done?" He crouched down in front of me and cautiously held both my hands in his. His touch was so gentle, it was hard to believe he was the same man who'd just turned on me. "I'm so sorry."

I managed to fight back the threatening tears as the throbbing subsided. "It's fine. Honestly, I'm fine." I pulled away, but he took hold of my non-damaged hand and helped me up, not letting go.

"God, Jules. I could've broken your hand. I'm so sorry." His eyes were filled with fear and self-loathing.

"You'll have to try harder than that to break me. I think my self-defence needs some work." I tried to lighten the mood again, but it didn't work this time.

His eyes darkened. He dropped my hand and ran his through his hair. "You shouldn't need self-defence around me."

"Look, Leo. You clearly don't want anyone in here for whatever reason, and that is your choice. You told me that when we were upstairs and kindly offered me a tour of the garden. I shouldn't have been so nosy coming in here without permission. Your body language is screaming loud and clear that you don't want me here, so let's just go outside and forget about all this. Okay?"

"I'll never forget hurting you. Never." He reached for my hurt hand and brought it to his lips, kissing it lightly. "Never, ever."

"I think I need to see the garden now," I croaked, not even sure if I could still find my voice. Leo's lips touching my skin had sent my whole body into a spin. *What would it be like if they kissed my lips?* There was something really dangerous about this man—dangerous, exciting, sexy and liberating. But I wouldn't actually cheat, and something told me Leo wouldn't either. He had a quiet integrity about him that made him even more attractive. When I was with Leo, I felt like I was in the presence of a real man—the kind of man I wanted to be with. Knowing that was impossible hurt more than the physical pain Leo had caused only minutes earlier.

I was in big trouble, and for the first time in my life, I wanted to ruffle some feathers. I wasn't looking for the path of least resistance. I should've been running away from the man who was making me question all my choices so violently. I should've been running from that house that made me feel so alive. Instead, I stepped out into the garden, the cool air making me shiver, and I allowed myself to imagine it was mine. *He* was mine.

Leo loosened up a bit once we were outside, but he would occasionally throw me a glance, riddled with angst. I wished he could just forget what had happened inside. I knew he was physically dominant and capable of hurting me far greater, but I also believed it was a one-off and had something to do with being in that house. I knew he was mortified, and his overreaction to my touch was based on something in his past. I didn't for a second blame him or feel threatened. Perhaps I was naïve, given the fact I barely knew him. Perhaps it was the masochist in me who revelled in danger. Perhaps it was the connection I felt to him every time he looked in my eyes and I felt like I was being seen for the first time. Perhaps I was losing my mind in the heady combination of everything the last few days had thrown at me.

A million thoughts flooded my brain. I knew I had to leave that house, that garden and that man, and I had to leave soon. I couldn't organise all my thoughts, and I felt panic-stricken. Overcome by what felt like a supercharged shot of adrenaline, I bent over and put my hands on my knees, trying to draw air into my lungs. My heart was fluttering too fast, as if I'd had too much caffeine. My palms felt sweaty, and I couldn't swallow past the choking lump in my throat. The garden looked foreign, and my mind couldn't reconcile what I was doing there. I was losing control.

# CHAPTER 13

## LEO

"JULIETTE. ARE YOU OKAY?"

I had walked ahead of her into the garden, eager to get out of that damned house, eager to escape. I'd hurt her. Regardless of my primal desire to protect her, I had turned on her in an instant and crushed her perfect little hand. I stood there staring at the overgrown hedges and the tangled mess of wisteria and wondered if she would really forgive me—if I would forgive myself. I turned around to see her bent over, struggling to draw breath, and immediately rushed to help her.

"I. Can't. Breathe." She could barely get the words out.

"You can get through this, Jules." I'd seen panic attacks many times, and I knew what to do.

"I. Just. Want. To. Breathe."

"Relax. Just listen to my voice, okay? I'm going to count to ten."

As I counted, I could see her breathing slow down and her body uncoil. God, she was so beautiful. She was strong and brave one minute, then a vulnerable, hot mess the next. Apologising one minute, then throwing sass the next. I'd never known a girl with so many layers of beauty and torment, but it felt like my soul had recognised its mate in Juliette's.

"I think it's time I went home. I shouldn't have come here." Her whisper snapped me out of my thoughts.

I'd convinced her to sit down in the shade under the large magnolia tree for ten minutes to ensure her breathing had completely returned to normal. We didn't speak in that time. We just sat in silence.

"I'll drive you home in your car. I can get the train back for my car tomorrow. I don't think you should drive."

She contemplated my offer for a few seconds before nodding her acceptance. Another hour with her was the added bonus to my peace of mind.

I drove Juliette home to her apartment in the city. We barely spoke, but for some reason, I knew her thoughts were as loud as mine. I parked the car and walked her to the lift in the lobby, feeling like it was the end of a first date when you don't quite know what to do. She pressed the call button on the lift then bit her lip, unable to look me in the eye. I wanted to bite her lip and I wanted her to invite me up. But I also wanted her to be single. She had enough shit going on in her life, and quite frankly, so did I.

"Why did you go into my house?" I suddenly had to know.

Her eyes snapped to mine and they conveyed so many things, yet I understood nothing. "I didn't know it was *your* house."

I cocked my head. "That wasn't my question."

Her smile warmed my heart, and I knew I needed to be responsible for many more of them. "I don't really know. I felt drawn to it somehow. Maybe *I'm* the stalker."

We both smiled. I really liked this girl, whoever she was.

"Thank you, Leo. And thank you for the lift." She clenched her teeth and scrunched her nose. "I'm sorry I've inconvenienced you."

"It's no bother."

I touched her arm briefly, and I could've sworn her body shivered. "Well, I guess I'll see you round, then?"

"No doubt we'll run into each other."

The lift door opened, and she walked in and turned around to face me. Our eyes locked for the last few seconds before the heavy grey doors closed, stealing her away from me.

I turned but only made it halfway across the lobby before the blood in my veins went cold—I was now face-to-face with Isabel Fontaine. She was a little intimidating when bossing her staff around, but at that moment, she looked more like the mythical creature Medusa with snakes for hair, turning everyone to stone.

"What are you doing here?" she hissed.

The cogs in my brain turned too slowly to make up a believable lie on the spot. I wasn't much of a liar anyway, and I'd done nothing wrong. "I just dropped Juliette home."

"And why, pray tell, would you be doing anything with my daughter?"

"She had a panic attack, and I drove her home in her car, as I didn't think she should be driving. I'm going home now."

She was silent for a minute, probably deciding whether I was telling the truth. I'd left out a few details, but I hadn't lied.

"Okay. Well, I'd rather you stayed away from her. I can't have my friends seeing her with my staff. People talk, if you know what I mean, and she's with Richard."

"I'm aware of her status, Mrs Fontaine."

"Juliette is unstable. She needs what Richard can give her and she needs to focus on securing him."

I just stood there listening to the biggest load of crap I thought I'd ever heard. Juliette was dealing with a psycho mother and a dickhead who didn't deserve to breathe the same air as her. My blood had gone from cold to hot and was reaching boiling point when she continued.

"I saw the way she was looking at you last night, and it was highly inappropriate. She needs to focus on the prize. You are a distraction."

*And the prize would be... Richard?* I wondered to myself. Richard was a prize douchebag.

"I just dropped her home. No big deal."

"Look. Richard plans to propose soon. It's what I've always wanted. I mean, what *she's* always wanted." It now appeared she was talking to herself, despite addressing me, mumbling almost incoherently. "We're so close. Richard and Juliette will be married soon." She opened her eyes wider and poked me in the chest. "If you mess this up for me, I'll kill you."

I felt awkward and wanted to get the hell away from the crazy woman. I was starting to get a clearer picture of Juliette's life, and it wasn't nearly as pretty as she was. "I'd better go."

"You're a liability. I could put up with my friends flirting with you, but not my daughter. She needs to focus on Richard, and I can't always be watching her."

"With all due respect, Mrs Fontaine, I don't think you're giving Juliette enough credit. She's a grown woman who can make her own decisions." I didn't care if I was speaking out of turn at that point. She probably wasn't going to hire me again anyway, so I had nothing to lose speaking my mind. "She's a strong and beautiful woman, and I don't think Richard is worthy of her. Not the other way around."

"I think you should return to whichever backwater you come from." Medusa hissed again, this time with an extra dose of venom.

"My pleasure." I walked past her towards the glass doors with my head held high. She had sucked all the air out of the room, and I didn't need to be around her another second.

"Stay away from Juliette," she shouted.

I didn't turn around. "No chance," I replied under my breath. I was going to walk away, but I *would* see Juliette again. My heart and soul wouldn't have it any other way.

# CHAPTER 14

## Juliette

"YOU'RE A LIABILITY. I COULD put up with my friends flirting with you, but not my daughter. She needs to focus on Richard, and I can't always be watching her."

I'd returned to the lobby to retrieve my mail and suddenly wished I'd let another day go by without it. I was startled and horrified to hear my mother's angry voice directed towards Leo when the lift doors opened.

"Shit, shit, shit," I whispered through gritted teeth.

I shuffled sideways to hide behind the enormous indoor plant feature to my right. The voyeur in me wanted to listen to their conversation before interrupting them.

I missed Leo's response but was again horrified by my mother's words.

"I think you should return to whichever backwater you come from."

"My pleasure." His response was absolutely warranted but nonetheless devastating.

"Stay away from Juliette," she shouted.

Instead of going back to the lift, I bolted for the door to the stairs and took them two at a time. I was on the fifth floor, and I barely acknowledged the pain in my muscles as I ascended.

With the searing memory of Leo's eyes on me, his brief touches, his burning energy pulsing from every pore of his body, I knew I needed to get my head on straight and make some hard decisions about my future. I was done with the crazy, sanity-preserving bullshit. I was done with the guilt that served only to fester in my soul and my withering idea of who I was.

I didn't think I'd ever felt more alone. I was a twenty-five-year-old woman living the life my mother had planned for me. I walked on eggshells, and it had gone on for too long. On paper, I was the perfect daughter she could be proud of, but in reality, I was just an illusion. As a young girl, I'd worn pink tutus with wings sewn onto sequined tops. She'd dressed me up as fairy princesses, and I'd worn veils, pretending to be a bride. I did ballet, drama and even a few modelling shoots for high-end kids' clothing companies. In the end-of-year ballet concerts, my mother would meltdown if I wasn't the little girl in the limelight. I'd feel ashamed and would vow to do better, even though I was more than happy to be a part of the backdrop.

I had never been perfect, nor a princess. As an adult, I wanted to get my hands dirty, drive too fast, go to illegal fight nights, wear comfortable clothes, and allow myself to feel the way I felt about Leo whenever I was around him.

The desire to let myself drown under the pressure had always been overwhelming. There was something about Leo that made me want to throw myself off a bridge and then swim upstream like my life depended on it, because in a way, it did. Leo, or maybe even just the idea of Leo, made me want to scale rock faces with my bare hands and then stand at the summit and scream his name. I had a steely bravery within me, screaming to find a way out and into my everyday life—I think I always had. It was stifled by oppressive parents who had told me I was weak, an ingrained guilt laid on me all my life.

A child's need to please their parents can last a lifetime. Pleasing mine was like being on a treadmill set to a speed I wasn't quite fit enough for, but the idea of stepping off was daunting. My mother controlled the buttons and knew when to push them. If she sensed me getting ready to slow from a run, she'd increase the speed or the incline. I stepped up every time, thinking it would make her happy. By even noticing, she was paying attention, and I took solace in that. My father wouldn't notice if I fell off the treadmill and broke my neck. Having no one care about me seemed far worse than the pressure of living someone else's life.

When the knock on my apartment door came minutes later, I braced myself, knowing I was about to make my mother cry.

She wanted a key, but I always managed to 'forget' to get one cut. Before opening the door, I looked through the peephole at her for a few seconds, enjoying the fisheye view as she impatiently awaited entry. The optical lens made her head appear abnormally large and her eyes bug-like. Her stern features were distorted, transforming her into a crazy caricature.

Taking a deep breath, I opened the door.

"Well, it's about time, Juliette," she huffed, storming past me into my apartment, which suddenly felt very small. "It's rude to let me stand out there waiting."

"Hello, Mother." I rolled my eyes.

"Don't use that tone with me. I'm very upset."

*Here we go,* I thought to myself.

She dropped the stack of bridal magazines on the coffee table and sat down gracefully on my lounge. She nodded her head towards the other chair. I complied with her wishes, knowing it was best we were both sitting down for this conversation.

"Richard and I are worried about you," she began. "He thinks you've lost sight of what's important and you really need to sort yourself out."

"Richard thinks that, does he?"

"Richard is a very smart man, Juliette. He takes care of the tricky money side of my foundation. I'm so lucky to have him. *We're* so lucky to have him."

"I know this isn't what you want to hear, but I can't be with Richard anymore and I certainly can't marry him." I looked at the floor and steeled myself before looking her in the eye. "I'm sorry."

"What?" Mother asked, going pale. "Don't be so ridiculous, Juliette. Richard is the best thing to ever happen to you." After a few-second pause where neither of us said anything, her eyes narrowed as she leaned forward and went for the jugular. "After everything I've done for you, you owe me. I need this."

I stood up and started pacing, unable to sit still for a second longer. "I don't love him, Mum. Sometimes I don't even like him. How can you want that for me?"

"Sit down, Juliette. I don't know where all this is coming from, but I don't like it. Has it got something to do with the muscled-up bartender?"

I stopped pacing and turned so I could look her right in the eyes. She needed to hear this.

"This is about *me*. Me!" I clutched my chest. "This has to do with *me* not wanting to be with someone I'm not in love with. And this has to do with *you* being far too invested in every aspect of my life. I'm a grown woman and I'm not a puppet." I took a deep breath before saying the words I'd wanted to say for so many years. "I'm not you, Mum."

She was already pale, but my words appeared to drain the rest of the blood from her face, and her eyes glazed.

I walked over and sat down next to her. Tears were welling in her eyes, so I put my hand over hers. "I'm not you, Mum. I never have been and I'll never be what you want me to be." I squeezed her hand and waited until she looked at me. "You have to see that."

She was mumbling to herself and refusing to look at me, so I continued my attempts to break through to her. She pulled her hand from mine and started nervously picking at a loose thread on her skirt. I wasn't even sure if she'd heard anything I'd said. It was unnerving. She appeared to be having some kind of internal meltdown, and I feared her face might crack.

"Sorry, Mum." I blew out a long sigh, knowing my determination had dissolved in a pool of emotional guilt. "Say something, Mother," I implored.

"You have more of me in you than you realise, Juliette, but I think enough has been said today." She stood up and smoothed her skirt down her legs. "You need to cool off. I'll expect a phone call from you tomorrow apologising for this unnecessary friction. I don't have time for your immature failings." She finally looked me in the eye. "Grow up, Juliette. Marriage isn't all hearts and flowers, and you're naïve to think it is. Richard is perfect for you, and I don't want to hear another word otherwise."

She turned and walked towards the door, stumbling a little on the edge of my rug.

Neither of us said goodbye.

For the rest of the day, I tried in vain to escape into my books. Leo was never far from my thoughts, and I kept finding myself reading the same lines over and over, wondering what he was doing at that moment. Was he thinking about me? Did he feel the connection I had felt?

I went to bed that night thinking about my life up to that point. If I looked at the positives, I had a decent job, I had somewhere to live and I had my health. Those were the things I could cling to in the light of day. At night, when everything felt more daunting and inexplicable, I found myself dwelling on how weak and pathetic I felt, allowing my life to be forged by anyone other than me. There was more to me than pretty dresses and polite conversation, but every year that passed me by, I was slipping further and further into that life, and it scared the hell out of me.

I let out the tears I'd been choking on for too long. I sobbed the big, ugly tears I'd always been too afraid to release. The flood gates opened, and my whole body started to shake. I screamed in frustration and beat my fists against my pillow.

# CHAPTER 15

*Juliette*

I CALLED TO APOLOGISE TO my mother the next day like the good daughter I was, but the seed of doubt had been planted in my mind. Was I helping her by pretending to be someone I wasn't? For as long as I could remember, I'd tried so hard to be what she needed me to be. I loved my mum. I wanted her to be happy, and that's what always drove me to accept the responsibility of preventing her breakdowns. My need for an adrenaline hit was at an all-time high.

To make matters worse, Richard was become increasingly attentive. He and my mother had clearly talked. I'd exhausted every excuse under the sun to avoid him, but he was waiting outside the gym on Thursday evening after my vigorous training session with Zac.

"How was your class?" he asked after kissing my cheek, appearing somewhat interested for the first time.

"Great, thanks." I took a deep breath and summoned the energy to converse. "How was your day?" I then summoned further energy to remain present for his reply.

"Fantastic. My speech on Saturday night definitely had its desired effect on the attendees." He put his arm around my shoulders as we started to walk, and I tried not to flinch. "I've signed three new accounts this week, and one of them signed up to the premium service."

"That's great. Congratulations." I tried to sound enthusiastic, but I was just irritated. He could've been talking about saving baby seals and it would've rubbed me up the wrong way though. I had to find a better way to handle it, or my life was just going to get a whole lot harder to tolerate.

As we crossed the bridge, Richard stopped. "I have something for you," he said as he reached into his pocket.

I stared at his pocket, horrified, because I already knew what it was going to be.

He opened his hand and sure enough, a small padlock lay innocently on his palm. I looked in his eyes, searching for anything genuine or true. I found nothing, and it made my heart hurt. I didn't want to even pretend we had an unbreakable love and, very clearly, neither did he. Why was he doing this?

"I got our initials engraved on it during my lunch break today." He sounded proud of this achievement. "Are you surprised?"

"I um... yes. Yes, Richard. I'm surprised. You seemed so against the whole thing just last week. What changed?"

"I don't want to lose you, Juliette, and if clipping a silly padlock on a bridge helps, I'll do it."

And just like that, I wanted to throat punch him. He had completely missed the point on every level, and I'd never felt more depressed about our relationship than I did at that moment.

Regardless of my lacklustre reaction, he clipped it to

the railing as I watched on, nauseated. The more I thought about it, the more irritated I became. He was an obnoxious narcissist, and he was making my skin crawl.

"So I'm supposed to throw the keys in the river?" He looked at me, holding them up. "Do you want to do the honours?"

Not a chance. "You do it. You went to all the trouble, after all." I tried to keep the sarcasm to a minimum.

I stood against the railing and watched the two small keys, bonded together by a tiny silver ring, sail through the air. Instead of the romantic moment I imagined it was meant to be, it felt like I was watching my self-worth plummet into the murky water and disappear. I needed to get away from there. I needed to escape before another panic attack took hold.

"I'm getting cold. Can we go?" I didn't wait for his response. I just walked away, choking on the enormous lump in my throat that seemed to have taken up permanent residency.

Over the next few days, I felt my rebellious streak gain traction, and I was finding it harder and harder to hide it. I was riding a rollercoaster of guilt as the seed of doubt began to shoot. One minute I'd be convinced breaking up with Richard was the only way forward, and then I'd spiral downward and fear the repercussions for my fragile mother. I couldn't just abandon my life as she knew it without seriously considering how badly it could impact her. I loved her, and part of me clung to the fact that she was so invested in me. How would I feel if she abandoned me?

By the weekend, I was almost beside myself with the constant flip-flopping of my poor tortured mind. Fortunately, there were no social engagements I was expected to attend, so I was free to drive the two hours north of Melbourne to Winton raceway for a little adrenaline therapy. I left at the crack of dawn on Saturday and arrived invigorated and determined. As I pulled my Mini into one of the designated parking bays, I felt my excitement level escalate, allowing my brain to finally compartmentalise my mother, Richard and even Leo, giving me a modicum of peace.

Supersprints took place on a racetrack and, whilst the rush of the drag came from the extreme acceleration, I got my Supersprint adrenaline from the never-ending quest to achieve a 'perfect lap' and in beating my personal best times. A number of cars of similar performance were sent onto the track at roughly five-second intervals for a specified number of 'hot laps,' which were electronically timed to thousandths of a second. My objective was to register the fastest lap time in my car's class over a number of five-lap sessions during the day. Achieving better times than guys in similar cars to mine was always icing on the cake.

It was a case of pushing myself and my car to our absolute limits on every lap. Brake ten metres too early at one hundred and fifty kilometres per hour—lose two tenths of a second. Brake ten metres too late—run wide, lose half a second. Miss an apex coming on to the main straight—lose a few kph mid-corner speed and kiss goodbye to a full second. It was all a question of concentration and consistency, and by the end of each session, I found myself drained and perspiring freely.

I'd only been to Winton once before and knew I needed to get myself up to speed for the first flying timed lap after the quick left-right dogleg corner leading to the start finish line straight. The trickiest part of the track was somewhat risquely called 'the Cleavage,' due to the obvious similarity of the double-dipping corner layout. The ninety-degree right hander onto the main straight was my favourite corner and also the most important one on the whole circuit. I knew that every extra bit of speed I could hold through here would be carried for the whole length of the main straight and help to compensate for my JCW Mini's relative lack of horsepower compared to my opposition.

My phone rang just as I was getting out of my car. Looking at the screen, I groaned.

"Hey, Mum." I cupped my phone with my free hand, attempting to muffle the sound of the cars revving in the background. This is the last place on earth she'd expect me to be, and she would be horrified I was participating in such a high-risk activity. She'd be even more concerned by how it would look to be alone at a racetrack full of men.

"Hello, darling. Where are you?"

"I'm out and about." I tried to sound upbeat and friendly. I didn't want to lie, but I would if I had to. "I'm flat out today, actually."

"Oh, okay." She sounded sulky and dejected.

"Sorry, Mum. Did you need something?"

"I just thought we could have lunch together today. There's a new restaurant in Prahran getting fabulous reviews."

"Oh... um..."

"Please, Juliette. We need to spend more time together."

"I come to the house every Sunday night for dinner," I retorted, perhaps a little too aggressively.

"I've talked Richard into leaving the office for a few hours to join us." She continued as if she hadn't heard me. "He's such a workaholic. It's Saturday, for goodness' sake. Such a good work ethic, that man."

Surely, after our recent conversation, she had to know that was a deterrent rather than an incentive. I stared at the sky, willing it to drop a plausible excuse into my brain. I drew a blank.

"I'm really busy today, Mum."

"You can be very selfish, Juliette. I don't ask you for much."

Tears stung my eyes and I paused before replying. "I'm sorry, Mum." When no response came after a few seconds, I glanced at the screen. She had hung up.

I put my phone back in my pocket and closed my eyes, trying to push the negativity away. When I opened them, I gritted my teeth. This weekend was mine.

"You made it," Jim called out, waving to me as I walked past his Subaru WRX towards the registration desk. "Of course." I waved back. "No place I'd rather be. Where's Shorty?"

"He's over at Smithy's car, fiddling with tyre pressures as usual."

I laughed. Shorty worked as one of the bookies at Flemington racecourse, but his passion was engines and he could easily be a top race mechanic. He could talk endlessly about the intricacies of ignition-timing and suspension settings—and frequently did. When it came to improving a car's performance, he could talk under wet cement with a mouth full of marbles, and it always made me smile. Listening to anyone talk about their passion is a joy, especially when the subject is something that interests me, too.

I signed in and quickly scanned the entry list. I saw Scott Henderson was in the same class as me and wondered if he'd show me any more respect since I crushed him at the drag race. Probably not—his ego would've assured him it was a one-off fluke.

"Good luck, Juliette," the lady behind the registration desk said as she checked off my CAMS licence details and handed me my race number. "You show those boys how it's done."

"Oh, don't you worry," I replied, grinning. "I fully intend to."

Back in the pits, I took my jumper off and flung it on the plastic table set up next to my car. I then retrieved my fire-engine-red race suit from the back seat and pulled it on over my jeans and t-shirt. As I zipped up the front, I rolled my eyes, hearing several wolf whistles coming from nearby.

"Lookin' good, Jules—I've always liked the Winton cleavage." Scott Henderson's face appeared in front of my car. "Shouldn't you be at home doing the dishes or something?" he added with a smarmy grin.

I climbed into my car, shaking my head at his backhanded compliment and blatant chauvinism. I knew he was just trying to get a rise out of me. I clicked my six-point harness at the front, pulled it tight and gave him my best hair toss. "Just keep checking your rear-view mirror, pal—I'll be all over you after a couple of laps." I looked him dead in the eye and cocked my head, inviting him to bite. Instead, he just mumbled something under his breath and shuffled off.

"You all set?" Shorty asked, tapping the bonnet. "Tyre pressures? Wheel nuts? Nothing loose inside the car? The scrutineers are really looking for trouble today."

I pulled my helmet down over my head, fastened the strap and gave Shorty the thumbs up.

Half an hour later, I'd been given the all-clear and was ushered onto the track for a single warm-up lap. I quickly tried to familiarise myself with the track. Accelerating hard down the main straight was actually the easiest part. Whilst making sure I snatched third, then fourth gear the instant my shift light indicated maximum revs, I also had time for a quick glance at my engine temperature and oil pressure gauges. Normal.

Perfect. The world outside was deafening, but the craziness inside my head was silent. The adrenaline rush forcing drivers to push harder and faster, otherwise known as the 'red mist,' had well and truly taken control, and I was out to win with no thought for anything, or anyone, else.

# CHAPTER 16

*Juliette*

WINTON WAS SUCH AN AWESOME high; it carried me through the next couple of weeks. I had crushed my previous best lap time, well and truly showing Scott Henderson and anyone else who doubted my abilities, that my drag race victory was no fluke.

When the next fight night arrived, I waited for the text message with even greater anticipation than usual. As a cab pulled up in front of me, I locked eyes across the street with a familiar-looking guy with white-blonde hair and pale eyes. I'd seen him at the gym the night before while I was warming up for Zac and had felt uneasy at the time. It had felt like he was watching my every move, but I'd forgotten about him as soon as I started pummelling the bag. The man across the street broke eye contact, pretending to be interested in a flyer stuck to the inside of the shop window he was standing in front of. *Weird.*

The whole process of getting to the fight was the same, but the adrenaline I thrived on hit me with a greater force. As much as I tried to deny it to myself, I felt anxious to see Leo again, at the same time knowing I should stay away. Nothing had actually changed in my life, and seeing him would be a reminder of what was out of my reach. Would he be there? It had been almost a month since I last saw him. He'd probably forgotten about me.

"Do you think Leo will show tonight?" Shorty asked as we jostled our way into the non-descript warehouse somewhere on the outskirts of the city.

"Word on the street says he'll be here." Jim shrugged his shoulders with indifference.

My heart soared and plummeted in quick succession.

I headed directly to the cage fence with Jim while Shorty, once again, went in search of his other mates.

"I'll be fine if you want to go with Shorty, Jim," I reassured my friend.

"I'm good, Jules. This is a networking opportunity for him. I'm just here to watch the fights."

Happy with his response, I started scanning for the fighters. I zeroed in on the huddles and strained to catch any glimpse of the one person who had claimed a piece of me. I closed my eyes in an attempt to block out the rising emotion of knowing however much I wanted to be what my mother needed, I had needs, too. I needed to see Leo.

The announcer's voice startled me, and I snapped my eyes open. Leo was in the cage right in front of me. I wanted to cry out with happiness, with fear, with a confused mixture of warring emotions and hungry desire. The bell rang, and the fighters tapped fists before taking their places and bouncing on the spot. Leo's opponent, Reaper, looked terrifying and mean. His head was fully shaved except for a plaited rat's tail hanging down the back of his neck. Tattoos covered the majority of his upper body and, judging by what I could make out, he was one angry individual. Fire-breathing dragons, swastikas, skulls, tombstones and a variety of other ink, no doubt designed for intimidation. There appeared to be some kind of tally system across his lower abdominals, and I couldn't help wondering if they were ink representations of his victims, lying dead in dumpsters and riverbeds. Although Leo was undefeated, I was sick to my stomach with worry.

The first few minutes were fairly uneventful, both fighters managing to avoid any serious blows. They were completely focused, and I was mesmerised by Leo's massive, rock-hard body, dancing with a ballerina's grace. Reaper had equally skilful footwork and, much to my horror, they appeared evenly matched.

"Hit him in the vagina!" yelled a swaying man three across from me. "Pussies!"

The crowd roared with laughter, clearly enjoying the entertainment of the excruciating build-up. The tension between the fighters rose, and I could sense an imminent explosion. The hairs on the back of my neck stood on end. Leo's eyes were like slits, and my whole body hummed with fear and excitement. He hadn't looked into the crowd once and, whilst I longed for his gaze, I didn't want to risk any distraction.

I'm not exactly sure what I'd been expecting, but it wasn't what transpired. Leo landed a hook to Reaper's body faster than my eyes could witness. Judging from the seemingly slow motion of the flailing body flung impossibly far, there was some extraordinary brute strength behind his fist. Reaper was left sprawled face-down on the khaki canvas. Murmurs around the crowd questioned whether he was faking, but I was convinced he wasn't. When he started to spit blood, I knew I was right. Leo was the winner by knockout.

Leo exited the cage. The first fight was over, and I

managed to exhale.

Within minutes, two new fighters entered the ring. Rusty had a shock of orange hair sticking out at odd angles. I couldn't decide whether he meant it to be styled that way or it was just naturally bizarre hair. His skin was pale, almost translucent, and dotted with a fine smattering of freckles. I bet he was a cute kid before he turned into a first-grade thug. Thumping his chest, he emanated guttural roars as he raised the volume of the room with his crowd-pleasing antics. At one point, he flung himself up the cage fence and straddled the top, arms flung into the air to the crowd's obvious delight. His opponent, Barb's husband Paul, had a much better shot this time, and I could see his sly smile only just visible to my keen eye. He obviously knew the showier the fighter, the less concerned he needed to be. This guy was almost an assumed pushover.

As expected, Paul had him down for the count in less than four minutes. Rusty would've no doubt been embarrassed had he been conscious when he was carted from the ring, a pool of blood in his wake.

A few boring fights later and Leo was back in the cage with Paul for the semi-final. The desire to leap into the cage and throw myself into Leo's arms was, at times, overwhelming. He was everything. Pure, unadulterated lust seeped from my pores and slid unashamedly towards him. I couldn't see straight and, at that moment, I knew I would be breaking up with Richard. Even if Leo wanted nothing to do with me, I couldn't go on the way I had been. I wanted more.

"Bloody hell," Jim cursed. "I have to take a piss. You'll be okay for five minutes?"

"Of course." I smiled at my overprotective friend. "No worries at all." He started the process of pushing through the crowd, and when I had lost sight of him, I turned back to the cage.

"Hello, beautiful." A deep voice whispered into my ear from behind, and cold chills ran the length of my spine.

I spun towards the voice and was met with a creepy set of pale blue eyes, shadowed by a grey hoodie, partially covering the now-familiar man's head.

"Who are you?" I demanded, irritated by his interruption and obvious stalking.

"Don't be afraid."

I was vaguely aware of the bell ringing and the fight beginning. A quick sideways glance and I could see Leo the predator stalking his next meal.

I turned back to Hoodie. "Puh-leease. I'm not afraid of you." My voice was even with honesty. "What do you want and why are you following me?"

"Somebody really doesn't want you here with the scum of society." His hand surprised me with its steel grip on my arm, and I flinched with the pain shooting up to my shoulder.

"Let go of me, you psycho." I pulled away roughly, which only served to increase the pain in my shoulder socket. His eyes had gone from showing no emotion to obvious enjoyment. He was getting a thrill out of our interaction, and I was getting increasingly pissed off. I took a quick survey of my surroundings and assessed I was on my own. Jim and Shorty were nowhere to be seen, and everyone else's attention was gripped to the cage.

"You're a feisty little number." He licked his lips as he raked his eyes up and down my squirming body. "I might give you a run later."

"Fuck off, you pig." My cursing made him chuckle, and I took the opportunity to slam my foot down hard on his, followed up immediately with a knee to the balls when his grip on my arm momentarily eased off.

Hoodie's screams of pain turned a few heads, and when I glanced up at the cage, I was horrified. Leo had seen me. We were riveted to the spot in a locked stare, and Hoodie took the opportunity to grab me roughly from behind. Leo's body coiled in rage, and he launched himself at the wire cage.

"Get off her!" he yelled. "I'll fucking kill you if you don't get off her."

He had to refocus. Paul had been given a reprieve and was stalking towards him, having taken a moment to recover with a blood puddle at his feet. I launched into counter-attack mode, starting with a rear head smash to draw his attention upward. I spun around when he released me and quickly slammed my foot down hard on his again. I shifted my hips hard and fast to the left and then struck his groin with all the force I could muster. Judging from the fact I was quickly released and he was bellowing in agony on the ground, it was a lot.

Smiling, I looked away from my victim and back to Leo, whose shocked look would've been cute if I weren't then watching Paul take his opportunity in what felt like slow motion. I heard myself scream Leo's name, and he thankfully reacted on instinct to the threat behind him. All the saliva in Paul's mouth flew sideways as he took a hard hit to the face, then a punch to the stomach. He dropped to his knees and tipped forward, landing with a loud thud. He was out, and I was pretty sure Barb would be warming up the car.

The crowd gasped and cheered as Leo was declared the winner and poor Paul was dragged off.

"You little bitch." Hoodie spat then groaned again. His aching, bruised groin would be a reminder for a while to leave me alone.

"Don't you speak another word to her, you fucking arsehole." From nowhere, Leo's angry voice startled me.

Stunned and muted, I watched in horror as Leo wrenched Hoodie from the ground into the air by his throat. With his breathing cut off, his legs flailed frantically.

Jim and Shorty appeared by my side, and I'd never been more thankful to see them.

"Please get that guy out of here before Leo kills him." I could hear the desperation in my own voice, and clearly they could, too, as they leapt forward immediately and pulled Hoodie from Leo's grasp in the nick of time.

"We'll get this good-for-nothin' out of here, mate," Jim assured Leo, who still appeared murderous.

"If I see you again," Leo said to Hoodie with a menacing tone. "You'll be eating your next meal through a straw."

Hoodie spat on the ground as he was dragged away, clutching his groin with one hand and cradling his throat with the other.

"Are you okay?"

I shivered at the sound of Leo's strained voice. With him right in front of me, sweaty, a little bloodied and bruised but no less intoxicatingly handsome, I had trouble formulating words.

"Did he hurt you at all?" he asked, sounding increasingly concerned.

"I'm fine," I croaked.

Leo ran his hands through his hair and dipped his head forward. "Fuck, Juliette." He sounded angry. He grabbed my hand and pulled me around the side of the cage, then away from the crowds towards the fighters' exit. We stopped in a small hallway with the sounds of men in pain for background noise. The rooms off the hallway must have been where the losers were trying to recover.

"What happened back there?"

"What? I took care of it."

"I saw that," he said through clenched teeth.

"Are you angry with me?"

"You shouldn't be here. It's too dangerous for someone like you."

"Are you kidding me? Too dangerous for a poor, defenceless little rich girl, you mean?"

"Clearly you're not defenceless, but why would you put yourself in danger like that?"

"I could ask you the same thing, Leo," I replied indignantly. "Speaking of, you better get back in there for the final."

"I called it a night."

"What? Why? You can't do that. I didn't need saving." I didn't know why I was being so petulant, but I could take care of myself. I didn't need anyone trying to be my knight in shining armour.

"No." His brow furrowed and his eyes dimmed. "I will lose the next fight if you're here. I won't be able to concentrate."

"Don't think about me when you're in there." I reached out and touched his arm, pleased by the goose bumps I felt on his hot skin.

"I've thought of little else for the past month." He stared at my lips with lust in his eyes. "I don't give a shit about the win."

His candid statement floored me. I wanted desperately to kiss him and find out what those perfect lips would feel like on mine. I swallowed hard, completely terrified by what I was feeling.

"I'm still with Richard." It was the truth and it had to be acknowledged, but it made me feel nauseous. I watched Leo's jaw clench and his eyes darken.

"What are you doing here, Juliette?"

"Watching grown men fight like animals. Same as everyone else."

"Okay then. *Why* are you here? You are not from this world. You live in a fancy apartment, wear fancy clothes and go to fancy parties with your fancy boyfriend. Then you show up here trying to fit in but failing miserably. You're the most goddamn beautiful girl I've ever seen, and there's little wonder guys are going to hit on you. Then what? He takes you out the back and rapes you, or worse? You got lucky this time, but what about next time? You don't belong here, Juliette."

"You don't know anything about where I belong," I seethed. "In case you missed it, I can handle myself. I train hard to be able to defend myself against scumbags like that, and I'm actually proud of myself for handling it. And I don't need you psychoanalysing me when you're the one with the big mansion in the country you can't set foot in without having a meltdown and nearly breaking my hand—then coming here and fighting like a man possessed. Why don't we discuss that while you're judging me and my reasons for being here?"

Leo recoiled from my harsh words. I felt instantly guilty for throwing in his face what happened in that house.

"I'm sorry." I screwed up my face, ashamed. "I didn't mean that."

An awkward silence stretched for miles between us.

"I'll let the promoters know I'm taking you home."

"They won't mind?"

"They won't be thrilled, but they can go fuck themselves if they try to stop me. They can tell the crowd I'm injured." He shrugged his shoulders. "I don't really give a shit."

"Okay." I couldn't look at him.

Leo returned in a few minutes, pulling a hoodie down

over himself and flinching mildly. Even undefeated, he had sustained a variety of injuries. You don't go into a cage with almost no rules and come out clean.

"Let's go." His authoritative tone was both irritating and hot. He took my hand possessively and led me out into the cold air of the very early morning darkness. His Jeep was parked close by, together with a range of other vehicles ranging from dinged-up shitboxes to the expensive and possibly stolen variety.

He opened the passenger door and waited for me to climb inside before shutting it with more force than necessary. He was clearly still pissed off with me. I watched him stalk around the front and then stop at the driver side. He just stared at me through the window, taking a few deep breaths as if he were psyching himself up to be in the car with me. I threw my hands in the air in annoyance and glared at him. I wasn't exactly sure what his problem was, but I didn't deserve his wrath. I hadn't done anything wrong, and he was the judgemental one.

When he got in the car, he did up his belt and turned the ignition. He still hadn't looked at me.

"Seriously. What is your problem?" I asked.

Without answering, he turned the engine off and leaned forward, resting his forehead on the steering wheel. After what felt like an eternity, he sat back and swivelled to face me.

"My problem, Juliette, is you."

I placed my hand on my chest. "I'm your problem? Why exactly am I your problem? Please enlighten me."

He just shook his head and started the car again. This time he put it in gear and took off.

I nearly said something about fifty times between leaving the fight and Leo pulling up in front of my apartment building. I was pissed off and completely confused.

"Well, thanks for the lift, I guess," I whispered, not having a clue where his head was at.

When he didn't respond, I reached for the handle.

"Wait."

I closed my eyes briefly and then turned, giving him my best glare. "I'm tired, Leo."

"Look. I haven't seen you in a month. It was a long fucking month. Can you stop glaring at me? I'm trying to explain."

"Fine."

"I think about you all the fucking time. I think about how I hurt you."

"We agreed at the time to forget it. I'm sorry I brought it up again. I don't usually speak without thinking like that. Why are you still dwelling on it?"

"Because I had no control over what I did to you, and I like being in control."

I didn't know how to respond, so I just sat there quietly, waiting to see if he would continue.

"Every day, I think about you staring at me through the cage, dressed in black, looking so out of place but daring anyone to send you away. Every day, I think about the next time I saw you, dressed in white lace, behaving like every bit the society princess you are. I feel like I'm in a constant state of whiplash."

"Thanks for summarising my fucked-up life, Leo. Much appreciated. Can I go now?"

"God, you're frustrating. Let me finish." He stared at me for a few seconds with raised eyebrows, probably making sure I wasn't going to interrupt. "I have my own shit to deal with, and whenever I see you, I feel like I've been in a head-on collision. I have no right to ask this, but I need you to stop going to fight night."

"Why?" I choked.

"There's something about you that brings out every protective instinct in me. I watched you take down that arsehole right in front of my eyes, but you're reckless and you're going to get yourself hurt. I need to be there and I need you *not* to be there." He shook his head, clenching his jaw. "I know you have a boyfriend, and I have no right to feel the way I do about you."

"How do you feel about me?" I whispered, my heart racing and threatening to leap right out of my chest.

Leo's shoulders dropped, and he rubbed his forehead with his fingertips. "I feel like we were meant to meet, like we have some intense connection drawing us together. Even though I barely know you, my heart gets ripped out every time I think about you with someone else, and when I saw that guy hurting you, I would've ripped *his* heart out without thinking twice."

"I feel it, too." Tears welled in my eyes at my own admission. "But have you thought about what *I* need? My bet is you think I'm a spoiled brat seeking attention through reckless activities." I felt rage boiling up from the pit of my stomach and, for the first time, I didn't restrain my inner voice. "You know what, you judgemental arsehole? I am so bloody sick of being judged, reprimanded, criticised and belittled. All I've ever done is try to be what others need me to be or do or say. You have no idea who I really am or what I go through every day trying to keep everyone happy. And you know what? It doesn't seem to make any difference. No one is ever happy with me. I'm still judged for what I am and what I'm not. No one gives a shit *who* I am." I gulped in a breath, choking back tears.

"Wow." He bit his bottom lip and shook his head. "Are you done projecting on me? Can I answer your question?"

Tears slipped down my cheeks. "I don't remember my question." A sob escaped from my throat in reaction to his gentle tone.

"You asked me if I'd thought about what you need."

"Oh, yes. I guess I didn't give you a chance, did I?"

Leo smiled. "No, you didn't. I learnt more about you from your rant though."

My cheeks heated, and I placed my cool hands on them briefly.

"I don't know for sure what you need or why you're there, but from what I've seen, you don't either. I think you're struggling to be two different people, and it must be exhausting. I don't think you belong with Richard, but as I've said, I don't like thinking about that. I think all this fighting is making you miserable."

I stared at him, rendered speechless by his summation. He wasn't judging me. He had paid attention and had come to conclusions based on everything he'd seen. I'd attacked him unfairly and he'd taken it calmly.

"I'm sorry, Leo," I said eventually. "I'm a hot mess. I think I should go."

Leo reached over and lightly touched my face, instantly reigniting the heat. "I'm sorry for being angry with you. You were really impressive back there."

"Thanks." I tried to smile, but my mind was jumbled.

"Take care of yourself, Juliette."

"You too."

I got out of his car and watched him drive away, feeling depressed and lonely.

# CHAPTER 17

*Juliette*

THE ONLY THING I ACHIEVED over the weekend was finding a dress to wear to Juniper's wedding next weekend. Determined to avoid the designer boutiques my mother insisted my dresses be bought from, I ventured past the inner-city urban edge of Brunswick Road to a shopping district with Sia. We hopped on the number nineteen tram heading north, and soon we were in the heart of Sydney Road shopping heaven. In a two-block radius, we were presented with a multitude of fashion stores filled with relatively inexpensive one-offs. Sia always told me it was hit or miss, but luckily for me, on my very first visit, I scored a home run.

Careful to stay away from whites, ivories and creams, I opted for a navy blue number with a sequined bodice, a layered skirt and a jewelled waist band. It was feminine, and in all honesty, wasn't dissimilar from something my mother would have chosen, other than the tiny price tag that included shoes. The difference was that *I'd* chosen it, *I'd* paid for it and if I spilt something down it, no one was going to give me a hard time. I was taking ownership of something as small as buying a dress, but it felt massive, liberating, and I didn't think I would ever love a dress more.

I struggled out of bed on Monday morning. I was sure I'd caught a few hours of sleep here or there, but I had so many thoughts running through my mind it was difficult to shut off. The recurring thought was that my adolescence and young adult life was a sham, glossed over by my futile attempt to save my mother. The worst part was that on some level, I'd known it was futile, but I'd done nothing about it. Actually, it was worse than that. I'd just dug myself in deeper by staying with Richard for so long.

I knew what I had to do. I didn't love him, I never would and I didn't think he loved me either. He had already seen my façade begin to crack. My feelings of guilt were solely for my mother and how miserable her life must have been to focus with such blinkered determination for her role of puppeteer. I would find a way to make her understand.

Two espressos from George later and I was as ready as I was ever going to be to face a new week. Crossing the bridge into the city, I was shocked to see council workers with bolt cutters removing the padlocks. Despite the sadness I felt for all the genuine love represented there, I was thrilled, and a small chuckle bubbled out of me. If I'd been looking for a sign, surely that would've been it.

When I got to my desk, I slumped down in my chair and sighed. It was going to be a really long day and it had only just begun. As if sent to taunt me, the first email I saw was from Richard confirming he'd pick me up after work at seven for dinner with our socially-acceptable married friends, Fraser and Stacy. Richard and Fraser worked together as financial advisers, and Stacy and I had gone to school together. I'd seen my mother's tight smile, and I could've sworn her blue eyes turned green when she found out Stacy was pregnant. I was happy for them, but I just didn't want the same things at twenty-five. I didn't want them with Richard at any age.

Thanks to my impossible workload, the day passed quickly, and at seven on the dot, Richard texted me. He was downstairs waiting. I shut my computer down and stared as the fading screen turned to black before gathering my things and heading to the lifts. I wanted nothing more than to just go home, change into my pyjamas and go to sleep with the covers over my head. Instead, I had to pull myself together and suck it up.

Richard was leaning against a 'No parking' pole, talking on the phone when I exited the building. I couldn't hear what he was saying, but he appeared flustered and more worked up than I'd seen him before. I moved closer, intrigued.

"It's all under control. I'll take care of it."

I presumed it was something to do with work, but it was unusual to see him rattled. He liked to be seen as the big man of the finance world, invincible and above everyone else. My career was of little consequence to him, and the only time he made any reference to it was with smutty secretary jokes. When he ended his phone call and looked up, he appeared startled to see me so close. His nervous expression disappeared and a mask came down, revealing smooth features and a fake smile. I could actually see it happening, and I wondered if I'd just been oblivious to it before. Perhaps I didn't know him any better than he knew me.

"Who was on the phone?" I asked without greeting him.

He looked guilty for some reason. "Oh, um, that was just a punter." He took a few steps closer. "Nothing for you to worry about."

If I'd known who was on the phone and that it was me being discussed, I might have pushed. I might have pushed so hard he would have hit the ground. Then I might have crushed his skull into the pavement, spilling his worthless brain matter into the gutter where it belonged.

"So, where are we having dinner?" I asked, happily changing the subject.

# CHAPTER 18

## Juliette

DINNER WAS MORE EXCRUCIATING THAN I'd expected. Stacy drivelled on and on about her pregnancy like she was the first woman ever to experience it. Intermingled with that riveting conversation topic, I also endured Richard and Fraser discussing the commissions they'd made that week. I could've sworn they licked their lips when they referred to their clients as 'punters' and the latest deals as 'money for jam.' Considering my mother's foundation was one of his major clients, it made me sick. Their attitudes were what gave financial advisers a bad name, and I was embarrassed I had just let their behaviour slide. I had an overused self-preservation mechanism. I heard words come from people's mouths and my subconscious knew when to nod, smile or make a polite, innocuous query. But I had never really listened. Until now.

"Hey, Juliette. I have a new joke for you," Richard said, gripping my thigh under the table when we were seated at dinner.

I cringed, pushing his hand away, knowing another

bad secretary joke was the last thing I wanted to hear from his mouth at that point.

"Richard," I said through gritted teeth. "I'd really appreciate you not belittling my job in front of our friends."

He laughed and took another long swig of his wine, either oblivious to me or pretending he hadn't heard.

Fraser and Stacy laughed nervously. I'd always just gone along with Richard's jokes at my expense. I'd never stood up for myself before. Richard was too busy swigging his wine and laughing. My mind was flooded with memories of all the little things he'd said during our relationship. A little jab here and there, his pretentious behaviour in public and our absolute lack of chemistry. I shuddered, remembering his rude behaviour towards Leo at my mother's Yarra Valley function. It all flooded in, and I felt a rage welling in my gut.

Slurring slightly, he began. "A secretary was helping her new boss set up his computer—"

I slammed my hand down on the table and cut him off. "I told you I didn't appreciate your rude jokes at my expense."

Richard waved his hand at me dismissively. "Don't be so sensitive, Juliette."

My thoughts turned into words, and they spilled out of my mouth before I had a chance to restrain them. "I was going to wait till later, but I want you to be sober enough to understand what I'm about to say."

Richard put his wine glass down and sat back in his chair, crossing his arms over his chest. "What's up, my love?" His asinine tone grated on me. *Patronising bastard.*

I turned to Stacy and Fraser, who were sitting rigid like stunned mullets. "I'm sorry, but I can't take one more second of this." I turned back to Richard. "We need to talk."

Without any obvious reaction good or bad, he wiped a few drops of wine from the edges of his lips with his linen napkin. He pushed back from the table and stood up. Leaning forward, he whispered in my ear, his wine-soaked breath making me flinch. "Don't you dare make a scene in front of our friends, Juliette." He gripped my arm so tightly I was confident he would leave a mark. "Let's take this outside." Without waiting for my agreement, he made our apologies to Stacy and Fraser then dragged me out of my seat, through the restaurant and out onto the footpath.

He didn't stop directly outside, and I quickly found myself in the darkened confines of a deserted alleyway running between the next two buildings. A dirty grey rat scuttled off, scattering onion skins over the damp cobblestones.

"What the fuck was that about?" Richard asked, pushing me roughly—one hand pinned my left arm to the cold brick wall while the palm of his other hand pushed against my chest. "You need to cool off, and then you need to go back inside and apologise for embarrassing me."

"Get your hands off me right now." I spat the words out, overcome by the desire to end him on the spot. "This is over. We're over. Do you get that? I don't want you touching me again."

He didn't let me go. His grip tightened on my arm while his other hand moved up to my throat, squeezing momentarily before slowly moving down my neck and chest. I knew I could have him writhing on the floor in seconds, but I wanted to hear him acknowledge we were over first.

His sneer turned into a thin-lipped smile as his knuckles grazed my breasts. "We're over when I say we're over, Juliette. What happened to Mummy's good little girl? You're so pathetic." He grabbed the hem of my skirt, wrenching it up.

Years of emotional abuse crashed down around me. He was right. My life was pathetic, and I'd allowed others to steer my life choices. I was taking control though, and he was making it increasingly easy to be sure of my decision to end our relationship. I heard his snide words loud and clear, and they were making me mad.

I reefed my left hand out of his and pushed him hard in the chest, out of my personal space. "Get off me, you son of a bitch."

The next thing I knew, I felt a hand connect with my cheek. The bastard had slapped me. *Who the fuck was he?*

"You're mine, Juliette." His voice was rough, and his eyes were almost black with a hatred I'd never seen before.

I took a few calming breaths as I watched his arrogant face smile in satisfaction at his perceived dominance. Banking on the element of surprise, I went for the sucker punch. My clenched fist, propelled by anger and resentment, landed in the solar plexus—the soft tissue between the middle portion of the chest and the abdominal muscles. I was quietly thrilled by his shocked expression and his struggle to draw breath. I had successfully winded him.

"Don't ever touch me again, Dick." I knew I should've run, but I took up a defensive stance and waited for him to recover.

He slowly stood up, rubbing his chest. "Your mother is right. You're unstable."

I took a step towards him and he took one back, glancing over his shoulder back up the alleyway. I hoped he was scared. He should've been. I had a lifetime of suppressed anger rising to the surface, and I had self-defence training to back it up.

"I'll pack up anything that's yours in my apartment and have it delivered to your place."

"This isn't over." He motioned between us.

"This should never have started," I replied, incredulous he would still want anything to do with me.

He began walking away from me towards the busy street. Halfway, he turned and spoke with a quiet confidence. "Watch your back, my love." He said *my love* with such hatred; the irony wasn't lost on me.

I stood in the dark alley and watched Richard retreat. I was sure his ominous words were just about him wanting the last word.

Checking my watch to make sure it wasn't too late, I called my father. Mum played Bridge on Monday nights, so I knew he'd be home alone.

"Juliette. Is everything okay?"

"Hi, Dad. I... I need you to keep an eye on Mum."

"What are you talking about?"

"She's going to be angry with me, and I don't want her overreacting."

"Why will she be angry with you?"

"I just broke up with Richard."

"Oh."

I hated having this conversation with my father. It was awkward, but he was the best placed to know if she was going into meltdown territory.

"I'll give her a call tomorrow, but just in case she speaks to Richard tonight, I wanted to let you know she might not take it well."

"I'm sure she'll be fine."

"Okay, Dad. Just giving you a heads-up. She was

really invested in our relationship."

"Okay. If there's nothing else, I really need to get back to work. Thanks for calling though."

I rolled my eyes and said goodbye.

# CHAPTER 19

## Juliette

"HOLY SHIT, JULES. YOU LOOK awful. Are you okay?"

Sia's greeting in the office lobby the next morning reinforced the reason I knew I should avoid all reflective surfaces for the next few hours at least. "Thanks. I haven't been sleeping well lately."

When the lift doors opened, too many people pushed forward to get in. Sia and I found ourselves jammed into the back corner like sardines.

"Too much crazy sex with your hot man," she whispered, trying to stifle a giggle.

I just smiled and shook my head. She couldn't have been further from the truth.

"Are you okay?" she asked, sounding concerned.

"Lunch today?" I asked as we got out on the fifth floor before going our separate ways.

"Of course. I'll meet back here around one?"

I nodded, making a mental note to ask her why she didn't want to come to my desk, then watched her saunter away, swaying her hips in an exaggerated fashion.

*Crazy girl,* I thought to myself.

Heath was in the morning meeting when I got to my desk, so I took the opportunity to call Mum. Even though I had finally done the right thing breaking up with Richard, I knew she would think otherwise, and I was worried about her.

"Yes?"

"Hi, Mum. How are you?" I said through clenched teeth.

"Fine."

"I presume you heard."

"Yes."

"Are you okay?"

"Look, Juliette. I'm a bit busy at the moment. The world doesn't revolve around you and your dramas, you know."

I shook my head. I really couldn't win.

"Okay, Mum. I'll speak to you soon, then."

She hung up, and I swallowed the lump in my throat. I would've preferred her to yell and scream at me.

~~~~~

"So what's up with you?" Sia asked when we were settled at a lunch table several hours later.

I looked down at my soup and stirred slowly. When I looked up, I could see genuine concern and I knew I needed to be honest with her. I *wanted* to be honest with someone.

"I broke up with Richard last night."

Sia's mouth dropped open and her eyes widened. "What? Are you serious? Why? What happened?"

"The short story is I met someone else."

Sia nearly choked on her noodles and had to take a

swig from her water bottle.

"Are you serious? Who? Where?" She leant forward and rested her elbows on the table. "Did you cheat on Richard?"

"No!" I was a little offended. "Nothing has happened. I just met someone who made me feel something I've never felt before, and it made me reassess a lot of things in my life."

"Sounds like you need to tell me the long story."

"We just want different things. I wasn't as happy as you thought I was with him."

Shaking her head, she paused for a minute. "So how did Richard take the breakup?" Did he have any idea?"

"He actually took it far worse than I expected. I've seen him get angry before, but he really flipped out when I insisted we were over. He got quite aggressive. At first I thought it was because I embarrassed him in front of his friends, but then he got angrier when we were alone. I don't get it."

"How aggressive are we talking?"

I instinctively cradled my cheek. It had been a limp slap, and the slight redness had faded. I'd managed to hide what was left of the mark with makeup. "Nothing I couldn't handle, but it was a wakeup call. I saw a whole new side to him."

"You know that's why a lot of people insist on a prenup before they get married? It's impossible to foresee how anyone will behave when things go sour. It's so easy to think both of you will be rational and fair if it doesn't work out, but if one party feels slighted, shit can hit the fan."

"Lucky we're not married, I guess." I laughed humourlessly.

"Hey, speaking of weddings, it's Zac and Juniper's this weekend. I'll let them know Richard won't be coming."

"Thank you. Hope that's not a big inconvenience."

Richard didn't like Sia. He'd only met her once but had deemed her beneath us because her family was working class. I was ashamed of how long I'd stayed with him.

"It'll be absolutely fine. As long as you're okay. I'm here for you. I hope you know that."

"I do. Thank you." I pointed at her with my fork. "Now tell me how it's going with Heath." I scrunched up my nose. "Spare me any details from the bedroom though."

"Oh, we called it quits. You were right. Total workaholic, but we had some fun. He has the most enormous penis."

It was then my turn to choke on my lunch before laughing so hard soup came out my nose. When I'd recovered, Sia filled me in on her short-lived, raunchy affair with Heath. It was far too much information for me, but she appeared happy. I wasn't sure how I was going to look my boss in the eye.

The next few days passed in a blur of rollercoaster emotions and too much work. By the time Thursday evening rolled around, I was ready to take out some of my frustrations.

"Steady on, Jules." Zac put one hand on my shoulder and stilled the swinging bag with the other. "Take it easy."

I'd been letting loose on the punching bag suspended from the ceiling. I was already dripping with sweat, and our session hadn't even started yet.

I stepped back from the bag, puffing, and Zac undid my boxing gloves. "I'm fine. I think I'm warmed up now." I smiled. I'd been imagining Richard's head when I put the full force behind every punch.

Mum had called me several times a day, leaving

increasingly irate messages, but she didn't seem to be melting down. I'd answered the first few times but soon realised the conversations were getting us nowhere. She thought I was making a big mistake throwing away someone as wonderful as Richard and was adamant I was going to come to my senses.

The fact that Richard and I'd had no face-to-face contact since we parted ways in the alley was a relief. I couldn't deal with the histrionics from both of them. Out of courtesy, I'd emailed him about Zac and Juniper's wedding to let him know his attendance was no longer required. I'd received no reply.

"Juniper told me about you and Richard splitting up." He put his hand on my shoulder. "Good riddance, I say. The guy was a dick."

I snapped my head up. "Really?" I'd never heard Zac speak badly about anyone, and his candour surprised me.

"I only met him that one time, but I got a bad feeling. I know you can do so much better."

It was good to know I had someone else on my side. I'd committed social suicide when I broke up with Richard, and that was actually fine by me. The likes of Fraser and Stacy had never been people I would choose to spend my time with. I'd always been really happy in my own company, but I was glad to have a few real friends.

Zac started the session slower than usual, perhaps giving me a chance to recover from my self-imposed gruelling warm-up. I'd been looking forward to seeing Zac all week, and I didn't want him to go easy on me—I wanted to be pushed hard. I didn't feel like falling apart. I did, however, feel anger towards my parents, towards Richard, but primarily towards myself. That was enough anger to push to the next level of my training.

"Holy shit, Jules," Zac said, shaking his head. It was the first time I'd managed to blindside him and, for a few seconds, I'd had the upper hand. It didn't last and Zac regained his superiority, but for those few seconds, it was exhilarating.

I left the gym that night feeling energised and happy. As I'd walked out the door, I automatically looked around for Richard. It was second nature, and when I realised what I was doing, I smiled knowing I wouldn't have to play along anymore. Practically skipping up the street, I became aware of the hair standing up on the back of my neck. It was hard to describe, but I felt watched and I couldn't help stopping to look behind me. There were plenty of people around, so it was impossible to know if anyone was actually following me. It was just an uneasy feeling I couldn't shake. Perhaps the guy from fight night hadn't gotten the hint after all.

"Can you spare a dollar?" I practically jumped out of my skin when I turned back the way I was walking and was confronted by a man holding his cap out to me.

I reached into my bag, grabbed some loose change and put it in his cap.

"Thanks, pretty lady. God bless you."

I smiled, then jogged the rest of the way home despite my tired muscles. Richard's parting words from the night we broke up had bothered me. *Watch your back, my love.* His display of aggression on Monday night replayed over and over in my head. He had been a stranger. Clearly, neither of us had shown our true colours for the full course of our relationship. I was starting to worry that his mask was shielding something far more sinister than my miserable and misguided quest.

# CHAPTER 20

## LEO

I'D SPENT ALL WEEK THINKING about her, and working on the stone wall at the farm did nothing to alter that. Juliette was irrevocably under my skin.

*Smack.*

It made no sense, but I knew there was nothing I could do about it. The physical attraction was clear as day—we were drawn to each other like magnets. She was drop dead fucking gorgeous, and the lust I'd seen in her eyes convinced me of our mutual desire.

*Smack.*

But it was more than that. Much more. I wanted to know every detail about her. That was a first for me.

*Smack.*

Was I that much of a masochist that I wanted a girl obviously laden with baggage, potentially unstable and attached to a man who couldn't be less like me? Plenty of girls had made their interest known, but none of them had registered anything close to what I felt when I made eye contact with Juliette on fight night, or when I touched her briefly, or when I saw her mask settling over her perfect features and turning her to ice. Perhaps it made perfect sense, and our lives were destined to collide exactly when they did.

*Smack. Smack. Smack.*

I dropped the mallet down on the rough earth and picked up my chisel and straight edge to smooth off one of the surfaces of the first stone I'd worked on in years.

I wasn't ready to work on the house yet, so I'd decided to start on the drywall boundary—one of the features I loved most. My grandfather had built it with his own hands, and my father had shown me the technique when it had needed repairs over the years we still lived there.

"Leo!" Bea's voice called out.

I looked up towards the house and saw her standing next to her yellow bug. "Over here." I watched her turn and acknowledge me with a wave before wandering over.

"I was just at Beans, and Kayla said you were headed here. I had to see it for myself. Never thought I'd see the day," she said with a sad smile.

"It's not such a big deal." I picked up my discarded shirt and wiped the sweat from my face and chest.

"It is a big deal, Leo."

I shrugged my shoulders. I knew Bea, and Angus to a lesser extent, struggled with the fact that I wouldn't talk about what happened five years ago, but verbalising it wouldn't change anything.

"Leo Ashlar bashing on rocks again. That makes me happy."

"I'm rusty as hell." I bent over and sifted through my tool box, looking for something I wanted to show her. I found it behind the mallet head tooth chisel. "I could do with a break."

We both walked over to the gazebo and sat down. I opened my palm for her, revealing a winged horse carved from stone. "I found him this morning when I went looking for my tools in the shed. Do you remember him?"

Bea took it from me, cradling it gently in her hands. "Oh my God. You were totally obsessed with Pegasus and all those Greek myths. I'd totally forgotten about this little guy. He was your favourite, wasn't he?"

I nodded as Bea's finger gently traced the intricate curves, her eyes glassy. A few tears slipped down her cheeks. "Where are all the others?"

"I'm not sure." I took the small horse back from her and wondered how something so small could hold so many memories. "I haven't seen them in a long time." I looked up to see Bea's tear-stained face.

"I'm sorry, Bea." I moved closer to her and touched her shoulder. I would've given her a hug if I weren't dirty and sweaty. "I didn't mean to upset you."

"No. No. I'm hormonal. I cried at a toilet paper commercial last night. I'm so glad you found him. He brings back such good memories of..." She couldn't finish her sentence, but I knew what she meant. Bea wiped her eyes with the back of her hand. "So you're here and you're fixing the wall. Does this mean you're ready to talk?"

I wiped my brow with the back of my arm and shifted on my seat. "There's nothing to talk about." I glanced up to the old, run-down stone house and closed my eyes, wishing looking at it didn't bring back such horrifying memories.

Bea was clearly unhappy, so I said the one thing I knew would cheer her up.

"I met a girl."

Her eyes lit up. "What?"

"I met a girl who... well, she kind of rocked my world." Images of Juliette were now a permanent fixture in my mind.

"Oh my God. This is amazing. When are you seeing her again?"

"Don't get too excited. She's got a boyfriend." I felt irritated to my core even thinking about him. "She's way out of my league, but she's further out of his league."

"Sounds like you're jealous." Bea's recently-teary eyes flashed with delight.

"Attached women are *not* my type, Bea. Plus she's from a different world."

"Well, it's great someone has finally made a small dent."

"I don't have a wall up, Bea. I just hadn't met the right girl."

Bea nodded. "Right girl, wrong time?"

"Pretty much." I stared at the floor.

Bea picked up her bag and stood up. "Angus and I have a wedding in the city at five. Family friends of Angus's. Honestly, I'd much rather stay home on the couch with a tub of ice cream, but we're committed. You know how much I hate the city."

"Have fun with that. I'm going to put in a few more hours here before heading back to the city. I'm working tonight."

"Oh yeah. The new gig. Where is it?"

"Just off Liverpool Street—it doesn't have a name. The manager just gave me directions to the door."

"Hey. How was Kayla doing this morning when you were there?"

"She seemed to have it all under control." I put my arm around her shoulders as we walked towards her car.

"You know she's completely in love with you, right?" She shook her head and laughed.

"She knows the score." I grimaced, remembering her trying to clean up some crumbs on my trousers and lingering too long on my crotch. "She appeared to be doing a good job for you, and that's the main thing."

"I'll have a word to her anyway. I don't want her flirting with you in front of my other customers."

I hugged her and held the door as she climbed in.

"We might stop by on our way home from the wedding. It's in the botanical gardens, so we'll be close by. Who knows the next time I'll back be there." She smiled.

"I'll text you directions. Have a great night, Bea."

I watched her car bump along out to the road, vowing I would fix the cobbled stone driveway next.

# CHAPTER 21

## Juliette

COMING HOME FROM FRIDAY NIGHT drinks last night, I once again got the feeling I was being watched. It was nothing concrete exactly, just a strange sensation backed up by no evidence. I had one more week to wait for fight night, and the need for it was palpable. I could've easily caught a cab home, but I refused to allow fear to infiltrate my psyche. Choosing the side streets and alleyways over the well-lit main roads, I purposely took the long way home.

I'd caught sight of a man in a dark grey hoodie, ducking out of sight when I looked his way. When I reached the river, I waited by a closed paper stand for him to appear again. Fifteen minutes passed and no one approached, so I gave up and wandered home, lost in my thoughts. *Was it the same guy? Why was he still following me? What could he possibly want?*

Sia and Juniper had insisted I spend the morning with them getting primped and preened for the wedding. I loved Juniper, but she reminded me of whom I was meant to be. She had dreamed of her wedding day all her life, and everything was going to be perfect. For her family to be able to afford such a premium venue, the wedding was being held in winter rather than the more popular warmer seasons.

Sia kept asking about the mystery man and the big changes in my life, but I remained tight lipped. Richard and I'd been together for three years and broken up for less than a week. It wasn't a case of getting over him, because I don't think I was actually ever *on* him. I just didn't want to talk about my love life. I was more than happy to concentrate on Juniper's. I headed home just after lunch and spent a few hours tending my little garden and reading.

The wedding ceremony was being held at Gardens House in the Royal Botanic Gardens at five, followed by a reception cocktail party. It was walking distance, but in my silver heels it felt like a marathon. With my overcoat shielding me from the cold, I made my way into the heart of the Gardens and found the beautiful double-storey Georgian house. A marquee had been set up on the manicured lawns, presumably for the reception, but guests were milling around outside with champagne, waiting for the ceremony to begin. They were incredibly lucky it was a clear day so it could be outside. There had to have been a rock-solid plan B.

My light mood was immediately darkened by an unexpected familiar voice. "You look beautiful, my love."

My head snapped up, and my posture immediately slumped before I managed to push my shoulders back. "What are you doing here?" I seethed.

"We were invited, Juliette." His feathers weren't remotely ruffled, and he was matter-of-fact with his response. "Of course I'm here."

I took a few purposeful steps to close the distance between us so I could get right up in his face. "These are *my* friends and we're broken up. I already told them you wouldn't be attending."

"Don't be ridiculous. We haven't broken up." He gestured between us, and when his hand touched me, I flinched. "I told you this isn't over until I say so."

"And I told you never to touch me again, you arrogant bastard." I took a step back. "Trust me when I tell you we've broken up. You complained incessantly about having to go to this wedding, and suddenly you turn up when you're no longer invited. I don't get it."

"You needed some space and time to cool off and see the error of your ways. Being the gentlemen that I am, I rose above your disgraceful behaviour and decided to give you another chance."

My hands flew up in frustration. "I don't want another chance. I don't want to be with you and I don't think you want to be with me. Why are you pushing this? It doesn't make sense to me."

"Juliette!" Sia called out when she saw me and came rushing over. "You look amazing. I knew that dress was killer." She turned to Richard and scowled. "I didn't think you were coming."

"Misunderstanding, I'm afraid," Richard replied, smiling disingenuously. "I hope Juliette's dramas won't cause any catering issues."

Before Sia had a chance to reply, her mother appeared looking flustered. "It's about to begin, Sia. You need to take your place."

"Sorry, I have to run." She looked at Richard. "This is my sister's wedding day. Don't ruin it, please."

I was humiliated and so incredibly deflated. Five minutes before I'd been congratulating myself on starting afresh and moving forward, and there I was, taking shit from Richard.

When Sia and her mother left, I took a deep breath.

"Just stay away from me tonight. I don't know why you're here, but Zac and Juniper's wedding isn't the time or place to discuss it."

Richard just laughed, an evil laugh, reminiscent of the night in the alleyway. It seemed he had other ideas about our breakup. He and my mother just didn't seem to be getting the hint that this farcical relationship was over.

I stormed off to find a seat so I could try to enjoy the ceremony. Rows of white chairs were set up on the other side of the house. Most were already occupied, but I spotted one with a handbag on it. I shuffled past a few guests lingering in the aisle.

"Excuse me," I said, trying to get the attention of the lady in the next seat with her back to me. When she turned around, I got my second surprise for the evening. "Bea! What are you doing here?"

"Jules?" She appeared as shocked as I was and quickly took her handbag off the chair so I could sit down. "I could ask you the same thing. This is my husband, Angus." She put her hand on the knee of the man sitting next to her. "Angus, this is Jules. She's my coffee-loving twin."

I leaned over Bea and shook Angus's hand. "Pleasure to meet you. So how do you guys know Zac and Juniper?"

"Zac's family and mine go way back," Angus informed me. "We haven't met his wife-to-be yet though."

"How do you know them?" Bea asked.

"My best friend at work is Juniper's sister, Sia, and Zac is my trainer at the gym."

She shook her head. "Wow. Small world."

"I've been noticing that a bit lately." I sighed, thinking of Leo and hoping my cheeks didn't look as hot as they felt.

"So where's your boyfriend?" she asked, looking

around.

"*Ex*-boyfriend. We broke up last week. Unfortunately, he's here, but I've told him to stay away from me."

"Oh. Jules, I'm sorry. Are you okay?" she asked.

"I really am." I didn't elaborate because I didn't want to talk about it.

"Shuffle up." Richard's voice cut through the mood.

I looked up into a smug face.

"Richard Sacks," Angus said in a surprisingly unfriendly tone, shaking Richard's outstretched hand. "This is my wife, Beatrix."

He nodded towards Bea.

"You know each other?" I asked, shocked.

"Gussie and I worked together for a while in the city. I heard you're stuck out in some tiny regional office?"

I glanced at Angus, who was rolling his eyes. Clearly, he wasn't a Richard fan either. The group of people who disliked my ex was getting bigger.

We all shuffled along to make room for him to sit next to me on the aisle.

The music playing through the speakers stopped and the Wedding March started. The audience fell silent and turned around, waiting to see the bride. Juniper passed us in a silver satin gown with shoestring straps and a fluffy stole wrapped around her shoulders. She was breathtaking. My eyes glazed over when I was hit with a sudden rush of emotion, and I felt like I might cry from seeing her so radiant and happy. And why wouldn't she be? She was marrying a really good guy whom she loved and was loved wholeheartedly in return. Zac spoke kindly about everyone, except Richard, but when he spoke about Juniper, it was with reverence, awe and a love I couldn't comprehend. My parents always appeared indifferent to each other, and my only long-term relationship had been a complete farce.

I watched the ceremony but didn't hear any words. My mind was drifting to a million different places at a hundred miles an hour. When everyone stood up and clapped, I was shocked back to reality and realised Richard had his arm around me. I quickly pushed him off and gave him my best glare. He just smiled. The MC announced there were drinks and canapés in the marquee while the bride, groom and families had their photos taken in the surrounding gardens.

As the evening wore on, I found it increasingly irritating that Richard wouldn't leave me alone. There were only so many times I could use the bathroom, but it was my favourite excuse, as he couldn't come with me.

"I need to go, too," Bea said.

"Don't be too long, my love," Richard said as we moved away from the group.

The toilets were on the ground level of the Georgian house.

"What's going on there?" Bea asked when we were out of earshot. "He isn't acting like an ex-boyfriend."

"I honestly have no idea," I replied. "He just won't accept we've broken up, and it's getting really irritating. I don't get it. We weren't good together."

"I hope I'm not speaking out of turn, but Angus said he was a real piece of work. He doesn't trust him."

My heart sank further, and I made a mental note to speak to my mother, given her charity was Richard's major client. Angus and Zac both saw something untoward about the guy when I'd been completely oblivious. I'd never considered myself to have a great radar for these types of things, but surely I could have had an inkling that there was something seriously off about my boyfriend of almost three years.

We returned to the marquee in time for the speeches.

Sia, as maid of honour, spoke first.

"Good evening, friends and family," she began. "Thank you for being with us today to witness my gorgeous big sister, who also happens to be my best friend, marry the love of her life, my new brother-in-law, Zac. Something not many of you might know is that Juniper was the Saint of Comedy. Despite the fact my sister wasn't named after the saint, I think it's fitting nonetheless. By the way, she wasn't named after the small evergreen shrub either." Everyone chuckled, and I wondered what she *was* named after. "Juni is the funniest, kindest and most loving person I know, and she deserves the happiness she found with Zac."

"Awwwwww," the audience sighed out loud.

I looked over at Zac and Juniper, and they kissed lightly on the lips. Then Zac kissed her cheek. They were such a beautiful couple.

"Anyway, I'm going to embarrass my sister now. We met Zac on a night out with friends. It was obvious to everyone there that they had an immediate connection. On our way home that night, she told me Zac was the one, he was her wonderlove. I rolled my eyes, obviously. 'Don't you mean wanderlust?' I suggested. Her reply has stayed with me ever since.

"'No,' she confirmed. 'Wonderlust is when you're not sure if you're lusting after someone or if you're actually in love. Wonderlove is when you're so goddamn sure you're in love, you wonder how you'll breathe without them. You wonder how your heart hadn't burst right out of your chest when you met. You don't wonder if they feel the same way because you know they do. Wonderlove is once in a lifetime, life-altering, it's blinding and it's worth fighting for. Zac is my wonderlove and I'm his.'"

"It's true," Juniper said, tears running down her face.

"It's obvious to everyone in this room that we're celebrating wonderlove here tonight and, my beautiful sister, I couldn't be happier for you."

Everyone clapped.

"Oh, and one more thing. You know you were named after Juniper berries that flavoured Mum's gin, right?" She held up her champagne glass to toast. "To wonderlove."

"Wonderlove," the audience repeated.

Everyone clapped as she left the podium.

I was having trouble getting Leo out of my head, and I realised how much I wanted to see him again.

"Are you okay, Jules?" Bea asked. "You look pale."

"I think I might get some fresh air," I replied, smiling half-heartedly.

Realising I hadn't seen Richard in a while, I glanced around the marquee. He had disappeared, and for some reason, that made me feel uneasy. I decided I would confront him away from the other guests in an attempt to get some answers. Excusing myself from Bea, Angus and a few others in our circle, I grabbed my coat and headed towards the exit. A waiter offered me another glass of champagne, which I took gratefully. A little extra Dutch courage couldn't hurt. It was dark and cold outside, and I wrapped my coat around me tighter. Looking both ways, I turned left and walked the long side of the marquee. As I rounded the corner, I saw him leaning up against a tree, smoking a cigarette. He puffed rings of smoke.

"How sweet. Missed me, did you?" His voice and manner dripped with sarcasm and made my skin crawl.

"Not a chance. I'm just trying to work out why you're here in the first place."

"Can you really not see what's going on? If you value your safety and those you care about, I'd suggest you get back on board with our relationship."

"What the fuck are you talking about?" I took a few steps towards him and saw his eyes blacken.

"I don't actually want to see anything bad happen. Just pull your head in and let's go back to the way things were."

I was rendered speechless as my brain tried to process his words. As they sunk in, I felt nauseous. Was he really threatening my friends' safety because I broke up with him?

"Let me go, Richard." I didn't want to fight with him again. I just wanted him out of my life. "We don't belong together, and the sooner you realise that, the better. We're over. I broke up with you, and even if you don't like it, bad luck."

He threw his arms in the air. "I knew that bartender was trouble. You're different since you laid eyes on him."

"Go to Hell, Richard." I started walking away, realising I couldn't breathe the same air as him for another second. Before I got too far, I was grabbed around the waist and shoved up against the closest tree.

"Listen here, you unstable little freak." He had both my arms pinned to the tree on either side of me. "You need to get down off your high horse and start playing ball."

"Or what?" I seethed, barely able to refrain from spitting in his face.

"Or—"

Richard was yanked off me before he could finish his sentence.

"What the fuck?" Angus was holding Richard in a vise grip, and Bea was standing next to him, stunned.

"Are you okay?" Bea asked, hurrying forward to check on me.

I pushed myself off the tree and dusted off. Bits of bark were stuck to the back of my dress, and my hair was no doubt a teased mess. "I'm fine, thanks." I stormed past all three of them and made for the ladies' room, desperately wanting to fix myself up and calm down.

Bea appeared next to me, and I locked eyes with her reflection. She put her arm around me and held my gaze. I felt strengthened by her show of solidarity and refused to let the threatening tears fall. "Angus and I are leaving. We're going to have a quick drink with a friend in the city. Will you come with us?"

I was ready to leave but not ready to go home by myself yet, so I nodded my agreement. "I'll just say goodbye to Sia, Juniper and Zac."

It took ages to leave as suspected. Sia was drunk and wanted me to stay and dance with her. It was almost midnight when, half an hour later, we were in Bea's yellow VW.

"I'm sorry about the dramas with Richard," I said, embarrassed by the whole scene we'd caused. "He's taking our breakup really badly."

"That was pretty fucked up, Juliette," Angus said, turning to face me in the back seat. "You should be careful, and if he threatens you again, call the police. Get a restraining order against him."

"I will." Richard had always been so harmless. It all seemed completely ludicrous.

We found a place to park the car, and Bea consulted her phone for directions. "Apparently this place is so cool it doesn't even have a name." She rolled her eyes, and I couldn't help laughing. She was so down-to-earth it was refreshing.

# CHAPTER 22

## LEO

THE BAR WAS A LITTLE out of the ordinary. The non-descript door in the alleyway opened up to an impressive setup. Exposed brick walls were painted white, and projectors were playing a mash-up of movies from varying decades and genres. When I'd first arrived, I'd recognised the airport scene from *Casablanca*. Instead of Humphrey Bogart and Ingrid Bergman's voices, Dooley Wilson's *As Time Goes By* was played through the sound system. I'd been told the bar had a really good reputation amongst the locals, not just because of the cool décor, but because it literally had no name. Personally, I'd take a cold beer at a pub over these overpriced cocktails, but I needed the money and it was double time after midnight.

"You're new." It was just after midnight when a glazed-eyed redhead leaned in across the bar, pushing her boobs together and batting her eyelashes.

"First night." Despite my sexual frustration, I had no interest. "What can I get for you?"

"You're fucking hot." Her words slurred.

I shook my head. "Okay, sweetheart. Maybe you

should have water?"

"How 'bout your number?" She ran her tongue over her upper lip then bit down on her bottom one. "When do you get off?"

I'd dealt with several of these situations in the last hour, and it was getting irritating. "Against club policy, I'm afraid." I had no idea what the policy was. Placing a tall glass of iced water in front of her, I hoped she'd get the hint. I couldn't get Juliette out of my head, making every other girl simply fade away.

She fished an ice cube out of the glass and ran it down her chest towards her cleavage. She was clearly not taking the hint. Suddenly, she was pulled back, shrieking as she lost her grip on the ice cube and it disappeared into her tight-fitting top.

"Have some self-respect." Bea stepped in front of my red-headed friend with authority, rolling her eyes.

"Nice timing." I smiled to see my friend, a little surprised that she had made it instead of heading home. "How was the wedding?"

"The wedding was lovely. A few surprises." She glanced over her shoulder into the crowd.

"Well, I'm a bit surprised you came. I thought you'd be desperate to get home."

"I told you we'd stop by."

"Hang on a sec. I'll see if I can take my break now." The Martin Scorcese masterpiece, *Goodfellas,* was playing out on the walls and through the speakers. It was a perfect choice because the music had an incredible way of telling the story. *Pure genius,* I'd thought. "Layla" wasn't deafening, but we were still having trouble hearing each other over the bar. "I'll bring a beer and a soft drink over. I presume you're driving?"

"Can you bring a cocktail, too? We bumped into a friend at the wedding. She's with Angus trying to find us somewhere to sit."

"Sure." I held up my hand. "Give me five minutes."

My break was overdue, so Adriana, the manager, reluctantly agreed to my request. The bar was busy but not that big, so it was easy to locate Bea in a bright red dress. She was waving to me from the lounges on the mezzanine level overlooking the bar. I made my way up the small flight of stairs, holding a tray of drinks. New Order's "Temptation" was playing, and I knew *Pulp Fiction* would be gracing the white screen behind me.

As I got closer, I felt the hairs on the back of my neck stand up. My body was on high alert. When Bea sat back down, I knew why. A vision in navy appeared opposite her. *Juliette.* She wasn't looking my way. She was laughing at something Angus had said. It gave me a moment to stare at her insane beauty. She had looked fierce at fight night, dressed in black and wearing her attitude like armour. At her mother's charity event, she had looked like an angelic goddess in white lace, tortured by something I didn't understand. When she had appeared in my house, the ugly memories trampled all over her beauty and smeared it like blood—painful, dark red streaks. Tonight, she surpassed anything my mind could have possibly conjured up, even in my wildest fantasies. She took my breath away.

When Angus looked up, so did Juliette. I must have looked like a deer in headlights, completely paralysed, but so did she. Seconds passed without a word spoken by anyone. At least I don't think there was. I was deaf and mute, induced by the shock I felt seeing her again. Then she smiled, and I could have died on the spot. It wasn't a coy smile or a fake smirk. It was a million-megawatt grin that made me want to drop the tray of drinks, leap over the couch between us and ravish her, body and soul. I suddenly understood the French idiom 'la petite mort' or 'the little death.' I'd thought at the time it was a ridiculous way of describing the post-orgasmic state. Yet there I was, believing it was possible to be rendered unconscious with ecstasy, and I was only looking at her smile.

Breaking the silence, Angus stood up and took the tray from me just as the music changed tempo and "Stayin' Alive" from *Saturday Night Fever* pumped out around us to the squealing delight of the Saturday night crowd. "Thanks, mate. Can you join us for a few minutes?"

I hadn't yet taken my eyes off Juliette, but his question finally registered with my brain and I shook my head to snap out of it.

"I've got ten minutes." I shook Angus' hand.

"Leo," Bea said. "This is Juliette. She stopped by Beans a month or so ago, and we bumped into her at the wedding."

Juliette stood up and closed the distance between us. "Good to see you again, Leo."

When I kissed her on the cheek, her breath hitched. My whole body lit up, knowing I had an effect on hers. I felt her breath release on my ear. It was the sexiest thing I'd ever experienced. I had completely forgotten she had a boyfriend to that point, and the realisation tore strips from me. I let her hand go and stood back. She appeared mildly shaken by our brief interaction and quickly returned to her seat and took her cocktail to her perfect lips.

"Um... Excuse me. You two know each other?" Bea demanded.

Juliette and I looked at each other, willing the other to explain.

"Remember the charity function I worked at last month?"

"Of course. I'm unlikely to forget the rare occasions you come home, am I?"

"Juliette was at that function, too."

"Oh!" Bea had the lightbulb moment. "That was the same day I met you." She then turned to me and mouthed, *She's the girl.*

I opened my eyes wide, silently begging her to shut up.

"I was on my way to my mother's function when I stopped by Bea's Beans," Juliette confirmed.

I sat down next to Bea, opposite Juliette and Angus.

"So, how's this for a small world." Bea was clearly delighted by the obvious sexual tension between Juliette and me. She knew about Richard though, so she had to know it wasn't going anywhere.

"It does seem to be happening a bit lately." I caught Juliette's eyes and she held mine.

"I love this song." Juliette shocked us all when she started singing along to the Jimi Hendrix freak power anthem, "If 6 Was 9." After a few lines, she noticed we were all just watching her. "*Easy Rider?*" She looked at us expectantly.

I glanced at Bea and Angus, but they were blank-faced.

"Dennis Hopper chose the songs for the film based on what he heard on the radio in 1968." My knowledge on the subject elicited another megawatt smile from the beautiful girl opposite me.

"Thank you." She held up her cocktail. "Cheers to that."

I really fucking liked this girl.

My ten minutes were up way too quickly, and I begrudgingly returned to the bar. They promised to come and say goodbye before they left. Bea was yawning, so it wouldn't be long. Every time I saw Juliette, I felt the same way—I wanted more.

As suspected, Bea came to the bar less than an hour later.

It was around one in the morning, and the music was louder and uptempo. There was no set dancefloor, but people were dancing wherever there was room.

"Juliette wants to stay." She had to shout to make herself heard. "We offered to drive her home, but she said she was enjoying the music. Can you keep an eye on her?" She winked, probably knowing watching her was no burden.

"Sure thing." I hoisted myself up on the bar and kissed her cheek. "Thanks for coming by, gorgeous." I looked over her shoulder and saw Angus.

"Thanks, mate," he shouted, but his words were muffled by Pulp's "Mile End." I glanced around expecting to see Juliette.

"I told her to check in with you before she leaves." Bea gave me a knowing grin.

"Okay. I'll look out for her. Safe trip home."

"She broke up with the douchebag boyfriend. He was at the wedding and isn't taking it very well, but she's officially single."

My mouth opened and closed twice before I could respond.

"I really like her, Leo. Good luck."

Five minutes later, I caught sight of Juliette walking absentmindedly towards the stairs leading to the mezzanine level. She was staring at her phone, grimacing at whatever she was seeing on the screen. I wanted to make eye contact with her, but she didn't look my way and I had a queue five deep in front of me waiting for drinks.

My shift ended at two. It was one forty-five, and I hadn't seen her since shortly after Bea and Angus left. My manager asked if I could do a last glass run, and I jumped at the chance to get away from behind the bar and look for her. I hoped she hadn't left without at least saying goodbye. She had looked upset by whatever she saw on her phone, and I was worried.

The whole bar was packed with moving bodies. The movies and the soundtracks had everyone on their feet, so I had to push and shove to clear a path through the crowd. I saw her before she saw me. She was dancing by herself, unaware of the three different guys clearly waiting for an opportunity to proposition the most beautiful girl in the room—the most beautiful girl in any room. I put the few glasses I'd collected down on the nearest bar table and moved towards her. She had her eyes closed and appeared lost in her own world, moving in perfect rhythm to the beats of Whitney Houston's "I'm Every Woman."

Before I made it to her, her eyes snapped open, and she immediately found mine. No words were required. We'd already said everything that needed saying with our heated silent exchange, and my need for her was now off the charts. My pace picked up, and before I could second-guess what I was doing, my body collided with hers and our lips meshed in a desperate tangle of desire and need. My arms encircled her lithe body, and we moved as one to music I could feel but my brain could no longer identify. I wanted to think only of this girl and how perfect she felt against me. Her arms had found their way around my neck and were pulling me impossibly closer.

Eventually, our lips moved apart and she stared up at me. Her arms were still around my neck and her body still moved to the beat. My body moved on instinct, and for the longest time, I knew what it meant to be at peace. My hands were clamped to her lower back, pinning her to me. A tapping on my shoulder killed my bliss, and I turned my head without reducing my hold on Juliette.

"What happened to club policy?" The drunk redhead from earlier was standing behind me with her arms crossed over her generous chest.

"I made an exception." I turned back and kissed the top of Juliette's head. Unfortunately, the interruption reminded me that I was still at work.

"My shift is about to finish. Will you wait for me?" She looked at me with her navy eyes, and I couldn't remember my question.

She took a step back, and I immediately felt the loss of her heat. "Okay." She appeared suddenly shy and unsure.

"Don't go anywhere." I kissed her again hard on the lips. I pulled back and held her face. "Promise?"

Slightly breathless, she promised she'd wait. I dashed around, collecting empty glasses at double speed, then depositing them behind the bar.

"Nice job, Leo. Can you work next weekend?" Adriana, my manager, asked as I was collecting my wallet, keys and helmet from the locker in the staff room.

"Absolutely." I had enjoyed working at the bar far more than I thought I would, and that was even before Juliette had shown up and the night had turned into the best of my life so far.

# CHAPTER 23

*Juliette*

I WAS LOST TO LEO. Completely lost. I'd all but forgotten about my earlier altercation with Richard. Leo had made me forget about the unnerving messages I'd been sent earlier. He'd made me forget my own name with his searing kiss, his steady heartbeat, his strong arms holding me to him and the way his body felt against mine as we moved in sync.

He wanted me to wait for him. *I'd wait forever* had been my first thought to his request, and then I'd remembered the shit storm of my life and hesitated. As if sensing my waver, Leo had kissed me again, reminding me how good his lips felt on mine and how I yearned for more.

"Let's go." Leo took hold of my hand and gave me no option but to follow him towards the exit. He was now wearing a very sexy leather jacket, and my brain was firing in every direction, trying to work out what I was doing. The several cocktails I'd drunk, the heady mixture of movies and tunes I loved, the ominous text message from my increasingly sinister ex-boyfriend, all combined in a whirlwind of battling emotions. All I knew for sure was I'd wanted to see Leo again desperately.

Leo led me further up the alleyway and ducked under a heavy chain into a small parking lot. There were a few small cars, one 4WD and a motorbike. It was then I noticed the helmet he was holding in his other hand. I couldn't hide the smile that involuntarily appeared plastered across my face.

"Is that yours?" I motioned towards the sexy black machine.

"Are you game?" He held up keys and raised his eyebrows.

"Are you kidding? Of course I am." I looked down at my dress and heels, wishing I were dressed more appropriately for my first ever motorbike ride. Yet the idea of being dressed completely inappropriately filled me with glee. I walked over to the bike and ran my hand over the curly pipework and leather seat.

I felt Leo's body behind me and his lips feather kisses across my neck while he held my hair back. I turned and kissed him hard, feeling the cold metal of the sexy bike on my backside. He lifted me and placed me on the leather seat, and my legs immediately wrapped around him. I could feel his desire pressing into me, and I knew for a fact I'd never experienced real lust until that moment. Every time I'd been in Leo's presence, I was reminded of our mind-blowing connection, and I couldn't seem to get enough. He was intoxicating, and I wanted to drown in him.

When he pulled back, he stroked my face and pushed my hair behind my ears.

"Comfortable?" he asked.

"Very." I stroked the leather seat. "What sort of bike is it?"

"She's a Ducati Diavel. My baby might look like a

cruiser, but the one hundred and sixty-two horsepower Testastretta engine will give you the ride of your life."

"That might be the sexiest sentence I've ever heard." I tried to keep a straight face to mirror his serious expression but couldn't stop myself from chuckling. Leo halted my chuckling by kissing me again, and I had no problem with that whatsoever.

"That's one way to shut you up." He grinned, and I was glad I was sitting down. The whole experience with him in the bar, and now being perched on his motorbike, was beyond anything I could've imagined. I didn't want the night to end. "Bea told me you broke up with Dick. Is that true?" he asked when we came up for air.

My body shuddered as I remembered his second act of aggression towards me. "Long overdue."

He helped me get down then reached into the side compartment and retrieved a second helmet. I held still while he pushed it carefully over my head and leaned in to do up the chin strap. He threw his leg over the bike and secured his own helmet in one fluid motion. Straddling the seat, he held his hand out for me to climb on behind him.

We hadn't discussed where he'd be taking me. I knew I had to sort out my own mess of a life, but for one night I wanted to let go of everything, be irresponsible and take something for myself.

Before he turned the engine on, he turned in the seat. "Shall I take you home?"

I reached forward and wrapped my arms around his waist, whispering in his ear, "Come home with me."

Without another word, the hundred and sixty-two horse power engine roared to life. We eased slowly down the alleyway and out onto Liverpool Street. The traffic was light, but Leo still had to manoeuvre between some cars and the occasional truck. I clung to him and rested my face on his leather-clad, muscular back, soaking up the raw power of his body and the bike between my legs. I felt the acceleration out of each set of lights. The adrenaline coursing through my veins made me giddy, and laughter escaped from me. I laughed so hard it made me squeal with unbridled joy. Leo's body shook, and I could hear laughter coming from him, too.

Leo found a place to park his bike easily outside my apartment building. We walked through the lobby and waited for the lift in silence. As soon as the lift doors closed on us, I found myself pinned up against the mirrored wall. Our tongues entwined in a lust-fuelled dance of intoxicating foreplay. When the doors opened on my floor, we were both breathless and needy. Fortunately, my key was easily located in my clutch, and I let us in quickly. Leo was on me again as soon as the door closed.

"Tell me what you want." Without waiting for my reply, he kissed his way along my collarbone.

My head hit the wall gently over and over as my body lit up from his touch.

"Tell me what you want, Juliette." He repeated his question, but this time he looked me directly in the eyes.

I slowly undid my coat and let it fall to the floor. I then unzipped his leather jacket and pushed it off his shoulders, allowing it to fall to the ground. I grabbed his head and ran my hands through his hair, standing on my tiptoes to reduce the distance to his gorgeous face. Then I whispered in no uncertain terms, "I want you."

His eyes flared with lust and a small groan escaped his lips as his hands moved to the back of my thighs and scooped me off the ground. His lips immediately found mine as my legs wrapped hungrily around him. We were on the move, but I was oblivious to my surroundings, lost in his kiss, his hands kneading my thighs. My apartment wasn't big, so he had no trouble locating my bedroom. A door was kicked open, and I squealed as I became airborne, thrown backward onto my soft bed. I landed with a bounce, giggling before Leo's muscular body crashed down on me again.

I unclasped my jewelled belt and flung it off the bed. Before it hit the floor, Leo grabbed the hem of my dress and roughly dragged it up and over my head. Desperate to feel him skin-to-skin, I did the same with his t-shirt then started work on his belt buckle. I was taking too much time, so he pushed my hands aside and ripped it off, flinging it to join mine on the floor. My hands greedily unzipped his trousers but were pinned to the bed above my head before I could make any further progress.

His mouth devoured mine. Our tongues intertwined in a frenzied collision of desire, and all I could think about was how much I wanted this man. I wanted him with every fibre of my being. One of his hands continued to hold both of mine in place while the other grazed down my body, leaving a hot, fiery trail. By the time he reached my inner thighs, I was ready to combust. His mouth found its way to my chest. His free hand moved from my thigh to my strapless bra, pulling down the cups to expose my breasts to his strong, sensual tongue. My back arched in ecstasy, allowing his hand to move under me and unsnap the clasp. I quickly found myself naked from the waist up, writhing, willing him to resume his attention. I was rewarded when his mouth closed down over my left breast, sending me into a tailspin of pleasure. My right leg hooked over his backside, pushing his hardness into me, and our groans tried to outdo the other as the heat between us hit fever pitch.

When his mouth moved to my right breast, my eyes rolled back into my head. I had never experienced anything close to this pleasure, and I was still wearing my underwear.

"Oh my God, Leo." I panted the words as my desperation for him to take me increased.

"I want to savour you." Both his hands roamed my body while his mouth came down over mine, and our kiss was tender, reinforcing his words.

With my hands now freed, I took matters into my own hands. I pulled at my G-string and wiggled it down my body before going to work on his trousers and boxers.

"Steady on, my little minx."

I was way too turned on to be remotely embarrassed by my forwardness, and it would have been fleeting anyway as Leo grabbed a condom from his wallet in his discarded trousers.

As he ripped the packet, I glanced down and gasped.

*Holy shit!* I thought, gritting my teeth with a mixture of fear and excitement at my impending impalement.

"Still in a hurry?" Leo asked with a smug grin, positioning himself between my thighs. His lower arms rested on either side of my head, and his thumbs caressed my cheekbones.

I answered by whipping my legs around and giving his backside a firm shove, pushing him straight into me. We were both caught by surprise as he filled me completely. My legs tightened around him, eager to hold on to the incredible sensations flooding my whole body. Leo hovered over me, staring with an expression of awe and rapture.

"You feel so fucking good," he whispered.

Rendered speechless, I grabbed his head and pulled him down, needing his mouth on mine so I could express everything I could through our kiss.

"I'm going to start moving now." He pushed in a

fraction further before retreating almost all the way out. "You feel so damn good, Jules."

I loved it when he called me Jules.

When he pushed back in, my head arched back and I willed him to keep moving. As if reading my mind, his pace picked up with each thrust. My mind was swirling in ecstasy, reaching heights I never knew existed. I could stay connected to Leo forever and want for nothing the rest of my life. When I looked up, his piercing blue eyes bored into mine with an intensity I couldn't quite handle. My head fell to the side and his thrusts halted.

"Look at me, Jules."

Wanting him to continue his sensual assault on my body, I raised my head back to his gaze.

"Are you okay?"

My eyes glazed at the extreme beauty of this man inside me. I'd seen the results of his fighting prowess bloodied on the floor. I'd seen his whole demeanour change in an instant and had him cause me physical harm in his beautiful house. Yet there was another side to him—warm, gentle and caring beyond which I'd never known from a man. I loved both sides equally, and I wanted all of him.

"Don't stop." I swallowed the lump in my throat and pushed my hips up. "Please."

My plea ended any further hesitation. I soared higher and higher, reaching for the summit I was now absolutely sure was there. Higher and higher. Leo was right there with me; his eyes, wild with lust, never left mine.

"Come with me, baby."

I leapt off the cliff and sailed through our own personal oblivion. I was home.

# CHAPTER 24

## LEO

NIGHTMARES HAUNTED MY SLEEP. I watched her fall asleep in my arms. We spoke no further about the fact she'd broken up with Richard, mostly because she was giving me nothing. I knew she had baggage; I just didn't know how heavy it was. With my own set of demons, I didn't know if I was strong enough to shoulder a bigger load. Would she even want me to? It felt like hours later that I fell into a restless sleep.

Through a hazy fog, I dragged my feet as if wading through honey along the hallway of my family home. I grazed my hands along the exposed brick walls and looked down to see them bleeding. Unable to stem the sticky red flow, I continued on at a painfully slow pace. Screaming was coming from the kitchen, and I just couldn't get there. My feet wouldn't let me run, however hard I tried. Too slow. Too hard. I wanted to call out, but my voice was muted. I wanted to be frustrated, but I was too tired and confused to try any harder. My subconscious was terrified, willing me to wake from limbo.

Eventually, my body found a way to the end of the

hallway, and I stood in the doorway of the kitchen. It wasn't our kitchen though. It was a kitchen I'd seen somewhere, but I couldn't work out when or if it was even real. It was all stainless steel and marble—ultra modern and expensive. My head moved slowly around the room, features blurring into unrecognisable shapes and colours. Then my sleep-trapped mind was bombarded by a recurring horror movie, warping slightly every time.

My lifeless body dominated my vision, completely covered in blood. I was standing there staring at my own dead body. I'd heard screaming but didn't know where it had come from. I scanned the room again, and this time the rustic country kitchen I'd grown up with had returned. A streak of blonde caught my attention, and my sluggish head moved towards it. Juliette. She was holding a knife, screaming? She was crazed. Her beautiful navy eyes were black as night, and her long blonde hair clung to her head in a damp mess.

"No!" I screamed, waking me from this new version of Hell. I sat up, sweat dripping from my forehead. Placing my face in my hands, I closed my eyes again, resting on my bent knees, and took some deep, calming breaths. As my heart rate decreased, I had flashes of the night before. I sat bolt upright and looked around, quickly realising I wasn't in my own room.

Oh shit.

Juliette had gone to sleep in my arms but now had her back to me and was as far as she could get without falling off the side of the bed. Her arms were wrapped around herself protectively, and I was swamped by an overwhelming guilt. I should've just dropped her off last night. I'd been driven by lust and built-up sexual frustration and had barely stopped to think where her head was. She'd just broken up with Dick, for fuck's sake.

There was something special about this beautiful, enigmatic girl, and I felt an unprecedented connection to her. I wanted more than a one-night stand, but her subconscious body language spoke of regret.

# CHAPTER 25

## Juliette

PHENOMENAL SEX WITH LEO WAS bittersweet. Sweet wasn't quite the right word to describe such a mindblowing experience, but I did feel the bitterness creep in and take hold of me. I'd wasted so many years shielding myself from anything likely to upset my mother. A onenight stand with a bartending motorbike rider, not to mention illegal fighting champion, would definitely upset her. My phone calls with my father assured me that Mum was coping. She'd stopped calling me and selfishly, I was relieved.

Leo made me feel worshipped. For one night, I felt like the centre of someone's world rather than a disappointment. As my consciousness faded, I fought against it, wanting to hold on to the blissful sensations of his hands stroking my hair, the occasional light kiss to the top of my head. I had fallen asleep cocooned in his arms, his muscular torso a surprisingly comfortable pillow, but I woke up the same way I did when I shared my bed with Richard—with as much distance as possible between us. Annoyed at myself, I rolled over, hoping to get a chance to unashamedly admire the hottest man I'd ever seen, but instead I found myself alone. His clothes were gone and my door was closed. He must have slipped out while I slept.

I thought waking up alone after a one-night stand would involve a slew of shame, but I was completely fine with it. I wasn't going to regret it, hang my head in shame or try to force it to be something more than it was—an awesome one-night stand. I'd never known lust before Leo, and it was far more amazing than I could've imagined and then some.

Leo had demons. A big part of me wanted to know what they were and maybe help him fight them. Can you help fight someone else's demons by bringing your own set into the ring? I had no idea. What I did know was that I had a whole lot of shit going down in my life that I needed to sort out.

I got up and pulled my robe around me. I needed coffee. It was then I realised I could smell coffee and hear some clanging coming from the kitchen. I hurried towards the smells and sounds and was confronted by an unprecedented sight I wanted to photograph and put in a frame.

Leo turned towards me, a loaf of bread hanging in one hand and a coffee mug in the other. He was wearing only his black trousers, giving me a full view of his defined abs. His expression was at first unreadable, but then I watched as his eyes moved down my body before regaining eye contact. The lust flashing in his eyes could bring me to my knees, and I was grateful to be leaning on the door frame.

He closed the distance between us without dropping his gaze and kissed me as if he had no choice.

"Good morning." His husky morning voice made it so.

"A hot man's made me coffee and a sandwich. It's a

great morning."

"I heard you were a coffee lover from Bea." He handed me a steaming white mug.

"I'm a self-confessed addict, but I don't care. I love it."

I closed my eyes and pressed the mug to my lips, inhaling the steam. Feeling his eyes on me, I peeked over my mug, still holding it to my lips. He was staring at me with unashamed intensity.

After taking a long draw, I put my mug down and reached for a sandwich.

"So, about last night." It wasn't really a statement or a question. It was just a group of words thrown out there for me to do something with.

I'd already taken a mouthful, so he had to wait while I chewed slowly for my thoughts on the matter. I swallowed and placed the rest of the sandwich down.

"Look, Leo. I know the score. It's okay." I was clearly struggling to maintain his eye contact and instead stared at my remaining sandwich while I continued. "I had a really good time last night, but I don't have wild illusions of this being a happily ever after. I just came out of a long-term relationship, my life is a nightmare at the moment and I really appreciated the escape from reality you gave me last night."

Leo's brow furrowed and his jaw tightened.

He looked like he had something to say on the topic but chose not to. We had both succumbed to a lust built up from the second we laid eyes on each other. It had felt so right. We just stared at each other. I wasn't sure of what to say or do.

"Let's go sit down while you finish your sandwich." His casual tone relaxed me. "I'll be offended if you don't finish my pièce de résistance."

"You like sandwiches." It was a statement rather than a question.

"My sandwiches are epic. Don't bother denying it."

I just nodded and smiled. The smile was all for him. We sat down next to each other on the lounge.

"Please don't feel you have to stick around." I glanced at him, then took a bite of the sandwich. I had no idea what he was thinking. "I actually thought you'd left when I woke up. I'm totally fine with what this is."

"Let's get something straight right now." I was a little taken aback by his tone. "Last night shouldn't have happened."

Even though I'd said I was fine with it, I couldn't help flinching at his words of regret. I put the plate on the coffee table and propped my leg up so we were facing each other.

His eyes softened slightly before continuing. "Don't misunderstand. I wanted you, but I never wanted a one-night stand with you."

"You didn't?"

He placed his hand on my cheek, and I instinctively leaned into it. "Your strengths and your weaknesses are black and white, Juliette. I wanted to see the colours in between. I wanted to get to know who you really are behind your masks, and sex has a way of complicating things."

I was both thrilled and saddened. His only regret was not getting to know me before our first sleepover. His eyes watched me intently.

Reaching between us, he took hold of my hand. "I think I've seen a little of it already." His killer smile disarmed me. "They are moments of pure heaven."

"Tell me?" My voice shook.

"I've seen moments when you let go, and it's breathtaking. I saw you laughing with Angus and Bea at the bar last night, and I watched you dancing by yourself, oblivious to everything and everyone around you. When you fell asleep in my arms, I knew I wanted to see a whole lot more of you, Jules."

I huffed out my held breath, and my free hand clasped one of my heated cheeks. "Wow."

"That's all you have to say?" Leo chuckled.

"Thank you," I whispered.

"What are you thanking me for?" He appeared confused. "If anyone should be grateful, it should be me thanking the powers of the universe for you."

My eyes cast downwards and my cheeks warmed. "You make me feel special and..." I paused.

"And what?" he pushed.

"You make me feel special and sexy." I sneaked a glance back to his face and found a look of shock. "I've never felt sexy before."

"Are you fucking serious?" He now appeared mad. He cupped my chin and forced my eyes to his. "You're an intoxicating vixen and you're sexy as hell."

"No one has ever really seen me like you do," I whispered, an unwelcome sadness now prickling my eyes.

He kissed me lightly on the lips and reminded me how we fit so perfectly together.

"Come with me." He held out his hand and I took it without hesitation.

Leaving the plates and mugs where they were, he led me back to my bedroom. Neither of us spoke as we walked, lust crackling between us.

When we stepped into my room, he pushed me up against the wall and kissed me hard, tugging at my robe and breaking our connection for only a few seconds before crashing his lips against mine. I wrapped my arms around his neck and pressed my body into him.

"Take me right here against the wall." His lust-filled

eyes drove me wild. "I want you right now."

"Badass Juliette is a massive turn-on."

He made it to the bedside table in a few strides and retrieved what he needed. Turning, he stopped dead, perusing my completely naked body. My robe pooled at my feet. His eyes stopped on my breasts, partially hidden by my long hair.

His trousers and boxers appeared to melt off his smoking hot body. Ripping the packet open, he sheathed himself in the few seconds it took him to cross the room. I felt possessive and desperate to claim him when he picked me up and propped me against the wall. I kissed him with a need I knew was mutual. I wrapped my legs around his waist and lowered myself in one smooth motion. There was nothing awkward about sex with this man. It wasn't strained or rushed. It was as natural as breathing and, in that moment, felt as vital as oxygen.

"Leo."

As I came, his name rolled out of my mouth from somewhere deep inside me, and I felt him tense then groan out his own release. I was done for. Completely owned by a man who, in a few weeks, knew me better than anyone ever had.

He lowered me to the floor and stroked my face. His piercing blue eyes sought mine. "How about a shower?"

He kissed me lightly on the lips then pulled me towards the bathroom, where he reminded me again how sexy he found me.

Showered, dressed and thoroughly sated, we relaxed on the couch, still tired from our late night. It was far too easy to let the outside world fade away with Leo's strong arms around me. While he spoke so openly about my life, he had his own unspoken issues. *What the hell had happened in his family home that made him so edgy? Was that the reason he fought with such ferocity at fight night?*

"So how is your mother taking your breakup?" His shoulders sagged slightly. "From what little I know, she really wants you to marry Dick. She seemed kind of obsessed by it."

"Ugh. I know. She has always had my life mapped out, and I've never made a stand against her before. She's giving me the silent treatment at the moment, so I'm not exactly sure how she's taking it. Richard is pissed off enough for the both of them though."

"You're an incredible woman, Juliette." He stroked my face. "Can't blame the guy for being upset about losing you, even if he is a complete douchebag."

"I've seen a very different side of him since I broke up with him."

"What do you mean?" Leo sat up a little straighter.

I'd hesitated telling him last night, and I still wasn't sure how much to share. He had already told me he felt protective of me.

"Tell me what you meant." His eyes hardened and he clenched his jaw. "Has he hurt you?"

"He just got a little rough. Nothing I couldn't handle, but it just seemed so out of character. I think he's worried about the impact on his business. He's a financial adviser, and my mother's foundation is his biggest client." I shook my head, still confused. "I don't know why he's worried though. Sometimes I think my mother likes him more than me."

"You stay away from him. I don't give a shit what his problem is. If he touches you again, I'll rearrange his ugly mug."

My thought process regarding the man sitting next to me was shooting off on a million different tracks. Leo was an enigma. With his prowess, he could fight professionally, but instead he fought illegally, risking his safety. If that paid better, why was he working for my mother or at bars?

I asked a question I'd wondered several times. "Do you fight just for the money?"

He looked at me and briefly closed his eyes. "It's complicated."

I leaned across and kissed him. It was meant to be quick, but he bunched the front of my t-shirt and held me close so he could deepen the kiss. It was completely futile fighting my body's natural reaction to him. *Was I being selfish?* I wondered as I closed my eyes, savouring the taste of him as his tongue explored my mouth. *He might be an undefeated fighter, but outside the cage was I dangerous and unhealthy for him? Would he be better off with someone who could ease his burden with a clear head and an open heart?*

Leo pulled back and held my face. "Stop thinking and kiss me properly, woman."

I smiled against his mouth, and then I kissed him properly.

"When can I see you again?" he asked when we finally came up for air.

Sighing, I contemplated my week ahead. I had to sort out whatever was going on with Richard. "I'll call you."

"Wow. Getting the brush-off already. Don't call me, I'll call you, hey?" Leo asked, raising his eyebrows.

"It's not like that, Leo. I promise." I placed my hand on his thigh, and his hand quickly covered mine, his thumb gently tracing the rises and falls of my knuckles.

"I was only kidding. You call me when you're ready, but considering you don't have my number, it's going to be hard."

I reached for my phone. "Tell me your number. I'll call you tomorrow night." When he gave it to me, I programmed it in and then dialled it. "There you go.

Now we have each other's numbers. Problem solved!"

"I'll speak to you tomorrow, then. No pressure." He got up from the couch and retrieved his other belongings. I went down with him in the lift, and we crossed the lobby. He held my hand the whole time as if he needed to maintain contact with me. We stepped outside and stopped beside his bike.

"I do want to see you again." I meant it.

He smiled and pulled me to him. "I really don't want to go." He hugged my body like I was the most precious thing in the world, and I couldn't help snuggling into his rock-hard chest. I was again surprised by how comfortable I felt against a wall of steel. We just seemed to melt into each other.

"And I really don't want you to go."

Leo moaned as his lips crashed hungrily into mine. I was the one to pull away and douse the flames of our hot connection. I didn't want reality to set in, but I needed time to think.

"Thanks for last night." I clenched my teeth in a half smile, cringing. *Had I just thanked him for sex?*

"You're very welcome." He winked as he slipped the black helmet over his head. "Bye, Jules."

I held my hand up to wave as he pulled away.

Walking into my apartment lobby, I glanced down at my old sweat pants and faded t-shirt and realised I must look a complete mess. *If only my mother could see me now. There'd be no mistaking me for a society princess in this outfit.* I waved to Barry at the front desk. A concerned look passed across his face as he waved me over.

"How are you, Juliette?"

"Surprisingly good." My cheeks warmed with the memories of just how good.

"Sorry to be a downer, but the night concierge told me Richard was here around midnight looking for you, drunk and angry. Can I presume you have parted ways?"

"Presume away. I hope he didn't cause any trouble."

"Nothing Joel couldn't handle."

"Please tell him I'm sorry. Richard isn't taking our breakup very well."

"You look after yourself." His serious expression was filled with concern. "Richard has an aggressive edge and I don't trust him. Never have."

Another man I trusted didn't like my ex-boyfriend. It was humiliating. I knew I wasn't in love with him, but I hadn't seen what everyone around me, other than my mother, seemed to see.

"I can take care of myself, but thank you for the concern. I appreciate it."

As I took the lift to my apartment, my phone buzzed with an incoming text from Richard. When I read it, my blood ran cold.

*Did you have fun last night?*

I replied immediately. *None of your business. Leave me alone.*

*You are my business, Juliette.*

With anger boiling in my veins, I hit the call button as I let myself into my apartment.

"The bartender, Juliette. Really?"

"You have no say in who I spend my time with now. Actually, you never did."

"You're mine."

"We've broken up!" I screamed, losing my patience. "It's over."

"Your mother is right. You're such a disappointment. I am still willing to forgive you though."

"Is this about money? You're worried about losing

your precious client?" I scoffed. "Trust me. Your business is safe. And if you do anything to jeopardise the Foundation, you'll have a lawsuit on your hands quicker than you can say 'money for jam.'"

I could hear Richard chuckling. "Your father would be so proud of you. Oh no, that's right. He doesn't give a crap about you."

I staggered a little and leaned against the doorframe leading to my bedroom. "Fuck you, Richard. Just leave me alone."

"Can't do that, princess."

After a short pause, I looked at my screen and realised he'd hung up. *Gutless dickhead,* I thought to myself.

I threw my phone on the lounge. Richard was becoming a bigger problem than I'd thought. I took a deep breath and closed my eyes, allowing my mind to relive the motorbike ride and every second with Leo after that.

# CHAPTER 26

*Juliette*

I MISSED SIA. SHE WAS going to be on leave all week spending time with family who'd flown in for Juniper's wedding. Richard left messages at regular intervals, alternating between declarations of love and flat-out abuse. It was exhausting. His emotional torment, together with an undercurrent of worry for my mother I couldn't switch off, was making it hard to breathe again.

As promised, I called Leo on Monday night when I got home from work, and just hearing his voice calmed me.

"You called," he whispered on an exhale.

"I told you I would," I replied, smiling. I took a deep breath in and relaxed as I, too, exhaled.

"How was your day?"

"It was okay, I guess."

"That bad?"

I sighed. *Did I want to let him share my burden?* I really wanted to see where this could go with Leo, and telling him more about my crazy ex didn't seem like a great way to go.

"Oh, it's nothing. Just busy at work. I'm fine. What about you? Tell me about your day."

He didn't respond.

"Hello?" I thought maybe we'd lost the connection.

"I'm here. Sorry. I... I was at the farm."

I sucked in a breath, unsure of how to respond. All I knew about that place was that it was his family home and no one lived there anymore. He obviously had some kind of negative associations with the place, but he was a closed book. "What did you do there?"

"I've been restoring the drywall and the cobblestone driveway."

"Wow. Leo, you're a man of hidden talents." I was brimming with questions, but I wanted him to offer things to me freely when he felt comfortable. I wanted to earn his trust.

"I come from a long line of stonemasons. My dad taught me the craft before he died."

My heart broke hearing him say the words.

"I'm sorry." I suddenly wished he was next to me so I could wrap my arms around him and offer physical comfort. "When did he die?"

"Five years ago." His voice was so quiet I could barely hear him. "But that's enough depressing stuff. When am I going to see you again?"

I smiled. "How about Thursday night?"

"I'm working at the bar Thursday night from seven, but maybe you could stop by?"

"Okay. I'll come by after the gym. I'll grab a shower there, so I should be with you before eight."

"Perfect. I'll see you then."

"Bye, Leo."

When my father called just as I was heading to the gym after work on Thursday evening, I picked up immediately, worried something was wrong with Mum. He assured me she was fine but asked if I could meet with him now. Despite really needing the session with the fight coming up in a few days, I agreed. Something in his tone was off.

Instead of going to the gym, I grabbed a taxi. A short time later, I rang the front doorbell on my parents' luxury townhouse in Toorak. I held no positive association with this house and didn't see my visits as coming home despite having grown up there. It was just bricks and mortar in a fancy location. It was better just to avoid the place as much as possible and when necessary, steel myself for a quick visit.

"Juliette." Jean, my parents' housekeeper answered the door with warmth that didn't belong in that cold house.

I returned her hug and stepped across the threshold. The black-and-white tiled entrance foyer felt drafty. I shivered, wrapping my arms around myself.

"Your mother's gone out, sweetheart."

"I'm actually here to see my dad."

"Oh. Okay. Well, he's in his office."

"Thanks." I tried to give her a genuine smile, but my mouth just twitched instead.

Dad's office was on the second level, so I trudged up the stairs, glancing at some new artwork I hadn't seen before as I ascended. When I reached his door, I knocked lightly.

"Come in." His deep voice sounded stern, and I considered turning around and walking back out. Instead, I pushed my shoulders back and opened the door. My father was sitting at his desk and didn't look up from whatever it was he was reading.

"Hello, Juliette. Take a seat." I felt like I was there for an interview. He had a way of making me feel like a hopeful applicant, applying for a job I was never going to get.

I closed the door behind me, walked slowly across the room and then sat down awkwardly on one of the Chesterfield leather couches. I crossed my legs, uncrossed them and then crossed them again the other way. Eventually, he finished whatever it was that had his attention, closed the book then walked over from his large mahogany desk and sat down opposite me on an identical lounge, removing his glasses.

His office was the largest room in the house. It was lined on three walls with floor-to-ceiling bookshelves. A ladder was attached to runners to retrieve the books on the upper shelves. With my intense love of books and reading, it was a room I should've loved. Instead, it made me feel small and worthless. Or perhaps that was just the other person in the room.

"Thanks for coming." We made eye contact briefly but both quickly found something else to look at. It was awkward.

"Is this about Mum?" I figured I might as well cut to the chase.

"How's work?"

Shocked he would ask and even more shocked that he genuinely sounded like he cared, I stuttered my response. "Fine. Good. Busy. Err... great." My cheeks burned as I stared at my fidgeting feet on hardwood floors. I was an adult with a respectable job. I shouldn't have let him make me feel like such a failure.

"That's good. I've heard you're doing a really good job."

I snapped my head up. "Really?"

"Of course. I'm well connected, Juliette. You know

that."

"Yes. I know that. I just... I just—" I uncrossed my legs and wrung my hands nervously in my lap.

"You just what?" He stood up and walked the few steps over to my couch then sat down beside me. "You just didn't think I'd be interested in my own daughter?"

I nodded. He'd never shown any interest before, so why now?

"Where's Mum tonight?" I asked.

"She's gone to the theatre with Carol. That's why I called you." He looked uncharacteristically nervous suddenly. "I wanted to talk to you in private about her."

"Well, I'm here. What's going on?"

"She wanted to go to Richard's house to talk to him. She's worried he won't take you back."

"What?" I sat forward, horrified. "That's insane."

"I know. I talked her out of it, and thankfully she had plans with Carol tonight to distract her."

"Seriously, Dad. Can you see how messed up this is? I'm an adult and I broke up with my boyfriend. It shouldn't be such a big deal to her."

"She's barely left the house lately. I thought she was okay, but I found her crying in the bathroom this afternoon. Your breakup is really upsetting her, and I don't like it when she's upset."

I shook my head, knowing where this conversation was headed. "So you want me to stay with Richard to make Mum happy? Put my life on hold? Again." My words burned like acid on my own throat. "Same as always."

I stood up and walked a few steps away.

He called out before I made it to the door. "Wait."

I whipped around, ready to unleash some of my pent-up anger, but the look on his face made my mind go blank. I hadn't noticed before, but when I looked closer, I saw the deep lines around his eyes and the marked increase of grey hair. No longer the vital and formidable man I always pictured in my mind, he just looked old.

"She's more fragile than usual at the moment, Juliette. I don't know what to do."

I walked a few steps back. "I can't keep living my life on her terms." I felt a lump in my throat the size of a tennis ball, and I took some deep, calming breaths to stop myself from crying.

"You've always been so good at smoothing the road, and you know how she can be. I just wanted to make sure you hadn't been hasty."

Swallowing my anger, I stood motionless, torn between my natural instinct to help her and my recent realisation that nothing I ever did made the slightest bit of difference.

"I can't." My voice croaked out in little more than a whisper. "I can't keep doing this." I repeated myself with more conviction. "I'm sorry, Dad." I paused before saying the next words. "It's your turn."

His shoulders slumped and he appeared defeated. "Please sit down, Juliette."

Despite my desire to walk away while my resolve still held, something about his plea had me walking back to the couch and sitting down obediently.

"Thank you." He looked me right in the eye, and I could've sworn I saw tears threatening. Surely not. My father had never shown that kind of emotion before.

"What is it, Dad? You're scaring me."

"I think it's time I told you the real reason your mother is the way she is." He wrung his hands in his lap, and I saw another glimmer of vulnerability. "Your mother is grieving."

"Grieving? Grieving for whom?"

"She's going to be really upset with me for telling you this, but I'm worried what will happen if you walk away from her."

"I'm not walking away from her. I'm walking away from Richard."

"Wait. You need to understand."

He paused for too long. My mind was spinning out of control.

"Many years ago, we lost a baby."

I sucked in a breath, completely blindsided by his statement. "Oh." It was all I could think to say.

"We were young when we got married. We didn't have much money and lived with her parents, your grandparents, on their farm. I was studying law and coming back to the farm each weekend. We were so madly in love and we were making it work. When she fell pregnant, we knew it wasn't great timing and I had hoped to graduate and get a job in the city before we started a family, but we were still over the moon." A sad and distant look settled across his face. "Our son died during childbirth." A tear slipped down his cheek. "The doctors had no idea why. It was just one of those inexplicable tragedies, but from the moment we were told, we became different people."

"It was a boy?"

"Yes. He'd be thirty-five now." He shook his head. "It's hard to believe."

I felt a sense of loss for a sibling I never had and never knew about my whole life to that point. "Oh my God, Dad. I had no idea."

"As soon as I graduated and got a job, we left the farm and she's never been back."

"I guess that explains why Grandma and Grandpa always came to pick me up when I went there."

"She never spoke of what had happened once we'd left the farm. I tried to bring it up, but every time she'd turn into an ice queen and make me promise to never tell anyone. She felt responsible, like she'd done something wrong, and she didn't want anyone to judge her. Your mother, God love her, has always worried far too much about what other people think."

"But then you had me."

"Yes. It was almost a whole decade later. I was working crazy hours and on the path to making partner. She immersed herself in charity work and the Melbourne social scene. Our new life was a far cry from the simple life we had as newlyweds. We had no financial concerns, and she appeared happy to be pregnant again but understandably stressed the same thing would happen. To be honest, I wasn't around a whole lot, but I know she could barely leave the house, and when she did, she'd have anxiety attacks. When you were born, I hoped she'd relax and be more like her old self."

"What was she like before it happened?"

Dad laughed and his whole body relaxed. "She was wild and free. A little reckless at times, but she loved life hard, and boy did she have spirit."

I felt a crucial part of my puzzle fall into place. Mum and I weren't as dissimilar as I'd always thought. In fact, from what Dad said, we were both trying to hide a part of who we were—the same part.

"She was the most beautiful woman in the world," he continued, lost in his memories. He appeared almost whimsical. "She still is."

I swallowed the lump in my throat. "I can't believe you've never told me this before." My heart broke for them, but a part of me felt angry that I'd never known about it. "I've lived my whole life feeling like I could never be who or what she wanted me to be. I've done everything I can for her. I've tried to be the perfect daughter, and all along you've both been hiding this secret from me that explains a lot of her behaviour. She has always been abnormally fixated on my life and especially on my relationship with Richard."

Dad hung his head. "I buried myself in my work, and to be honest, I thought everything was fine. You always appeared happy."

"Looks can be deceiving, Dad."

"That's true." He blew out a long breath. "I guess I've brushed a lot under the carpet. Witnessing her fall apart today gave me a bit of a wake-up call. I'm going to insist she sees a therapist. I should've done it a really long time ago. She thinks you're being reckless, and it's dredging up a part of her life she has blocked out."

I stood up. "I'll call Mum tomorrow and try to smooth things over, but I'm not getting back with Richard."

Dad looked suddenly pale. "Please don't tell her I told you."

*Wow.* She really held so much power over him. "She's barely talking to me anyway, so I don't think it'll be a problem." I smiled, trying to lighten the mood a little.

"You and your mother are the loves of my life." His sincere admission shocked me. He'd never been one for displays of affection or voicing his emotions. "Perhaps I should've been more involved in your life, but I focused on providing financially instead."

"Don't beat yourself up about what's in the past, Dad. Let's just figure out a way to move forward."

I walked slowly through the door, down the stairs and out the front door, my mind now swirling with the information I'd learned in the last hour. The cold night air hit me smack in the face, and I almost fell down the two steps leading to the footpath. I decided then and there to confront Richard about what was going on. He needed to cut ties with my mother regardless of the financial repercussions.

In the time it took me to walk to Richard's house, I was fired up enough to sort this craziness out once and for all.

His lights were on and, despite the sheer blinds, I could see movement in his front room. He wasn't alone, but my eyesight was insufficient to identify his company. He lived in a townhouse, similar to my parents' but smaller. Behind a wrought-iron fence was a tiled courtyard. The lack of garden was another similarity to my parents' place—cold and unhomely.

I stood in the cover of darkness and looked in. To my surprise and outrage, Richard was with a woman. Why was he so intent on getting me back when he was busy getting it on with another woman? It was hard to tell exactly what was going on between them, but it appeared somewhat intimate. I couldn't see her face, but I didn't need to. The overwhelming emotion was relief. He was obviously moving on with another blonde and would hopefully stop harassing me. Feeling like a voyeur, I turned my back on them.

Reaching into my bag, I pulled out my phone, scrolled through my contacts and hit send. I'd told Leo I'd be at the bar by eight, and it was now almost nine. I wanted to let him know I was on my way.

"You've reached Leo, leave me a message."

I glanced back to Richard's lounge room. Part of my brain registered the fact that I needed to leave a message for Leo, but the rest of my brain was exploding into a million tiny fragments of grey matter.

"No. No. No. NO!!!"

# CHAPTER 27

*Juliette*

I FELT A LOT OF things in those seconds I stood outside staring at my mother entwined around my ex-boyfriend, a man twenty-five years her junior, but nausea overwhelmed me. Bile rose from my stomach and burned my throat as my empty stomach continued to retch violently. *What was he thinking? How long had it been going on?* I wondered, completely enraged and sickened but unable to stop trying to process it. As each wave of nausea subsided, betrayal was there waiting to step to the forefront.

And her. After what Dad told me, I had a better understanding of her, but I'd spent most of my life trying to talk and act 'appropriately,' weighed down by the guilt she showered on me. I'd tried harder. I'd towed the line. I'd enabled her. But this was too much. Way too much. This was the final straw and I saw red. My teeth ground together as a sweat broke out on my forehead. My ability to think rationally slipped away as newfound raw emotions took hold of my whole body.

I stormed up the front steps and pounded on the

door. Eventually, the outside light came on, and when the door opened, I was greeted by Richard wiping lipstick from his face with wide eyes. The gutless bastard's reaction was to close the door on me, but I jammed my foot to stop its path. He tried to kick at my boot, but I threw my shoulder into the door and pushed against him, managing to gain entry. I leant against the closed door and glared at him, shooting venom from somewhere inside me I'd never tapped before. I was experiencing rage, the likes of which I'd never known. Perhaps I'd been bottling it up or sweeping it under the carpet. Either way, the bottles were exploding and the carpet was being pulled from under my feet.

Richard glanced backward briefly, and I had to laugh at the situation I found myself in.

"Who are you looking for, Dick?" My sarcastic chuckle would irritate him more than the nickname he hated.

"Don't call me Dick."

"Really?" My anger rose and my laughter died. "I don't think you're in a position to make any demands on me. You never were, you son of a bitch."

"You're in way over your head, Juliette." His voice was low and threatening.

"Speak up. I can't hear you properly. Are you worried Mummy Dearest will hear you?"

The look of shock amplified as the realisation I knew about his disgraceful affair dawned on him.

"I won't let you ruin this for me," he seethed.

"Holy shit!" I mumbled, more to myself than to him. "What is wrong with you?"

"You should go." He tried to reach past me to the door handle. "And stay away from that bartender, or he'll be removed as a problem."

"What the fuck are you talking about?" My hands and feet felt freezing cold, and my mind started to spin out of control. "Tell her to come out now so I can talk to her."

He ran his hands through his hair and looked at the ceiling. "I am not going to lose my biggest client now. I've worked too hard for this."

"You're out of your mind." I spoke through clenched teeth, barely containing my rage.

"I saw an opportunity and I took it," he said, trying too hard to sound casual. The vein popping out of his forehead was a dead giveaway for his high stress level. "That's what successful people do to get ahead. You were part of the deal."

"What do you mean I was part of the deal?" I asked, becoming more and more disgusted by the second.

"It seemed like a good deal to date the beautiful daughter of the most connected family in Melbourne. For a long time, you were a bit dull and compliant, but you were pretty to look at and didn't take up a lot of my time."

"Are you serious?" I asked, completely gobsmacked.

"I got the lucrative charity account and a pretty trophy wife-to-be," he continued, as if he were discussing a business deal, which essentially he was. "She has it all mapped out. She has big plans for the wedding. She's often rambling about hiring the Australian Centre for Contemporary Art in South Melbourne and theming the whole extravaganza in pink. You know what she's like."

"Her dream wedding," I uttered in complete disbelief.

"Richard!" my mother's shrill voice called from upstairs. "What's keeping you?"

I held my hand over my mouth, fearful of further retching. I spoke through my hand, closing my eyes as the gravity of the situation rolled over my broken soul. "You are a despicable human being."

He was silent for a few moments, and I could see the

cogs turning in his head.

He had the audacity to touch my arm, and I flinched away violently. "I'd gladly stay away from you and your fucked-up family, but your Mum's account is my golden ticket," he whispered, but his intensity was deafening.

"Fuck you." I hoped I burst his ear drum with my hate-filled words.

"That's no way to talk to your future husband, Juliette." My mother appeared right behind Richard, and her voice cut through the room like a knife.

Richard and I both jumped, clutching our hands to our hearts in perfect sync.

"What's going on, Mum?" I asked tentatively, suddenly afraid of a woman I didn't recognise.

"I'm trying to salvage a situation you seem determined to destroy." She was swaying as she spoke, and her eyes couldn't focus. "I'm so tired of cleaning up your messes. I give such simple instructions."

"What?" My voice was barely audible. She was drunk or high or maybe both. Had she always been like this and I just hadn't noticed the extent of her delusions? Or is this what I'd avoided for so many years trying to do exactly what she wanted, forging my own miserable fairy tale, solely to please her? "I think you should take a break and go home to Dad."

Mum scoffed and flicked her dyed blonde hair over her shoulder. "That old man is such a bore. 'Calm down. Take a break. Leave Juliette alone.'" She said it in a deep voice, cocking her head from side to side, trying to mimic my father. "I don't want to take a fucking break." She put her hand on the wall to steady herself and took some shallow breaths.

I stood up straight and walked towards her. "You need help, Mum. I've tried to help you, but clearly I've just made it worse."

"Stop talking." She put her hands over her ears and closed her eyes. "Stop talking. Stop talking."

"Come on, Mum." I stepped forward gingerly and lightly touched her elbow. "I'll take you home."

Her eyes opened, and she looked at me with such hatred I was in no way prepared for. "I said stop talking!" she shouted at me before she closed her eyes and resumed her ramblings as if nothing had happened.

I pushed my shoulders back but was unable to stop a few tears from slipping down my cheeks. Clearing my throat, I turned to Richard, who was white as a sheet—his eyes were out on stalks and his slack jaw trembled.

"I need to get her home." I'd take charge of this horrible situation before I fell apart completely. "Seriously, Richard. You need to leave her alone. She needs professional help. Go find another sugar mummy to feed your client base."

"Not going to happen just yet, princess."

I got right up in his face. "Look, you disgusting snake. You've done as much damage as you're going to do. I'll have my father remove you as her adviser in the morning." I turned my back on him, intent on helping my mother.

"I can destroy her."

His words made me falter. I turned back to him and steeled myself. "What do you mean?"

"I have no problem publicising my affair with her or this little meltdown she's having." He sounded so smug I wanted to punch him.

"It wouldn't reflect well on your career."

"Au contraire, mon amour. I have nothing to lose and I've done nothing wrong. I also have some compromising evidence I'd be happy to release."

Arsehole.

"So I don't tell my dad and you keep your mouth shut?"

He smiled and actually let out a little chuckle. "It's actually pretty damn perfect. Mummy Dearest can be shuffled off to a looney bin, leaving me in charge of the account."

He was making my skin crawl with his callous excitement.

"Can you help me get her home at least? She won't let me near her."

"Fine. Whatever. Anything to get the pair of you out of here."

Mum allowed Richard to put his arm around her, and she suddenly looked like a scared young girl. It was horrifying.

I turned on my heel and opened the door, allowing them to walk through ahead of me. We walked slowly back to my family home in silence. From the way she slumped into Richard's side, Mum was either sobering up, coming down off a high or she was simply exhausted. Staring up at the luxury townhouse I had called home for my entire childhood, I realised I was attaching another unpleasant memory to its four walls. The difference this time was, for the first time, I didn't feel directly responsible for the situation. Her behaviour wasn't on me.

I rang the doorbell and waited a few minutes. Richard stood behind me, holding up Mum, who was still resting her head on his shoulder. Her eyes were closed and she looked peaceful. Jean would've left for the day, and Dad was probably holed up in his office. I rang again.

Eventually Dad opened the door, and when he glanced behind me and saw Mum with Richard, he looked confused. "Isabel? What's wrong?"

He stepped outside and moved towards them.

"What's going on, Juliette?"

"Mum wasn't with Carol." I wondered if any conversation could be more awkward. "She went to Richard's after all."

"Sorry about this, Richard. Thanks for helping bring her home and for your discretion."

I wanted to throw up listening to him apologise. He had no idea and I couldn't tell him. Not yet, anyway.

He gently took Mum from Richard, who then took a few steps back and tripped over his own feet. I didn't laugh because nothing about that situation was remotely funny. Mum moved away from us and walked into the house as if on auto-pilot.

"She was acting crazy, Dad. She really needs that help."

The silence was palpable.

"Thanks for bringing her home, Juliette."

"I just want her to be happy, Dad."

"I'll call you tomorrow, okay? I'll get her the help she needs."

I nodded, smiled, then turned away.

Richard was waiting for me on the footpath, staring at the ground with his hands in his trouser pockets. When he saw me, he looked up. "So we have a deal? You're not going to tell him?" His voice was even, but his face was pale.

"No. He needs to focus on looking after her for now." I looked at my ex-boyfriend with disdain. His primary concern was always himself.

"I hear that bartending lowlife thug nearly lost his first fight because of you."

My blood ran cold. "How would you know that?"

"Your mother. She knows where you are at all times. It's become an obsession."

"For how long?" I was seething.

"Ever since the Yarra Valley function when you stepped out of line and she saw the way you looked at the bartender. She freaked out and I had to console her in the middle of the night to stop her drinking herself into a stupor."

"Are you serious?"

"She's had you followed ever since, and let's just say she's pissed. I'm pretty sure she's been doing background checks on what's-his-name."

"Leo. His name is Leo. She's not pissed. She's just lost touch with reality."

"Whatever, Juliette. I don't actually care anymore. That charity is worth hundreds of thousands of dollars to me and keeps me at the top of the adviser rankings. As long as I hold on to that, I don't give a shit about you or your crazy family."

"Trust me, Dick. I got that already."

I went home feeling lighter in some ways and heavier in others. I could've ended up married to Richard and worn a mask for the rest of my life. And worse, Mum wouldn't be getting the help she needed.

Knowing my mother had suffered in virtual silence for thirty-five years opened a whole new wound in my heart that I hoped would heal alongside hers.

# CHAPTER 28

## LEO

I'D BEEN AT THE FARM all week working on the stone wall, fighting to keep the constant flow of memories and regrets at bay. Stonemasonry had been my family's business for generations, and I'd worked alongside my dad during school holidays to earn some cash. He hoped I'd join the Ashlar & Son stonemasonry business when I finished school. The '& Son' part hadn't been the case since my grandfather died a decade ago. I wanted to be a doctor, and I'd studied damn hard to ensure I could follow that path. When I graduated from high school, Dad presented me with a shiny new sign for the business, hoping to change my mind. When I'd told him thanks but no thanks, he had respected my decision. Both he and Mum had given me their blessing to follow my own dream, but to this day I wish I'd followed his instead.

Angus and I had accepted places at the University of Melbourne and shared a flat in St Kilda—the same one I still lived in. Angus had wanted to work in finance, so he was doing a Business Economics degree, and I was studying day and night to be a doctor. I'd been living the dream until the day my whole world turned into one big fucking nightmare.

By Thursday evening, a shift at the bar was a welcome distraction. It was quieter and more relaxed on a weekday evening, and I found myself humming along to the music, again playing backup to the movies on the walls. Everything reminded me of her. When "I'm Every Woman" came on, I glanced towards the door, hoping she'd walk through it. I set about stacking the glass washer and refilling the bowls of nuts on the bar. When my shift ended at eleven, I was pretty gutted she hadn't shown up.

"I might have more work for you if you're interested," Adriana said as I pulled my helmet, wallet and keys from my locker in the staff room.

"Yeah, I'm interested. That'd be great." I needed some extra income if I was going to do more work on the house.

"Okay. Tony just gave me his notice, so you can take over his shifts in a couple of weeks."

I scrunched my face up, knowing I would have to say no. I closed the locker door and turned to face her. "Tony's on the door, not the bar."

"No one's going to mess with you, Leo. Trust me. That's all the experience you need." She had misunderstood my concern and slapped me on the shoulder, laughing.

"I'd prefer to stick to the bar if that's okay?"

"Let me know if you change your mind." Shrugging her shoulders, she left the room.

I hit the voicemail button on my phone. Juliette had left a message probably with the reason why she couldn't make it.

Adrenaline surged through me as I listened. It was confusing and a little horrifying. It was a long pause followed by her voice repeating the word 'no.' She sounded traumatised by something.

*What the fuck?*

I bolted out of the bar and sprinted up the alleyway to my bike with my phone to my ear.

"Hello." Her croaky voice answered. I was relieved to hear it.

"Juliette. God. Where are you? I just got your message. Are you okay?"

"Leo. I'm sorry, Leo." She sounded like she might be crying, and my desire to have my arms firmly around her was excruciating. "I called before... I'm sorry I didn't leave a message."

"Please don't apologise. Where are you?"

"I'm at home."

"I can be there in five minutes."

"Joel will buzz you up and I'll leave my door open."

I rode dangerously fast. My mind was focused on her voice. She sounded desperate and broken. If anyone had hurt her, they were going to pay. I nearly toppled the Ducati sideways when I pulled up outside her building.

When I entered her apartment, I immediately heard her sobbing on the lounge.

"Jules." I announced my presence as I didn't want to startle her.

She sat up so I could see her, and I immediately rushed forward. Her face was red and puffy, but she was still breathtakingly beautiful. I sat down next to her and pulled her onto my lap, hugging her close to my body. Her arms wrapped around my neck, and she buried her face in the crook of my neck. I could feel her body begin to relax, and the sobs subsided.

"What happened, Jules?" I whispered into her hair. "Did someone hurt you?" I clenched my teeth waiting for her response, knowing if they had, I'd hunt them down and kill them.

She shook her head against me then sat up and wiped her eyes with her sleeve. "Not physically."

"What does that mean?" I was seething. From the beginning, my instinct had always been to protect her.

"I'm sorry, Leo."

"What? No. Stop apologising." She wouldn't look at me, so I cupped her chin and forced her eyes to mine. "What happened?"

"I don't really feel up to talking about it at the moment." She tightened her arms around me. "Can you just hold me for a while?"

I kissed her head. "I'm glad you called me." I hesitated before continuing. "I missed you this week."

"God, Leo. My life is such a mess." She sat up and ran her hands through her hair and appeared defeated. "I don't want to drag you down."

I waited until she looked at me. "Life can be messy, Jules. I know all about messy and how angry, bitter and alone it can make you feel." I stroked her cheek with the back of my hand and stared into her beautiful navy eyes. "But this right here." I gestured between the two of us. "This feels like the most pure and honest thing I've felt in a really long time, and I think you feel it, too." I took hold of both her hands and brought them to my lips, kissing her fingers.

She gasped and her eyes glazed, but she didn't interject.

"You're a strong and beautiful woman. I've seen it with my own eyes. Don't let anyone or anything take that away from you."

Juliette leaned in and pressed her lips against mine. I wanted to devour her, but I needed her to take the lead here until I had a better idea of what was going on. I needed to know who or what had upset her.

"Thank you," she whispered against my mouth. "Can you stay? I don't really want to be alone tonight."

I kissed her again lightly. "Of course I can." I hugged her to me and stroked her hair. "Come on. Let's go to bed."

When we got to her room, she removed her clothes and pulled on her pyjamas.

"I'm just going to grab a shower. I smell like beer."

I was desperate to have her in my arms again, so I had a lightning-quick shower and returned to her room within minutes, but she was already asleep. I pulled the covers back and quietly joined her. She was facing me, so I could marvel at her beautiful features. I couldn't resist stroking her face and moving the loose strands of her hair away from her closed eyes. There was something very right about being in her bed, and I surprised myself how content I was just being there with her. For the first time in my life, sex wasn't the only reason to be in bed with a girl.

Juliette found comfort in my arms. When I was with her, I felt important somehow. I'd never blamed my past for anything. It was weak to use the past to justify your mistakes or shortcomings. I had spent the last five years trying to make peace with what happened in that house, and the first snippet of hope I'd felt was with Juliette. Clearly we both had demons, but no one gets a free ride. Everyone has baggage—things they wish they could change—and God knows there are things I'd have changed, but that was impossible.

Before sleep found me, Juliette started speaking. Initially, I thought she had woken up, but her mumblings were incoherent and obviously part of a dream or perhaps a nightmare.

"No. No. No. Mother. No. I can't. Mother. No. Don't

hurt him. Please."

There was something really tormenting this beautiful girl, and I was going to be there to help her.

# CHAPTER 29

*Juliette*

I WOKE UP EARLY—HOT and disoriented. Then I realised it was because a hot man was lying half across my body and was wrapped around me. The night before came flooding back. I buried my face into his neck and inhaled, willing his intoxicating scent to somehow push thoughts of my horror night away. I allowed myself a moment to enjoy being with this gorgeous man who seemed to value my existence.

When Leo stirred, I tried to move away from him as he oriented himself. Strong arms gripped me and soft lips kissed my neck. Desire shot through me as he feathered kisses along my jaw and cheek before finding my lips. The outside world was all but forgotten when he looked in my eyes and smiled.

"Good morning, beautiful."

"Morning." I didn't know much about anything at that point, but I did know I liked waking up with him. "How did you sleep?"

"Best sleep ever. I might have to keep you."

"Thanks for staying."

"My pleasure. Anytime."

Our clothes were quickly discarded. I was becoming accustomed to his body, every rock-hard inch of it, and I was enjoying sex more than ever before. In hindsight, sex with Richard had been more like a chore to tick off the to-do list. If we skipped a week here or there, we barely noticed. With Leo, I couldn't get enough.

Completely sated, I stretched out my body into star position when he got up to discard the condom in the bathroom. When he came back to bed wearing nothing but his black boxers, he gathered me into his side and put his arm around me protectively; his thumb rubbed my knuckles and squeezed my hand. For the millionth time, he stole my breath.

"Can we talk about last night?"

I sighed, knowing I couldn't avoid it forever.

"Tell me what happened that upset you so much, Jules."

"I want to tell you everything, but I'm afraid you'll run screaming for the hills."

"Try me. I can guarantee I'm not going anywhere."

I propped myself up with pillows and Leo did the same.

"Last night my whole life got tipped upside down and shaken up." I told him all about my conversation with my dad, and he listened intently. He was a really good listener, I discovered.

"So the voicemail message you left on my phone. What was that about? You sounded traumatised by something."

I didn't really want to tell him, but I wanted to be completely open with him. "I caught Richard and my mother together."

"Jesus Christ. No wonder you were upset. I'm sorry,

Jules."

"She's in a bad way, Leo. Breaking up with Richard seems to have triggered a complete meltdown. She had me followed, for God's sake." I shook my head at the ludicrous things I was telling him.

"She had you followed?"

"The guy at fight night. I'd seen him at the gym and on the street a couple of times."

"What?" He sat up and looked murderous suddenly. "You recognised the guy who attacked you? Why didn't you tell me?"

"You were pissed off at me for being there. Remember? It didn't seem important. Anyway, she's going to get help now, so it should be the end of it."

"Take the day off work and spend it with me." His eyes reinforced his demand with an intensity I'd only ever witnessed on this man. "I'm worried about you."

"You don't have to worry about me. You saw me defend myself and win." I grinned, remembering the look of shock and pain on his face.

"Fuck, Juliette." His harsh tone wiped the grin from my face. "This isn't a joke. He could've really hurt you."

"I'm sorry." I tried to keep a straight face. "I'm not afraid of danger, and if I'm honest, I get a thrill out of it."

"It's one thing to enjoy the rush of adrenaline. It's another to take on guys twice your size and think you're invincible. Next time there could be a lethal weapon or backup or a million other scenarios I'd rather not explore." The crease in his already-furrowed brow deepened. "It will catch up with you one day, and I don't want to see that happen." He cupped my chin so I was forced to look at him. "I won't see that happen."

"I guess I've never really cared before. I train and study hard, so I'm far from being a sitting duck, and adrenaline has always made me feel so alive."

Leo grimaced. "You're being too flippant with your safety, and that pisses me off."

"Look. Last night I watched my mother seducing my ex-boyfriend." I shuddered at the memory. "I'm not really sure I'll ever get over that, but learning to fight and searching for adrenaline have been the only ways I've found to help deal with everything life has thrown at me." I paused, not sure whether I should tell him about my first competitive fight at Lilydale next weekend. "Sometimes adrenaline feels like an addiction I can't shake. I love it, and I don't care if I'm putting myself in danger. That's kind of the point."

"I get that, Juliette. Trust me. But you need to rein it in a bit and not get yourself in situations you can't control."

"I'm going to my first competitive fight next Saturday evening." I just ripped the Band-Aid off, scrunched up my nose and waited for his reaction.

"What the hell, Juliette?" His whole body went rigid against me. "Why would you want to do that?"

"Fighting is my bliss. I love training with Zac, and he wants to see if I have what it takes in the ring. I want to feel that rush."

"Where is the fight?"

"Lilydale."

"Lightning Fight Centre?"

"Yep. The night starts at seven thirty, and I'll be on early, as it's my first fight. I imagine I'll be done and dusted by eight."

Leo blew out a long breath and, despite the angst radiating off his body, a look of resignation overshadowed. "Well, if I can't talk you out of it, I'm coming with you. I know a few people there. If I think it's getting out of hand, I'll drag you out, and there'll be nothing you can do about it."

"Thank you." I climbed into his lap and straddled him. "I'd love you to be there."

Letting out a long breath, Leo responded with a simple command. "Call your boss."

"If it means that much to you." I shrugged my shoulders.

"*You* mean that much to me." He held my face with his strong hands and looked me in the eye, smiling. "I thought I was going to have to work a lot harder than that."

"I'm easy. What can I say?" I raised my eyebrows, eliciting another smile from this outrageously gorgeous man. Even first thing in the morning, he looked amazing. I loved his hair, mussed during sleep. I ran my hand over the rough stubble on his cheek. The man was just flat-out bloody gorgeous, and the more time I spent with him, the more convinced I was of his integrity. My ignorance to Richard's true nature had really rattled me, but I had my eyes wide open now and they were seeing the man I wanted to give myself to completely.

"You make a phone call, I'll make coffee."

He kissed me, and when he pulled back, I grabbed his bicep. "Don't you want to stay in bed a little longer?" I hoped he would understand my implication.

He answered by pushing me onto my back and staying in bed a lot longer.

Later, I shamelessly ogled his incredible body as he walked out of the room.

I spoke to Heath, who wasn't thrilled with my last-minute request but agreed begrudgingly. I'd taken no annual leave in almost twelve months. No sooner had I hit the red circle on my phone than it started ringing. It was Dad.

"How is she?" I asked.

"Not great. I'm not going to lie."

I shook my head. "Well, I appreciate your honesty."

"I've put in a few calls and have managed to secure a place for her at Dartmoor West Wellness Centre. It comes highly recommended by Dr McGibbons."

"That's really great, Dad. When is she going in?"

"Monday. I'm going to take a few weeks off work so I can spend as much time at the centre as needed. It's time I got my priorities in order."

"That makes me really happy, Dad." I felt a heavy load lift from my shoulders. "Really happy."

"I'll keep you updated."

"Thanks, Dad. Bye."

# CHAPTER 30

## LEO

"WHERE ARE YOU TAKING ME?" she asked, standing next to my bike and strapping on her helmet.

"For a start, you haven't seen where I live. I could do with a change of clothes if that's okay with you?"

"Course. I'd like to see where you live."

~~~~~~

"St Kilda?" she questioned when I pulled up outside my apartment building.

"Why so surprised? Too upmarket for a thug like me?" I pulled her to me and tickled her sides, knowing it would be torture for her, but it would make her laugh.

She laughed, and the sound made me happy. "Not at all. St Kilda has some dodgy parts."

"Oh, thanks a lot, funny girl." I tickled her, making her laugh harder.

"I was going to say it's my favourite suburb in Melbourne before you jumped to conclusions, Mr Chip-on-his-shoulder." She smirked and I couldn't resist kissing her, because I could never resist kissing her.

"I was brought up in the country and longed for city

life. Once a year, Dad brought me to Melbourne and took me to Luna Park and the beach. We'd fish off the pier and eat ice cream. St Kilda became my favourite place in the world."

I took her hand and led her up the steps. I lived in a two-bedroom apartment on the ground floor of an interwar building that, quite frankly, had seen better days. "It's not fancy, but it's all I need."

Juliette stood in the middle of the main living room and did a full three-hundred-sixty-degree turn. She said nothing as she took it in. An old but extremely comfortable lounge chair was up one end with the TV, and an overflowing bookshelf and a table and chairs were set up by the back window up the other end. The kitchen was through a door on one side, and opposite it, a door led through to the two bedrooms and bathroom. It was a simple design.

"I love it." She said it like she meant it, then took a seat at the table overlooking the shared garden to the rear of the building.

"I'm glad." I sat down opposite her and waited until she looked at me. "Stay here with me this weekend."

"I'd like that." Her cheeks reddened slightly as if I'd just asked her on a first date. Then it occurred to me we'd never had a first date. We'd stumbled from one drama to the next, and our time together had been uncertain and fragile.

She sat forward in her chair and rested her elbows on the table. "How long have you lived here?"

I looked to the ceiling and counted in my head. "Eight years. I've lived here since I finished high school. Angus was my housemate while we were at uni, and then he ditched city life and headed home."

"You were at uni?" she asked, but her cheeks immediately reddened, embarrassed by her question.

"Sorry. I didn't mean to sound surprised. That was rude."

"Not at all. I went to uni for a few years but didn't finish my degree." I wasn't ready to tell her the reason I withdrew. "I've been working events and bars ever since. Plus the fights help pay the rent, too."

"I wanted to live on campus, but my mother wouldn't let me. I lived at home until I graduated and got a job."

"So why didn't you get an apartment in St Kilda when you were earning your own money if you like it here so much?"

"My city apartment was a university graduation gift from my parents."

"Wow. That's some gift."

"I know." She shifted on her chair and fidgeted with the end of her long ponytail hanging over her shoulder. "It was ridiculously extravagant and I didn't want to accept it, but refusing it would've ruffled feathers. My mother didn't like having her feathers ruffled. It would've been viewed as a childish act of defiance if I'd refused it. Mum used it as another example of all they did for me and brought it up if I ever put a foot out of place."

"So accepting the apartment was a double-edged sword?" I wondered out loud. "Part of you didn't want to owe them anything that could be used against you, but the little girl in you still yearned to please your mum and dad?"

She nodded. "They were like two opposing forces. Dad wanted me to be independent whilst Mum wanted my absolute obedience."

"Men are wired differently from women."

"I get that, but there's a balance. Neither of them ever really made me feel loved unconditionally."

"And you think risking your safety fighting and

whatever else you probably do to fill the void is the only answer?"

She sat back and crossed her arms over her chest. "Here we go again."

"I'm just trying to understand you completely, but I'm sorry. Today was meant to be about having some fun." I stood up and walked around the table, crouching down next to her and taking hold of her hand. "I want to take you on a first date. Where would you like to go?"

She placed her hand behind my head and leaned down to kiss me. "I think we're past the first date stage." She smiled against my lips.

I sat back so I could look her in the eye. "We might have muddled things up a bit, but I'm trying to rectify the situation here. You kissing me like that just makes me want to throw you on the bed and steal your virtue."

Juliette threw her head back and laughed. "Pretty sure that's long gone."

"You know what I mean." I jumped up, kissing her on the way. "I'm going to get changed. Help yourself to anything in the fridge or cupboards. I want a first date with you." I desperately hoped Google was going to come to my rescue. Romantic dates were a foreign concept for me, but I was willing to give it a crack.

"Hey, Leo," she called out as I walked towards the bathroom. I turned back. "I'm glad I took the day off."

"Just so you know, I was going to talk you into it one way or another."

She stood up and sauntered towards me. Fuck, she was sexy.

She put her arms around my neck and whispered in my ear. "Now I wish I'd said no."

How was it possible this girl had never felt sexy before? She didn't take my breath away—I gave it to her willingly. The realisation hit me and warmth spread through my body. I was falling in love with this girl.

I kissed her hard. "I'd prefer you said 'yes.' Really loud." I rested my forehead on hers and kissed her nose.

"I'm sure that can be arranged." She chuckled then kissed me with an urgency I hadn't felt from her before.

I stumbled over towards the bed, and we fell down onto the soft covers together. There was no time for laughing. It was just a blur of clothes and shoes being tossed and flung from our lust-fuelled bodies.

I loved the way her body fit against my much larger frame. She was strong and confident yet soft and responsive to my touch. What started as a crazy desire to take her hard and fast didn't last the second I had her naked beneath me, staring up into my eyes. I made love to her the way she deserved. All her life, she'd never felt good enough, and I wanted her to know she was so far beyond good enough. She was making me feel things and consider things I had thought were impossible. I wanted to lose myself in her body, in her smile and in her soul, and then maybe I'd find my way home.

# CHAPTER 31

## Juliette

"STUDLEY PARK BOATHOUSE? REALLY? WITH everything you know about me, is this really what you thought the ideal first date would be?" I asked, somewhere between confusion and amusement.

"Did you think I'd take you to mud wrestling?"

I put my hands on my hips but couldn't help smiling. I had a strong suspicion this would be the first result in a 'Romantic dates in Melbourne' Google search. "Well, that might have been closer to the mark."

"Settle down, angel." He grabbed my hand to help me keep my balance as I stepped onto the small row boat. "I've got this."

"Just so you know, if there's a flock of swans and a thunderstorm on this date, I'm going to throw myself overboard and swim to shore."

"I have no idea what you mean by that, but I'll take my chances. Do ducks count?"

"Yes! Ducks count."

"Guess I shouldn't have bought the duck food, then?"

He laughed, and I couldn't help laughing, too. He was so hot when he was being cute.

When I was safely seated opposite him, he pushed off the side with one oar and then got into a steady rhythm. I questioned why I'd mocked this date. I had a front row seat to the hottest man alive making good use of his muscles. He was wearing dark jeans and a black V-neck sweater over a white t-shirt. I cursed the season, wishing he would ditch the sweater.

"Tell me about Beatrix," I suggested as Leo rowed effortlessly down river. The serenity was all-consuming and lent itself to real conversation, something I realised I had actively avoided with Richard. "Have you known her all your life?"

Leo smiled. "Bea, Angus and I grew up together. We were like the three amigos as kids and the bond just stuck."

"Were she and Angus childhood sweethearts? Were you the third wheel or did another girl infiltrate the trio?"

"Actually, Bea and I had an on-again off-again relationship through high school."

"Oh! What happened? She's lovely and gorgeous." I felt a mild pang of jealousy.

"We were great friends, but the chemistry wasn't there. I wanted to go away to uni and then see the world, and she wanted to stay home and run a café."

"And make the best coffee in the world."

"That's it." Leo adjusted the oars so they were safely inside the boat. We just drifted with the gentle current. "Angus and I were best mates and decided to apply to the same uni."

"Time for you and Angus to sow your wild oats?" I cringed. Another ridiculous pang of jealousy hit me. The idea of him with another girl made me see red.

Leo laughed. "Are you pissed at me for being with women before I knew you?"

"No!" *Yes.*

Leo threw his head back and laughed mercilessly. "You are so cute." He leaned forward and kissed me and I kissed him back, because I could never resist kissing him back. "You do realise it was you with the boyfriend when we met, right?"

"Tell me the rest of the story." I pushed him lightly on the shoulder.

"Okay, bossy boots. So it was one drunken evening in our first year, Angus confessed his love for Beatrix. I'd had no idea he was so into her, but as it turned out, he had been broken-hearted, fearing his chances with her were gone because of me. Over many, many beers and several manly hugs, I insisted we were just friends and he had my blessing to pursue her."

"Wow. Poor Angus."

"The next morning, he drove home and declared his love on her doorstep. Apparently, she burst into tears and they never looked back."

"Happily ever after."

"Pretty much. He went home to the Yarra Valley every weekend."

"And what about you? Actually, don't tell me." I held up my hand and turned my head to the side. "I don't want to hear about all your girlfriends."

"Not much to tell, really." His expression softened and his eyes blazed with passion. "I didn't know what I was waiting for until I found a lost soul who belonged to me."

I gasped. I had no experience with romance, but in my heart, that was the most perfect thing anyone had ever said to anyone.

A noisy flock of what looked like magpies drew my attention to the bushland lining both sides of the river. It was hard to tell if they were fighting or mating. I smiled. *Who needed swans?*

I turned back to the gorgeous man sitting opposite me and sighed.

"Are you going to say anything?" he asked.

"I think you need to turn the boat around and paddle us back to shore."

Leo looked worried. "Did I say something wrong?"

"No. You said the most right thing."

"I don't think that's grammatically correct."

"You're questioning my grammar when I'm trying to tell you how much I loved what you said?"

Leo chuckled, his beautiful eyes the lightest I'd seen them. "So why do you want to leave?"

I leaned forward, resting my elbows on my knees and cupping my face in my hands. "Because I want to sit on your lap and kiss you, and when that happens in the movies, the couple tip the boat and fall overboard."

"Well, you were the one who threatened swimming to shore."

"I wasn't serious. The water would be bloody freezing."

"So, you just referred to us as a couple." Leo raised his eyebrows and his expression was unreadable.

My cheeks immediately flushed. "Um... well, I didn't exactly. I said couples in movies."

Leo's face erupted in laughter. "I'm kidding. You're mine. I'm yours. It's a fait accompli, Jules."

"Seriously." I shook my head, unable to hide my goofy grin. "You need to stop saying stuff like that while I can't show my appreciation properly."

"We have plenty of time for that, beautiful girl."

He did, however, turn the boat around and start rowing back the way we'd come.

"So a romantic boat ride wasn't so bad after all?" he asked as he helped me onto the small jetty. "I know it wasn't exactly an adrenaline junkie's dream."

"It was okay," I taunted, looking back at him over my shoulder as I sauntered away.

Strong arms hugged me from behind and soft lips kissed my neck. "I guess I'll have to up my game."

I turned to face him and wrapped my arms around his lean waist. "I guess you will, Mr..." I stared at him. "I don't know your last name."

"Ashlar."

The name rang a bell somewhere in my mind, but I had no idea why.

"We really do things the wrong way around, don't we? I think I just agreed to be your girlfriend without knowing your last name. Who does that?"

"We do. We're fucking perfect, Juliette. Don't question the order of things. Just enjoy the ride."

I stood on my tiptoes and kissed him. He was right. We were fucking perfect.

"So what now, Leo Ashlar?"

"Now I want to make out with you at my apartment, and then I have to be at the bar at eight."

"Work? Really?" I was disappointed. I wasn't ready to be apart from him.

"Come with me? I'm not ready to be apart from you just yet."

"Okay. I'll give Sia a call and see if she wants to meet me there. She can help me fend off your female groupies." I remembered watching as every girl had ogled him last time I was there. At the time, he hadn't been mine and I hadn't known if he ever would be. This time would be different.

Leo took my hand and led me back to his Jeep.

# CHAPTER 32

## Juliette

ON THE DRIVE BACK TO Leo's apartment, I felt peaceful. I loved being with Leo. He was so easy to be around, not only because he was so easy on the eyes but because I could breathe around him. For the first time in my life, someone was really taking the time to get to know me without an agenda. Life had turned around for me in a relatively short period of time. It was just over a month ago that I had first laid eyes on the incredibly gorgeous, and seemingly untouchable, Leo Ashlar. The impact that moment had had on me was unforgettable and set in motion the end of my life as I knew it. I had barely been living. I glanced over to Leo, who appeared to be deep in thought himself as he drove.

Obviously sensing my gaze, he stole a quick glance and smiled before returning his eyes to the road. "What are you thinking about?"

"Honestly, I was just thinking about how much my life has changed since I met you."

"I'm going to assume you mean for the better."

"Absolutely for the better." I suddenly felt emotional.

"I was drowning and I didn't care."

He glanced at me again with a concerned expression but didn't say anything. We were stopped at a T intersection. Turning left would take us to his home, but he went right and I knew where we were headed.

～～～～

"Chocolate?" Leo guessed.

"How did you know?"

"I didn't, but the way your eyes just lit up, I'm thinking I got it right."

"Chocolate is the answer to the problems in the world that coffee can't fix."

"I thought alcohol would rate a mention, too, as a problem solver?" He handed the money over to the teenager working the ice cream cart.

"You make a good point. Chocolate, coffee and wine—solving the problems of the world, one guilty pleasure at a time."

Once we had our ice creams, Leo took my hand and we walked along the St Kilda pier and stopped halfway along and leaned against the railing. It really was the most incredible view of Port Phillip, and the sunset was casting a peach glow over the bay.

"It used to be all about the sunrise for me, but now I prefer the sunset."

I managed to smudge ice cream on my face from laughing. "Leo Ashlar. You are a soppy romantic. How was it that you didn't pick up on my reference to the Nicholas Sparks' novel *The Notebook* back at the boathouse?"

"Excuse me." He smiled, but only briefly. "My reason isn't romantic, I'm afraid." He stared out across the water.

"I'm sorry for laughing." I touched his arm and he

placed his hand over mine, holding it in place. "Tell me why you love the sunset," I whispered.

"Tell me first why you felt like you were drowning and didn't care."

I exhaled a long breath. I'd never talked about it before, and part of me was scared to verbalise the dark thoughts I'd always had. Leo, however, made me feel so safe, and I loved that he cared. I stepped up onto the bottom railing so I could lean over the top and peer down at the dark water below. "I use my mind and my body to escape." The water swirled below and I closed my eyes, mentally imagining tipping myself forward and tumbling down until I splashed through the rough surface. "I imagine myself plunging into water, and I enjoy the sensation of sinking into the darkness. It's completely silent and I can shut out the voices."

"That's fucked up, Juliette."

I snapped my eyes open and looked into the fearful eyes of Leo.

"I didn't actually do it. Obviously," I retorted, upset by his angry reaction. "I just imagined it and I found it relaxed me."

"You find it relaxing?" he asked, clenching his jaw.

I stepped down off the railing and started walking away. He grabbed my arm before I made it two steps. "Where are you going?"

"I just opened up to you with something very personal and you shot me down." My eyes glazed with disappointment.

"Life isn't something you throw away because it gets too hard." He took my hand in his and brought me back to the railing. "When most people feel their hand is being forced, their instinct is either fight or flight. Mine is fight. With you, it's both. You run towards danger to escape. Even your imagination is reckless and suicidal."

The intensity of his eyes made my pulse quicken. "Open your eyes, Juliette. Stop seeing the darkness as your way out."

"You love the sunset. Isn't that the prelude to darkness?"

"You can be quite depressing." He chuckled lightly. "The night is lit up by a billion stars. If you focus on the black sky, you're missing the light show."

I looked up into the darkening sky and saw a few evening stars. I'd never noticed them before. "You're a surprising man, Leo Ashlar."

"Come on. I have to get changed for work, but tomorrow night I'm going to take you to a light show."

# CHAPTER 33

## LEO

I DESPERATELY DIDN'T WANT TO go to work. It had been a big day for us, and I wanted nothing more than to be alone with her. Instead, I had to work in a busy bar and sneak as many moments with her as I could.

"Give me fifteen minutes?" she asked, kissing me before disappearing towards her bedroom.

We'd stopped by her apartment on the way to the bar so she could get changed. While she was in the shower, I called Angus.

"Hey, mate. What's up?"

"I'm taking Jules to the farm tomorrow night. Any chance we can crash at yours if it gets too late to drive home?"

"Course, mate. You know you're always welcome, and I know Bea will be stoked to have Jules here."

I heard Bea in the background querying him.

"Leo?" Bea had taken the phone from her husband. "That girl is a very positive influence on you."

"It's not a big deal, Bea."

"It's a massive deal. For five years you barely set foot on the place, and since you met her—"

I cut her off. "No big deal."

"I'm happy you found her, or maybe she found you. Who knows? Maybe you'll talk to her about what happened."

"No," I snapped then immediately regretted my instinctive reaction. "Sorry, Bea." I paused to swallow the lump in my throat. "I don't need to talk about the past."

"Okay." There was silence for a few moments. "We'll see you tomorrow night, then."

I hung up with a knot in my stomach. I knew at some stage I would have to tell Juliette about what had happened, but we'd only just found our way to each other and she was dealing with her own dramas. I saw no reason to bring it up anytime soon.

She reappeared in black skinny jeans and a black tank top that was loose on her. I was relieved she wasn't in anything too revealing, given I'd be stuck behind the bar most of the night and couldn't lay my claim when the men swarmed. She sat down on the couch to put on strappy high heels, and when she leaned forward, I caught sight of her bare back.

"Your top appears to be missing the back section." I was only half-joking.

Juliette laughed and continued to do up her shoes. When she stood up, I grabbed her and pulled her close. My hands roamed her bare back, and the front of my jeans tightened. She was so damn sexy. Her hands found their way up my back and her lips found mine. When our kiss deepened, I groaned. I was going to be late for work if we took this any further.

"How am I going to focus on making cocktails all night?"

"Sia and I could go to another bar if you don't want to be distracted." She raised her eyebrows and grinned.

"No chance. At least at my bar, I can fight off anyone who tries to touch you." The idea of another man going anywhere near her flared a possessive streak I didn't even know I had. I kissed her again, wanting to savour the taste of her. "We really need to go."

She moved away from me and turned, looking back over her shoulder as she walked towards the door, smiling seductively. She knew the power she had over me. I bowed my head and groaned again before following her out the door.

# CHAPTER 34

*Juliette*

SIA MET US OUT THE front of the bar.

"Are you sure about this place?" she asked as she gave me a hug. "I'd never have found it without directions.

"You'll see. It's really cool inside." I stepped back and reached for Leo's hand.

"I think we need a few introductions here." She raised her eyebrows, glancing at Leo and then our interlinked hands. "Jesus, Juliette. I'm off work for a week and you've found yourself a much hotter man." She shook her head and chuckled.

My cheeks heated. Sia had thought Richard was hot, but she'd never really had a chance to get to know him. Good looks fade with a bad personality.

"Sia, Leo. Leo, Sia." I gestured between them.

Leo released my hand and then stepped forward to shake hers. "Pleasure to meet you. Juliette says really good things about you."

"She better! I'm awesome!"

We all laughed at her humility.

"Hey, Sia." A stunning blonde girl approached, holding hands with a guy who looked like he could be a male model.

"Aspen, you made it." Sia kissed her on the cheek. "And Jason. Aspen told me you were flying down from Sydney today."

"How are you, gorgeous Sia? Thanks for letting me tag along." He kissed Sia on the cheek.

Sia had such a beautiful, magnetic personality. Everyone couldn't help but love her. She introduced Leo and me to her friends, and I was struck by the warmth I felt for them immediately. They both looked me dead in the eye when they shook my hand.

My mother had always 'encouraged' friendships with the daughters of her social network, and I just never found any real connection to any of them. Sia felt like my first real friend, and I'd barely seen her outside work. My mother had blown a bubble for me to live in, and it had taken me twenty-five years to burst it.

"I'm going to have to clock on, Jules," Leo whispered into my ear and kissed my neck, making my whole body hum. He then turned to the group. "Are you guys ready to go in?"

Everyone nodded.

"Hey, Tony," Leo said to the bouncer. "These four are with me."

Tony nodded and let us pass.

"I'll find you on my break, okay?" Leo kissed me unashamedly right in the middle of the bar. I wrapped my arms around his neck and deepened the kiss. I loved how he groaned into my mouth, clearly not wanting to let me go. Hopefully all the single girls in the room had watched me stake my claim.

He disappeared behind the bar, and I turned to see Sia smiling radiantly. *Wow!* she mouthed.

My cheeks flamed again, but I couldn't help returning her smile. I was completely smitten for the first time in my life.

"Seriously, Jules." She hooked her arm through mine. "He is a god and seems lovely, too."

"My shout, ladies," Jason offered. "What are you drinking?"

"Corona with lime," Aspen, Sia and I said in unison then looked at each other and chuckled.

"Well, that's easy," Jason said, shaking his head and smiling. "You girls find somewhere to sit, and I'll find you with the drinks." He kissed Aspen lightly on the lips then turned and headed for the bar.

All the lounges were taken, but we found some bar stools around tall, round tables in the back corner of the ground floor.

"So, how do you two know each other?" I asked, glancing between Sia and Aspen. I'd heard Sia mention her name before, but I didn't actually know anything about her.

"When I moved to Melbourne from Sydney, I didn't know anyone. I answered a share-accommodation ad, and lucky for me, it was Sia's ad." She looked fondly at Sia. "She took me under her wing while I got my bearings. I stayed with her for... how long?" She looked at Sia.

"About six months, I think. Then your super-hot big brother gave you an apartment in Brighton, and I was ancient history." She rolled her eyes but smiled warmly.

"My brother is a property developer and is far too generous."

Jason appeared with the drinks, and we all clinked bottles. "Cheers."

"So you and Sia work together, I hear." Aspen continued with our conversation.

"For three years now," I replied. "And she was dating my boss for like five minutes."

Aspen chuckled. "Oh, she told me about him. Enormous p—"

"Oh my God," I cut her off and laughed at the same time. "I'm still trying to block out that visual. Change of subject, please," I begged. "How long have you two been dating?" I asked Jason and Aspen. They were a gorgeous couple.

They looked at each other and smiled.

"Bit over six months," Jason said, clearly besotted with his beautiful girlfriend. "We're doing the long-distance thing at the moment, which is killing me."

Aspen leaned over and kissed his cheek. "Jason's in Melbourne for work. He's a kickass Sydney architect."

"How long are you here for this time, Jason?" Sia asked.

"A week this time, but I'm seriously considering moving here." He looked directly at Aspen. "I really love Melbourne."

Aspen blushed, and Sia groaned but laughed at the same time. "Oh my God. I'm surrounded by lovebirds."

I decided to change the subject for Sia's sake. "Aspen's a beautiful name. Are your parents skiers?"

"Funny story," she said with a grimace more than a smile. "I thought I was named after the North American ski resort, and my brother, Ryan, always teased me that it's where I was conceived because our parents holidayed there."

"Oh God. No one wants to think about their parents like that." My mind flashed back to the conversation with my father when he had told me about the way Mum used to be. Apparently they had been madly in love when they first got married. It was hard to reconcile that with the awkwardness I had often felt between them growing up. I really hoped they could find a little bit of their old selves if they got some help. Grief really can have some devastating long-term effects I was only just beginning to understand.

"Well, my mum told me the real reason for my name on the day she married my stepfather, Jonathan, earlier this year. I was named after the Aspen tree."

I scrunched up my nose and tried not to laugh. "Really?"

She nodded her head and laughed. "Should've heard her try to justify it. *They're beautiful trees, darling. They benefit from fire. They're resilient.*' Blah, blah, blah."

I laughed and was still laughing when I felt strong arms encircle me from behind. I knew it was Leo immediately from his unique scent—an intoxicating mixture reminiscent of pine trees. I inhaled and basked in the perfect feeling of being in his arms.

"Having a good time?" Leo asked the group.

"I'm surrounded by drop-dead gorgeous women," Jason replied. "Best night ever."

"Cheers to that." Leo clinked his water glass with Jason's beer bottle.

I placed my hands over Leo's arms and reached back and kissed him. "Aspen was just telling me about her name. You know, I've never asked my parents how they came up with my name." I turned my head back again. "How about you, Leo? I bet your mum loved Tolstoy, or the zodiac maybe?"

Leo's whole body tensed briefly. He tried to shrug it off by releasing me and taking a seat at the spare bar stool. I looked at him questioningly.

"I... um... can't remember. It's probably a family name or something."

"My round," Aspen announced, standing up.

"I'll come and help you," Jason offered.

Leo stood up, too.

"Are you okay?" I whispered when he kissed my cheek. "Did I say something wrong?"

"No, beautiful." He cupped my face with his hands. "You're perfect. I'll come back when I can."

I watched him walk away, knowing something was off.

"Wonderlove," Sia stated, and I turned back to see her dreamy expression. "You're going to marry that guy."

A part of me wanted to laugh, but her speech at Juniper's wedding was said with such sincerity, I knew she really believed in seeing the difference between lust and love.

"It's all new, Sia. I am happy though. He's a really good guy."

"And fucking hot," she added with a wink.

Jason and Aspen returned with drinks, and we spent the next few hours chatting and laughing. It was the most fun I'd had possibly ever. I was surrounded by genuine people, and I had the whole weekend with Leo ahead of me.

"Let's dance!" Aspen exclaimed, grabbing my hand. "Come on, Jase. Sia, get your butt on the dance floor."

The four of us headed to what had become a dance floor. The music was so infectious that people were dancing everywhere, but a large group had converged near us and was creating a buzz of energy. Jason and Sia were really good, natural dancers. They had an effortless rhythm and seemed to really enjoy it. It was impossible not to have a great time with these three.

"So you and Leo are one hot couple," Aspen shouted in my ear. "The guy is completely smitten."

I looked at her a little shocked. My cheeks turned into

hot fireballs, and I shook my head.

"Don't be embarrassed. I've seen the exact look before."

"What do you mean? We only just started dating." Shouty conversations are always a little hard going, but I was taken aback by what she'd said.

"My brother, Ryan. He's planning to propose to his girlfriend, Holly, next month on her birthday. They had a rough time for a while, but seeing them together, it was obvious they were crazy about each other."

Butterflies, too big to be real, turned my stomach upside down. I glanced towards the bar and caught Leo's eye. He smiled and waved but was flat out with customers. I closed my eyes and allowed the music to consume me.

A few hours later, I felt Leo's lips on my neck, feathering kisses down my sensitive skin from behind and snapping me out of my dance meditation. "Ready to go?"

I turned into him and put my arms around his waist, looking up into his gorgeous face. "I'm ready." I meant it in every way.

He kissed me and our tongues went to war, driven by our mutual desire.

Aspen, Sia and I retrieved our coats and bags and met Jason and Leo out the front.

"So nice to meet you," I said to Jason and Aspen, giving them both a hug. "Hope we can catch up again before you go back to Sydney," I directed at Jason.

"Me too," Jason replied, his arm firmly around Aspen.

"What are you lovebirds up to this weekend?" Sia asked Leo and me.

"I'm taking Jules to my farm in the Yarra Valley tomorrow night."

"Really?" I asked, excited to go there again, invited

this time.

"I promised you a light show."

"You are out of this world."

"Should I take that as a compliment?"

I whispered in his ear. "Without a doubt, and I plan to show my appreciation in about fifteen minutes' time." I winked at him and heard a low groan come from deep in his chest. He gripped my hand and started pulling me away from the group.

"That sounds amazing." Aspen winked at me and gave me an 'I told you so' look.

"Bye, guys," I called out as we parted ways.

# CHAPTER 35

# LEO

"I HAD SUCH A GOOD time tonight," Juliette said as we walked into my apartment. "I can't wait to spend the rest of the weekend with you."

Juliette was finding herself, and part of that was being surrounded by genuine people. Bea and Angus were the most down-to-earth and loyal friends I could ever have, and they already loved her. Seeing her so happy at the bar with Sia, Aspen and Jason, I knew they, too, were the type of people she needed in her life. I wanted that for her.

She'd told me she'd never felt sexy before we met. My jaw clenched thinking about her with her ex-boyfriend, Dick. His name suited him perfectly, but I felt almost grateful to him. His loss had changed my life, and I'd never take her for granted. She was special and she was mine. There was no sexier sight than her.

"You know what I can't wait for?" I asked, raking my eyes down her body.

She smirked, but her eyes were filled with lust. "I've got a pretty good idea."

I was on her in two seconds flat. Our physical

attraction was there from the moment we saw each other, but now we were more. So much more. I couldn't get enough of her, and it wasn't even just about getting into her pants. I wanted to talk to her, get to know her, help her and maybe one day, I would open up to her.

"Come with me." I held out my hand, and she took it without hesitation.

She chuckled as I dragged her towards my bedroom. "Are you going to have your wicked way with me?" she purred.

Standing next to my bed, I cupped her face in my hands. "I'm going to worship you the way you deserve to be worshipped."

Her beautiful navy eyes blurred and I kissed her, wanting her to know how important she had become to me. Resting my forehead on hers, I whispered, "Tonight is all about you."

She groaned and I smiled.

"Get on the bed."

She lay down, never taking her eyes from mine, and I watched her in awe. She was spectacular. I climbed on top of her, my face an inch from hers. I was going to enjoy bringing her pleasure. I kissed her lightly on the lips before venturing to her neck. She tried to reach for my belt buckle, but I grabbed her hand and clamped it down by her side.

"My pants are staying on tonight."

She groaned again. I enjoyed the sound so much.

My right hand grazed her body from her neck, across her breasts, and then slowly undid her jeans. When I lowered the zip, her hips raised, allowing me to slip the jeans down over her perfect backside. I released her hand and quickly removed her jeans and underwear, throwing them off the side of the bed.

I pushed her sexy black top up, exposing her perfect

breasts.

"Take your top off," I instructed.

She obliged immediately, and I could see her nipples immediately harden under my gaze, waiting for attention. I wasted no time sucking each one, slowly torturing her with my tongue. Her back arched off the bed, and I could feel myself getting harder by the second.

I stroked her toned stomach, trailing light kisses everywhere I touched and slowly making my way south. As if sensing where I was headed, her whole body tensed. When I reached my destination, her head shot up off the bed.

"God, Leo," she panted. "No one has ever done that before."

"Good," I replied, plunging my tongue into the most intimate part of her beautiful body.

"Oh my God!" she half-whispered, half-shouted, convulsing beneath me.

I was in heaven and wanted to bring her this pleasure more than I'd ever wanted anything. Before long, she was writhing and screaming my name, her body shuddering in waves of ecstasy. Watching her come apart for me was the most incredible experience of my life. She kept her eyes closed, and her grin remained in place as she came down from her orgasmic high. I made my way back up the bed and lay down next to her, reveling in her afterglow.

Eventually, she opened her eyes and then turned on her side to face me. "Thank you. That was... fucking incredible."

"God, you're so beautiful, Jules." I pushed some of her hair, which had fallen across her face, behind her ear.

"I can take care of you, too," she whispered, grazing her hand across my straining trousers.

"Not tonight. I wanted tonight to be all about you, and

I meant it."

"I want you, Leo. I want you inside me right now."

There's not a straight man alive who could've resisted that invitation from her, especially with my uncomfortable hard-on doing most of the thinking.

"You are incredible, and there's no place I'd rather be."

I wrestled my pants off as I reached for a condom in the bedside table. After I'd rolled it on, I looked her in the eye to make sure her conviction was still there. If anything, she looked more lust filled and fiery. How did I get so goddamn lucky to find her?

I moved on top of her, and her thighs opened further to accommodate my large frame. Juliette's hands went to either side of my face and pulled me down to her. When my lips were almost touching hers, she whispered, "I want it hard and fast."

Hearing those dirty words from her beautiful mouth sent most of the blood from my body surging south, and I slammed into her in one motion. Juliette's head arched back against the pillow, and her hands gripped my biceps. Her arched back made her mouth-watering breasts rise invitingly towards me, and I didn't hesitate to tease her nipples with my tongue, licking each one slowly, in sharp contrast to the increasing speed with which I was slamming into her.

"Yes. Leo. Yes. Leo." Juliette alternated between those words and became increasingly breathless as we both powered towards our release. When it came, it was like nothing I'd ever experienced. We both shattered together, and I knew beyond any doubt that I never wanted to be with any other woman ever again. She was everything.

"So much for keeping your pants on," she mocked.

"Hey. I tried. It's not my fault you can't resist me."

She tried to punch me in the arm, but I grabbed her hand and kissed her hard on the mouth to shut her up.

Eventually, we managed to prise ourselves apart and take a shower. When we climbed back in bed, we resumed our position of lying face-to-face, mere inches separating us.

"When I'm with you, I feel brave," she whispered. "Brave enough to be myself for the first time." She reached for my hand and intertwined our fingers.

"What were you so afraid of?" I asked, squeezing her hand and rubbing my thumb over her knuckles.

She paused as if trying to collect her thoughts. "I was afraid my mum wouldn't love me anymore if I wasn't everything she wanted me to be. It sounds really silly to say it out loud. I'm an adult, for goodness' sake."

"There's nothing silly about a child loving their mum." A knot formed in my stomach and I felt the room sway. "You've carried around far too much guilt, and it's about time you let it go."

"Risk-taking has always been a coping mechanism, but it was all about the adrenaline rush. Taking a risk with my own life was calculated. Taking a risk with hers was unimaginable and, until you, never felt worth it. She's always been there for me and, despite her obsessive ways, I knew she loved me."

"Love between a parent and a child should be unconditional." My heart ached in a way I hadn't allowed it to in a long time. The lump in my throat was constricting my breathing. I didn't like this line of conversation. "Controlling your life has probably kept her grief at bay all these years, and now that you're not allowing that anymore, she'll finally confront it." I picked up her hand and squeezed it. "You've done her a favour, Jules.

"You never talk about your mum." She said it so

quietly I guessed she already sensed it was a touchy subject for me. A subject I didn't like to think about, let alone talk about.

"She's dead."

Juliette squeezed my hand tighter. Having her so close to me was starting to feel more like a need than just a want. She wriggled forward and moulded herself so perfectly to my body. Her head nuzzled into the crook of my neck. "Tell me about her?"

I kissed her head and sighed. "Not tonight, angel." I kissed her head again, sensing her disappointment in her slumped shoulders. "I'll tell you about her one day."

She looked up at me with trusting eyes. "Whenever you're ready, I'm here for you. Okay?"

"Go to sleep, beautiful girl."

I hugged her to me and breathed in time with her until I knew she was asleep. I couldn't help the uneasy feeling I had that she was putting her trust in me, and I had no real intention of opening up completely to her. I was doing her a favour sparing her the ugliness. Five years ago, I'd lost both my parents in a way I couldn't talk about. There was no point dredging up the past. I'd told her the only thing she needed to know about my mother: she was dead.

# CHAPTER 36

## LEO

"CAN WE TAKE MY CAR to the farm?" Juliette asked as we lay in bed the next morning, unwilling to untangle ourselves from each other.

"Sure. Why?"

"I love to drive and don't get much of a chance to in the city."

"Okay. We'll get the tram back to your apartment and go from there later this afternoon."

She snuggled in closer and kissed my chest.

"Hardly worth having a car in the city. Motorbikes are much easier."

"You have the Jeep though."

"It was my dad's. I just can't bring myself to sell it. I'd planned to sell it and even placed an ad about a year ago but pulled it as soon as I started getting enquiries. It's crazy, really. It's expensive to run and service, but it's just sentimental I suppose." I shook my head, knowing how ludicrous it sounded. "I should sell it."

"It's not crazy at all." She hugged me tighter and kissed me lightly on the lips. I was again reminded of the peace this girl brought into my life with her simple comfort.

I threw a few things in a duffle bag, and then we caught the number sixteen tram back to the city. A short walk from the tram stop took us to her apartment on Southbank.

"Pack warm clothes for tonight. It'll be cold at the farm. We might stay over at Bea and Angus's if it gets too late to drive home, so maybe pack your toothbrush."

"No sexy lingerie?" she purred, winking at me seductively.

She was killing me. I pulled her to me and kissed her. "I've changed my mind about the farm. Let's just stay here all weekend."

"I'm sorry," she groaned as I continued my exploration of her neck. "I really want to go back to the farm."

I kissed the delicate skin on her neck because I knew how much it turned her on. "Are you sure about that?" I said between kisses. "We can have a lot more fun here."

She groaned as I continued my sensual assault across her collar bone and grazed my knuckles over her breasts.

"You promised me a light show," she croaked out on jagged breaths.

~~~~~

My knuckles whitened as I death-gripped the grab handle while she deftly blipped down a gear and took a corner at a pace I would have thought utterly suicidal—except that she executed it perfectly. "Fuuuuck, Juliette."

"What?" she asked, smiling nonchalantly and humming along to P!nk's "Raise Your Glass." "Did you know P!nk is my idol?"

She wasn't kidding about how she loved to drive. I was observing more of the real Juliette behind the wheel.

"No, I didn't know that. She is pretty badass though, so it does make sense."

"She is totally badass, but I reckon she's so much more. She's beyond talented, a fierce mother, a poster girl for feminism but most of all, unapologetic for being herself. It's like she is who she is and doesn't give a crap what anyone thinks."

"Okay."

She laughed, probably knowing her assessment of the singer was lost on me.

"I've always loved her music," she continued. "But I never really listened. I always felt so inspired and motivated by her, but then I'd ignore my inner voice the second my mother said 'boo.'"

Juliette spoke quite calmly, even though she'd just taken another corner at warp speed. I braced my core muscles, closed my eyes briefly and tried not to think about how fast the next corner was approaching.

"Are you feeling inspired now?" I asked, opening my eyes. "Inspired to keep us alive, I hope."

She glanced over to me and smiled, the light reaching her eyes. "Trust me."

"I do, but I'll be happy when we get there in one piece."

She threw her head back and laughed. "No sweat."

My beautiful girlfriend handled the car with the casual competence of a professional race car driver. It was incredibly sexy.

"You're a bloody good driver. I reckon you could take on the pros."

She glanced at me and scrunched up her nose. I suspected it was one of the things she didn't publicise openly.

"Do you think I'm reckless?"

I shook my head. "Pushing limits and feeling the rush is obviously a part of who you are. You have to embrace it and own it. Trying to hide who you are was making you reckless. Those suicidal thoughts of yours just pissed me off."

"I like driving fast," she whispered. "Like—I *really* like it." She glanced at me again and bit her bottom lip.

I laughed. "Pretty sure I already worked that out."

"Maybe you'd like to come to the track with me some time?"

"You race? Seriously?" That I had to see.

"You could meet Jim and Shorty, my race buddies."

I clenched my jaw. Juliette would turn heads anywhere she went, but a racetrack would be awash with testosterone. "I'll be there." Damn straight I'd be there.

The farm came into view, and when she pulled up at the gate, I jumped out to open it. "Park next to the house. You can enjoy my handiwork on the driveway."

As we rumbled over the cobblestones, I felt the familiar pangs of tension roll through me. When she turned the car off, she faced me. "Are you okay?"

I nodded. I was nervous about being there, but I could do it for her. Her big eyes were willing me to open up to her, but she was better off not knowing.

"Let's get out of the car and go for a walk. Last time we were here, I didn't get to show you around properly."

We jogged down the garden to the drywall boundary, eager to warm up a little. Juliette had her cream coat, a scarf and a beanie on, and she looked stunning. The sun was dropping in the sky, and the cold air made her cheeks rosy.

"Wow!" she gasped, the cold air puffing from her mouth. "You've done an incredible job, Leo." She ran her gloved hands over the stone. "Is this the end of your property?" She indicated the grassy field beyond the wall.

"That field is part of my property, but only to the first fence. Beyond that belongs to my neighbours." I grabbed her hand. "Come on, I'll show you."

The grass was dry and a little crunchy underfoot. It hadn't rained in a while.

"I really love it here, Leo." She couldn't stop looking around. "Open space, pine trees, grazing horses. It's heaven."

"I like being here with you." It was true. Being with her made me so incredibly happy. I pulled her to me and hugged her close. She put her arms around my waist and rested her head on my chest. All was right in the world.

"I love this time of year," she said, pulling out of my arms and skipping ahead. "Cold weather has always been my favourite."

"Me too." I loved seeing her like this. She looked so happy and free. I never wanted to see her in pain or fighting to be someone or something she wasn't. "What else do you love?"

She stopped and looked at me quizzically. "Actually, lots of things."

"Tell me your top five."

We took off again at a slow pace. I kept glancing at her deep in thought with her eyes casting up to the sky, then down to her feet, then back up again. She was mesmerising.

Halfway across, one of the horses in the field lifted its head and wandered over to us. He was a beautiful bay gelding with black dapples on his rump and a white star on his forehead.

"I love horses. Cold weather is my number five and horses are number four." The old boy closed his eyes as she stroked between them.

"Do you ride?"

"Not for a long time. My grandparents have a farm on the Mornington Peninsula. I learnt to ride on a pony they kept for me."

"Well, this old boy belongs to Bob and Wendy, my neighbours. I let them use my field for their horses. I'll ask if we can borrow him sometime. I'm sure they won't mind."

A smile that could light up New York City erupted on her face.

"Getting dirty in the garden."

"What?" I asked, confused.

"That's my number three. I love being on my hands and knees getting dirty in the garden. I love digging the soil and watching things grow."

I swallowed hard and couldn't speak.

"What's wrong?" she asked.

"You shouldn't use the words 'getting dirty' and 'hands and knees' in the same sentence. My brain can't cope."

She smacked me on the arm and laughed. "Pervert."

"Your fault." I pulled her to me and kissed her. I couldn't keep my hands off her.

"Kissing. That's my number two. I love kissing you."

"Well, I'm glad you clarified." I kissed her again.

We walked in silence for a while before she stopped and turned. "Why me?"

"What do you mean?"

"You've known me less than two months, and for a lot of that time, it's been far from smooth sailing." She locked her eyes with mine, and I swore I could see right through to her soul. "So, why me? Why didn't you write me off the moment you saw me at the charity event with Richard?"

I huffed out a loud breath. "If you beat me back to the wall, I'll answer your question."

"Two questions." She held up two fingers. "I want answers to two questions."

"And if I win?"

"You won't." She took off at a sprint, catching me by surprise. I stood there dumbfounded for a couple of seconds before I realised she was making serious ground. Her long legs were a blur, but I could tell she was laughing at the same time, which was slowing her down. I gave her a few more seconds just so I could enjoy the sight of that beautiful girl leaping over rocks and waving her arms around.

I took off after her. My legs were fast and strong from rigorous training, but I didn't catch her. I didn't really want to. I enjoyed the back view of her almost as much as the front. She stood at the wall, puffing but laughing jubilantly.

Picking her up, I threw her over my shoulder and walked through the back gate and to the gazebo. She was laughing and pounding on my backside.

"Put me down, you caveman," she demanded.

I deposited her on the seat and collapsed next to her. She stood up and climbed onto my lap, straddling me before kissing me passionately, wriggling in my lap when she could no doubt feel my desire for her.

"Spill it, Ashlar. Question one. Why me?"

She pushed down harder on my crotch, and I groaned but chuckled at her unnecessary tactic. A deal's a deal.

"It started at fight night," I confessed.

"When you saw me getting attacked by the guy?"

"No. The one before that."

"You mean when you just glared at me through the cage and then disappeared?"

"That's right."

She climbed off my lap and sat down on the seat next to me.

"Does that freak you out?"

She looked up from what she was staring at on the floor. "No. I'm not freaked out. I'm blown away. There's a difference."

I stood up and paced a few times, gathering my thoughts before standing under the wooden archway, looking up towards the house. "Some dickhead in the crowd called out to me as I was leaving the cage. It hit a nerve and stupidly I saw red. I wanted to find him and pummel his face into the ground." I turned my head to face her.

"I remember." She stood up and walked over to me, reaching for my hand.

"I scanned the crowd, hoping he'd call out again when my eyes came to rest on you. Everything other than you faded away. Sounds corny, but you looked like an angel, and I no longer felt the urge to hurt that guy. I felt calmer than I'd felt in years, and somehow I knew you were someone special." I squeezed her hand. "I knew we'd meet again."

"Probably didn't guess it'd be the next day at my mum's snobby charity event, huh?"

"No," I chuckled. "When I saw you in that white lace dress with Richard, I was dumbfounded. I had an overwhelming desire to protect you from whatever was happening in your life that made you appear so downtrodden."

"Oh," she mouthed.

"Then you appeared in my old bedroom." I pointed towards the house. "The sassy smartarse ready for a fight."

"I was trespassing and I accused you of stalking me."

She covered her face with her hands.

"You asked me why you? And I'm telling you, I've never been more intrigued, more confused, more frustrated or more turned on by any girl in my life. It certainly hasn't been a classic boy-meets-girl love story, but here we are."

"Here we are." She hugged me tightly and I kissed her head.

"I'll throw the question back at you. Why me?"

"You're really hot, and I wanted to get in your pants." Her deadpan expression was ruined by the light dancing in her eyes that turned into a laugh.

She had such an incredible way of laughing with her whole body, and it was infectious. I lunged for her and tickled her sides, eliciting pained laughter.

"I'm kidding," she huffed out between laughs. When she'd composed herself she continued. "The moment we locked eyes across the cage changed my life." She took a few deep breaths. "I felt something fundamental shift inside me, and from that moment on, my worlds began to collide." She kissed me gently and spoke against my lips. "You and I were meant to meet when we did. You saved me from myself. I feel that in my bones."

"I love you, Juliette." The words fell out, and I realised quickly that I didn't care. I loved her and I wanted her to know.

A gasp escaped her lips before I crushed them with mine so she didn't feel pressured to say the words back. It was a kiss unlike any before. She pushed me back before we got too carried away. "Are you going to let me respond, or are you just going to kiss me to death?"

"That's how I'd like to go." I tried to hide my inner turmoil with a cocky grin.

"If you're going to be a smartarse, I'll keep it to myself." She tried to escape, but I tightened my arms around her.

"You don't have to respond."

"I love that you love me," she started.

"Seriously, Jules. You don't need to say anything." I wished at that moment I hadn't told her how I felt. I didn't want to scare her off.

"I'm not finished."

"I love how you make me feel important and special."

"There's no one more important to me than you."

"Can you please stop interrupting?" She smacked me lightly on the chest. "It's getting annoying."

She was so fucking beautiful. "Sorry."

"I love that, despite the demons that so obviously haunt you, you were willing to show me the beauty you know shines brighter here."

She really loved the farm and that made my heart ache.

"I love your body." She ogled me shamelessly and I chuckled, thankful for her ability to bring her light to my dark. She was flush against me.

"I love your heart." Her face turned serious as she touched my chest in the middle and could no doubt feel my heart rate quicken under her touch.

She placed her other hand on the side of my face. "I love your mind and how you make me smile every time I think of you, which is pretty much all the time, by the way."

She took her hand from my chest so both were cupping my face, and then she reached up to kiss me. She pulled back, and the look in her eyes gave away what she was about to say before she said it.

"I love you, Leo. All of you. You're my number one."

My lips crashed down on hers in a kiss to end all kisses. Our tongues entwined in a frenzied collision of lust and love. I couldn't wait to get her home and naked. When we came up for air, I held her for a long time, enjoying the serenity I felt with her safe in my arms.

"Come on, gorgeous," I whispered. "We can't stand around all day. We have jobs to do." I smacked her lightly on her butt. "I noticed a tree fallen down around the other side of the house. I'll need the chainsaw from the shed to cut it up. I might even let you have a turn."

"Wait! I have another question."

"Oh right. You do. Hit me with it."

She appeared suddenly unsure, shifting from one foot to the other before looking me in the eye. "What happened in this house?"

My blood ran cold. It was the question I dreaded the most. I felt the blood drain from my face. I flinched when I felt her hand on my arm.

"You don't have to tell me. I'm sorry for asking." Her voice was soothing and calm.

I squeezed my eyes shut and tried to calm my mind. When I opened my eyes, I told her my truth. "I lost both my parents in that house five years ago."

"God, Leo. I'm so sorry." Her voice was full of sincerity and warmth. "Thank you for telling me. I can't imagine how hard that must have been for you."

She had no real idea just how hard. "I'm sorry, Jules. It's in the past, and I don't see the point in dredging it up."

She nodded, and I was grateful she didn't push for details.

~~~~~

It was after five by the time we'd finished chopping and stacking the wood. For a city girl, Juliette had no fear of getting her hands dirty. She was so fucking perfect.

"Come on," I said, grabbing her hand. "I'll put the chainsaw back in the shed and grab some torches. It'll be pitch black here in under half an hour."

The moon would rise around nine, so we'd have a fantastic view of the night sky until then. Everything was going to plan.

# CHAPTER 37

*Juliette*

"Umm... Leo. Mother Nature is calling. Is there an outside toilet?"

Leo looked around the shed, cursing to himself. "There isn't." He glanced at the house. "You can use the downstairs bathroom, but I don't know what state it's in. Sorry. I didn't think." He appeared completely mortified, and I'd never wished to be a boy more than I did at that moment. "Do you want me to come with you?"

His reluctance came through loud and clear. "It's fine, babe. Thanks," I said, hopping from one foot to the other. I'd left it to the absolute last moment to ask. "I'll just take one of those torches."

I could see the indecision on his face. He was clearly tortured letting me go in there alone, but he'd probably have been more tortured to go in with me given what happened the last time we were in there together.

Shaking his head as if he were disgusted with himself somehow, he spoke so quietly I could hardly hear him. "There's a key in the pot next to the back door. Go through the kitchen, and the bathroom is the second door on the left down the hallway."

"Thanks. Back in a sec." I scooted quickly towards the house, glancing back at Leo just before I went through the shed door. His usually powerful demeanour appeared crippled by fear. He stared at his feet with his hands in his pockets and rocked nervously from heel to toe. I hated to see him hurting, but my bladder was pulling rank.

The last time I was here played in my mind. Leo telling me that both his parents had died in the house shed a lot of light on why he was so edgy. I didn't know the circumstances, but he was obviously still grieving and the house was a tangible reference point for his grief. He still loved it; otherwise surely he would've sold it.

When I let myself in, the scent of freshly-cut lavender invaded my senses. I really didn't enjoy the smell, but that was beside the point. Why would there be fresh lavender in the house at all? Shining the torch around the country-style kitchen, I found the offending arrangement. A large vase filled with flowers in exclusively purple tones sat proudly on the bench. Lavender was the overwhelming scent, but I also recognised hyacinths, morning glory and some beautiful irises.

I'd barely looked around last time I was there, but I was sure it had been dusty and disused. By contrast, it was now spotless. With my screaming bladder, I didn't hover and quickly made my way into the hallway, shining the torch ahead of me, thankful for its light. The first thing I noticed was another vase of flowers sitting on a wooden sideboard halfway along the exposed stone wall. It was similar to the one in the kitchen but a bit smaller. I had a quick smell, recoiled as the lavender hit my nostrils, then scurried to the toilet before things got embarrassing.

The bathroom, like the kitchen, was spotless, with a distinctive smell of disinfectant. Someone had cleaned it that day, and I said, "Thank you" out loud. So desperate to take care of business, I hadn't noticed the note stuck to the mirror above the vanity. After I washed my hands by torchlight, I pulled off the paper and picked up the torch. It was for me, and when I glanced at the bottom, I smiled when I saw Bea's name.

> *Dear Juliette,*
>
> *When Leo told me he was taking you to the farm, I thought I'd take care of a few housekeeping issues.*
>
> *First things first, there's a battery-operated lantern on the vanity. Just flick the switch.*

*I shone the torch across the vanity top and located said lantern. I flicked it on, and the room was illuminated by a soft glow. I continued reading.*

> *There's another lantern by the picnic basket in the kitchen. It's full of everything you'll need for a winter picnic. I took a wild guess and assumed Leo would forget to bring food.*

I kept reading as I started walking back down the hall to the kitchen, so incredibly touched by what Bea had done for us.

> *I think you're just what Leo needs to help him face his past. The fact you are there at all speaks volumes. He won't talk about what happened, and I think it's eating him alive.*
>
> *Bea*
> *xx*

What on earth happened here? I wondered, staring at her note.

I picked up the basket and lantern and hurried outside to set up the picnic in the garden. When I laid the blanket out, I rushed back inside for the other lantern along with the flowers. When I stepped back outside, I picked out the lavender and carefully placed them by the back step. Once I was happy with the way it looked, I returned to Leo. He still looked nervous and fidgety.

"Was it okay?" he asked, looking up and exhaling when I re-entered the shed.

"Better than okay, actually." I wasn't sure how he was going to react to Bea's gesture. "The bathroom was spotless, and clean towels were hanging on the rails. There were vases of fresh flowers."

"Purple flowers?"

"Too much lavender," I replied, scrunching up my nose.

He shook his head and clenched his jaw. "Beatrix."

I took a step forward and touched his arm. "She's a really good friend. I have to say I was relieved to see toilet rolls." I chuckled nervously.

"I'll be sure to thank her." He bowed his head. "That sounded sarcastic. I am genuinely grateful to her for your sake."

"She really went above and beyond." I took his hand and led him outside. I'd left the light lanterns next to the picnic so it was easy to find in the otherwise pitch-black garden.

Leo remained quiet as we approached the lights.

When we were standing next to the blanket, I stated the obvious. "She left us a picnic and these lanterns."

"She knew I'd forget." I could hear the smile in his

voice.

"I'm actually really starving now." I released his hand, stepped forward and knelt next to the basket. I patted the ground next to me. "Come on. We had ice cream for dinner last night. This can be our first dinner date."

"Hmmm... It's freezing cold and I forgot to bring food. I'm not setting the bar very high." He sat down on the blanket, shaking his head.

I shuffled forward on my knees to hand him a sandwich. He looked down at the sandwich in his hands but wouldn't look at me. I placed my hands on either side of his face and waited for him to raise his eyes to mine. "You're here and I'm here. I'm as happy as I can be."

A small smile was all I needed, and I gave him a big one in return. "Eat your sandwich and stop with the feeling sorry for yourself."

Leo chuckled. "Bossy Juliette is very sexy."

We devoured the sandwiches Bea had provided and washed them down with a beer. I couldn't think of a time I'd felt more content. When we were done, we packed everything back into the basket.

"So, are you ready for the after-dinner show?" Leo switched off the lanterns, then lay down on his back.

"I think it's a bit cold for that?" I shivered involuntarily.

"Lie down next to me, Jules."

When he asked me to do something with that sexy-assin voice, it was impossible to deny him. I lay down on my back, looked up and gasped. "That's quite a light show."

The night sky was now an inky canvas, shot by thousands of tiny light bullets. I stared, completely spellbound—understanding for the first time how the city lights and pollution had deprived me of something truly wonderful.

"Pretty incredible, huh? Mother Nature was on my side tonight."

I glanced at him briefly and nodded enthusiastically before returning to the panorama above.

"Those two really bright stars," I said, pointing in the general direction. "What are they?"

Leo shuffled as close as he could to me, and I felt his warmth against my side. He pointed to the sky. "They're actually planets. The one that appears lower is Venus, and the other one's Jupiter."

"And that one there?" I pointed to one halfway between Venus and Jupiter.

"That's not a planet. It's called Regulus, and it's actually four stars quite close together. We're seeing it tonight with light rays which left Regulus way back in 1937."

I tilted my head to the left so I could look at him. "You know a lot about this stuff, don't you?"

He closed his eyes briefly and took a deep breath. "My mother was fascinated by the stars."

"Oh really?" I was inwardly thrilled to hear him mention his mum again. "Was she into astronomy or astrology?"

"Before I was born, she was a Classical Studies professor. Her interest was primarily Greek mythology and the names they gave the twelve constellations."

"That is fascinating," I said sincerely.

"She was obsessed with it. My bedtime stories were The Odyssey and The Iliad."

"Oh. I love those books."

"Me too." He exhaled a long breath as if this subject was making it difficult for him to breathe. "She moved to the country to be with my father and gave away her career."

"So you became her student?"

"Kind of. I guess. I loved the myths and legends, but I began studying astronomy on a more scientific basis. Constellations are just groups of stars with no real association to each other; they're usually hundreds of light years apart."

We lay together in silence. He moved his arm under my head so I could snuggle into him, stargazing on a cold winter's night but cocooned by his warmth.

"I could stay here all night," I sighed. "Will you tell me more about the stars?"

"Last night you asked me about my name."

I held my breath, remembering how his whole body had gone rigid.

"I did," I whispered, studying his side profile.

"That star you picked out—Regulus. It's the brightest star in the Leo constellation."

"Oh! Wow." I turned my head skywards again.

"You know Leo is the Latin word for lion?"

"I didn't know it was Latin."

"Okay. Well, that group of stars were perceived as a lion by ancient civilisations as far back as 6000 BC."

"What about the Greek myth?"

"Have you heard of the twelve trials of Hercules?"

"Vaguely. I can't remember much about them though."

"His first trial was to find and kill the enormous and powerful Nemean Lion with the impenetrable hide."

"Oh, that rings a bell."

"Hercules manages to corner the lion in a cave, stuns it with his club, then strangles it with his bare hands. To prove his victory, he must bring the pelt of the Nemean Lion back to King Eurystheus. He works out the only way to get the pelt is by using the Lion's own claws to cut it from his body and ends up using it as his own personal armour."

"Keep going." I was completely mesmerised by his storytelling.

"There are multiple versions of how that story connects to the constellation. Most legends assume it is done in homage to Hercules, but then why would it be of the lion he defeated?"

"That's right. It was an honour to ascend to the stars. I remember that."

"Right. My mum only ever told me one version. Queen Hera had a very strong connection to the lion. Angry at her husband, Zeus, she sent it to live in Nemea where there is a shrine to Zeus. Anyone wanting to worship Zeus had to get past the gigantic and almost indestructible lion. When the lion was hunted down and killed, Hera allowed him to—"

"Ascend to the stars." I finished his sentence, completely absorbed.

"There are a lot of other explanations for the Leo constellation, but that's the only one my mother was interested in."

"Can you show me the other stars in Leo?"

"I can try. It's low in the sky and will drop below the northwestern horizon soon. So you can see Regulus about halfway between Jupiter and Venus?" Leo pointed to the sky.

"Got it."

"From there, you go up in the shape of a backward question mark. That's the lion's head. It's marked by Algeiba and Adhafera."

"Okay," I said unconvincingly.

Leo chuckled. "Back to Regulus. Take a straight line to the left, and you get to a triangle of stars—Chort,

Zosma and Denebola. The lion's rump."

I laughed. "You lost me at Regulus, I'm afraid."

Leo hugged me to him and laughed. "Thought I might, but you did ask."

I snuggled into him and put my arm over his chest. "I did. Thank you."

"I haven't really looked at the stars in years." His voice was shaky. "I forgot how much I liked it."

I cranked my neck back so I could look up at the sky without letting him go. "What do you believe in, Leo? Do you think maybe your mum and dad are up there amongst the stars?"

His body shuddered, and I immediately felt like I'd said something wrong.

"Everything okay?" I asked, willing him to drop the guard that just shot up.

"Are you too cold?" he asked, pulling his arm from under me and sitting up. "We should probably get going."

"I wasn't cold until thirty seconds ago." I felt dejected. Every time I felt like he was opening up, I seemed to say something to make him shut down.

"Did you hear that?" I asked, sitting up, startled and suddenly on high alert.

"The crack?"

I nodded.

"We're in the country, princess. It was just a branch breaking."

I relaxed, knowing he was right. It was just so incredibly quiet compared to the city.

"Okay. Sorry. I might just use the bathroom again before we head off."

"I'll pack the basket into the car."

He pulled me to him and kissed me hard on the lips.

"What was that for?" I asked, breathless.

"Do I need a reason to kiss the woman I love?"

I shook my head and smiled. "I'll see you at the car in a minute."

# CHAPTER 38

## LEO

As I ROUNDED THE CORNER of the house, I stopped in my tracks.

"Don't take another step."

Standing in front of the Mini was a man I recognised from fight night. He was the one who had attacked Juliette, and he was pointing a handgun at me with a sly grin on his face.

Memories of him being rough with Juliette unleashed my rage. I clenched my fists and took a step forward.

"I said, not another step." His voice lacked absolute authority even though I heard him pull back the hammer. The slight reservation was all I needed to know he wasn't about to shoot me.

I raised my hands above my head as I took another step forward. I didn't want him to perceive me as a threat, but I needed to get closer.

"What do you want?" I seethed, stopping my progress to engage him. The most common mistake in situations like these is being too confident. The second most common is fighting back, unless you are trained to disarm, which I was. My biggest concern was ending this before Juliette came back, and I knew I didn't have long.

"Where's the little blonde bitch?"

"She's none of your concern, mate. Just tell me what you want. Then no one gets hurt." I took another step forward.

He waved the gun around aimlessly. "I don't give a fuck about you or the stupid bitch. I just want my money, and that means I need to deliver a message to you, and only you."

"Who put you up to this?" I edged forward whilst keeping the conversation going. "Maybe we can come to an arrangement." The only arrangement I was planning was the rearrangement of his face.

"Have you ever shot a gun before?"

"Of course I have."

He was lying. His eyes glanced to the left, his mouth was tense, his lips pursed and he rubbed his nose with his gun. He had amateur written all over his body. I was obviously stronger than him, and he'd been at fight club, so he'd seen me fight. He shouldn't have let me get so close to him.

I had one chance and I acted without hesitation. Before this amateur fuckwit knew what hit him, I moved myself to the left, out of the discharge line of the gun. It is slower for a man to aim to the firing side of his body than to the support side.

In a blur of rapid movement that caught him completely off guard, I grabbed his wrist that was holding the gun with my left hand and simultaneously grabbed the barrel of the gun with my right, pushing it in towards him. I rolled it against his thumb, being the weakest point of the hand, and he squealed like a pig.

I was in control and forced his hands down towards his body, dropping the arsehole to his knees with the weapon now facing him. Clearly in pain from a twisted wrist, he released the gun and I took a step back.

"Hands in the air, motherfucker." When he'd obeyed my order, I pointed the gun at his head. "How did you find me here?"

He spat at the ground in front of me, aiming for my shoe but falling short. What a complete loser. I hit him across the side of his head with the handle of the gun. He yelped and toppled to the ground, sobbing like a baby. I stood over him and asked again, completely calm.

He managed to get back up on his knees, looking pale and defeated. "I've been paid to make you an offer," he mumbled.

"Speak up, douchebag. I asked how you found me."

"I saw you get in the car with blondie, but I lost you on the way here," he continued. "She's a fucking maniac on the road. I had to track her phone's GPS. My employer is offering to pay you handsomely on a monthly basis. The only condition is that you stay away from the girl."

I shook my head at the ridiculous offer. "Well, you can go back to Dick. I'm assuming it's Dick who sent you. Tell him to man the fuck up. I'm not taking money to stay away from her. He missed his chance and I will fight for her. I'll fight and I'll win."

I removed the magazine and racked the bolt, rendering the gun unloaded and safe in under a second.

I nodded my head. "Get up."

When he was standing in front of me, I bunched his hoodie in my left hand and spoke calmly, but with the absolute authority of a seriously pissed-off man protecting his girl. "Get the fuck off my property and, if you value your life, stay away from me. More importantly, if you get within ten miles of Juliette, I'll kill you and make it look like an accident."

"I don't want anything else to do with that psycho

bitch. Either of them. But little blondie will end up dead if you don't accept the offer. I'm just the messenger. Next time there won't be any warning." He flicked a business card at me with a number printed on it. It landed in the dirt. "Text this number with your answer by ten tomorrow morning."

I punched him in the face before I could consider what he meant by 'either of them.' "I don't like being threatened, and last time I saw you, I told you to stay the fuck away from me or you'd be drinking dinner through a straw."

"You two deserve each other." He spat blood on the dirt in front of him. "This job wasn't worth it. Just text the fucking number and get your money. Then your little girlfriend doesn't get hurt."

"Tell Dick to go fuck himself. Now, get off my property."

He scurried off up the driveway like the sewer rat he was. I watched him slip through the gate in the light of the half-illuminated moon.

The whole episode was over in minutes, and it was only after he'd gone that I realised I had instantly discounted the sewer rat's threat to her life. *Should I consider the possibility the threat was real?* Richard was money driven, and money makes people do terrible things—desperate things. I could protect her when she was with me, but what about when she wasn't? Juliette was far from defenceless, but she had a tendency to put herself in risky situations.

I had just enough time to pick up the card and stash the gun in the shed before Juliette returned.

"Everything okay?" she asked.

"Absolutely. Let's get out of here."

"Are we going to stay with Bea and Angus?"

I stroked her face gently and felt my protective

instincts take hold. I couldn't let anything happen to her. "I really love you."

Her eyes softened. "I love you, too."

"Do you mind if we head back to the city instead of staying with Bea and Angus?" I kissed her neck and whispered in her ear. "I want to hear you say that really loud over and over."

"I can get us back to the city really fast," she panted.

She wasn't kidding. No doubt she broke the speed limits, but I had to admit, she drove with the precision of a pro, barely having to slow down to take corners. The gear changes were smooth and deliberate, maximising the small car's power and agility.

When we got back to my apartment, I climbed out of the car and stretched my limbs. There was enough room for me to fit but not enough to be comfortable.

I met her at the front of the car and we walked in hand-in-hand, sexual tension crackling between us.

# CHAPTER 39

*Juliette*

THE SECOND WE WERE IN his apartment, I found myself
being dragged to the bedroom. Not that I was
complaining. He pushed the door closed with his foot,
kicked off his boots and pulled his jumper and t-shirt off
in one go. His lips were on mine in five seconds flat. His
tongue pushed into my mouth and danced seductively
with mine. I pushed him back, wanting to take some sort
of control this time. Leo groaned, clearly frustrated to
lose his grip on me.

I unbuttoned his jeans, swatting his hands away when
he tried to pull me back to him. I slid his jeans down,
bending lower and lower with them until they were
pooled at his feet. When I tapped his ankle, he stepped
out of them and I thought I heard a faint chuckle.
Kneeling, I kissed the light smattering of hair just above
his boxers and was rewarded with a low, drawn-out
groan. I could see his boxers straining, and I couldn't
resist running my hand over the tented bulge. I looked
up, and his incredible eyes locked with mine, glazed with
lust, desire and what I now knew to be love.

I pulled the boxers down over his impressive erection, and he kicked them off without hesitation. Before I had a chance to make my next move, I was pulled up to him and kissed passionately. I was fully clothed against his nakedness, and I enjoyed the sense of power I felt over this man.

"You have far too many clothes on." Briefly pausing our kiss, his gravelly voice sent desire shooting through my entire body.

When he started to pull at my top, I halted his progress.

"Tell me you love me," I whispered, placing my hands on his bare chest to keep him at bay.

"I love you." His intensity was a major turn-on.

I took a step back and removed my layers of clothing one by one, not letting him help me, despite his best efforts. Reaching behind my back, I unhooked my bra and slowly removed it, enjoying the heightening sexual tension between us. Leo took a step towards me, but I pushed his chest gently with my pointer finger. "Patience."

He shook his head and another frustrated groan bubbled from him.

I hooked my fingers into the top of my underwear and slowly slid them down, not losing eye contact with Leo, who looked like he might explode any second. I retrieved a condom from the bedside table and stalked back to him, ripping the packet open. "We really need to both get tested so we can stop using these."

"Agreed." His voice was croaky and barely a whisper.

Completely naked, but not feeling remotely vulnerable, I sheathed him with a confidence I'd never felt before. I wrapped my arms around his neck and crushed my lips to his. He lifted my left leg and placed it around his waist, and I felt his hardness rub against me exactly where I wanted it.

"I need to be inside you, Jules." He picked up my other leg and carried me to the bed. I was no longer in control and I didn't mind.

He lay me down on the bed and positioned himself between my legs, then thrust into me. I opened my mouth to cry out, but his mouth swallowed the sound.

"Your turn," he whispered mid-thrust.

"Don't stop, Leo," I practically begged.

"Tell me you love me."

I placed my hands on either side of his face and said the words I could only ever imagine saying to him. "I love you."

He pushed into me deeper than ever before, and my head arched back against the covers.

"I fucking love you, Leo," I repeated as his mouth moved to my neck, then to my breasts, where they roamed with an agonising slowness that drove me insane. He kissed them, sucked them and licked them as if he had a direct line to my brain and knew exactly what would send me over the edge. I couldn't help repeating his name over and over as my body surged to climax.

The man I loved was a god in every way. For the first time in my life, I felt like my life was on track and I fell asleep, wrapped in his arms, with a smile on my face.

～～～～

I woke up the next morning and was instantly aware that Leo wasn't beside me. My watch on the bedside table told me it was just after ten.

I found one of his t-shirts to put on, then padded barefoot into the lounge room. I found Leo standing by the window, staring at his phone. He was gripping it like he wanted to crush it with his bare hands.

"Morning," I said softly.

He turned around, startled, and I saw pain in his eyes. He'd obviously been deep in thought. "Morning."

I closed the distance between us and hugged him. "I missed you when I woke up alone."

He kissed the top of my head, then stepped out of my embrace. "I'm sorry."

He appeared pensive and distracted. His body language wasn't welcoming me the way I expected, particularly after last night. Something had changed, and a cold dread consumed me.

"Something's wrong. Please don't shut me out." I reached out and touched his arm. "Not now. Not anymore."

He stared back out the window as if contemplating the problems of the world. "I just have a lot on my mind." He stuttered his words as if saying them out loud caused him physical pain.

Undecided whether to push him on the subject or not, I set about making coffee, because coffee makes everything better. When I handed him a steaming mug, he still wouldn't look at me.

"How about we go out to breakfast?" I suggested hopefully.

He nodded his agreement, but it appeared more out of resignation than consent. I got dressed quickly and returned to find him still staring out the window. There was something really troubling him, and I hoped he would share his burden with me over breakfast.

We walked the few blocks to St Kilda beach and found a café with a free table. In summertime, it would have been near on impossible, but the cold season didn't attract as many tourists to the beachside suburb. He held my hand, but conversation was stilted for the first time.

There was definitely something off with Leo. If he hadn't declared his love for me the night before, I'd suspect he was seriously reconsidering us or worse, trying to find a way to say goodbye. It was deeply unsettling and completely confusing.

When our breakfast arrived, I'd had enough of the inexplicable awkwardness between us. "I'm not trying to pressure you, Leo, but are you sure everything is okay? Have I done something wrong?" I twisted my napkin in my hands. "Are you regretting what you said to me last night?"

He snapped his eyes up to me and appeared pained, but he didn't deny it. My heart plummeted and I felt sick to the stomach.

When he didn't say anything, I shook my head and waved to the waiter for the bill. I sat there in silence just staring at him.

The bill arrived, and I snatched it up before Leo could. Grabbing my coat and bag, I walked to the front counter to pay, not caring if he came with me or stayed at the table. I didn't really want to deal with his mood any longer and needed some fresh air. *How could you go from 'I love you' and making passionate love all night to this?* I didn't get it. It occurred to me that I had glossed over his secrets and his demons. I'd thought it didn't matter when he opened up to me because our connection was so strong. I'd thought I could help him get over whatever was in his past. Perhaps I'd been mistaken.

My phone started ringing in my bag as I dropped my change in the tip jar.

"Hi, Dad." I stepped out of the café as I answered. I wasn't really in the mood for him either, but I did want to know how Mum was getting on.

"Hi, sweetheart. How are you?"

"Fine," I lied.

"Are you busy?"

I glanced back to the table. Leo was still sitting there with his elbows on the table and his face in his hands.

"Umm, no." It felt like the truth.

"Can you come over now?"

"Why?" I asked, concerned. "Is Mum okay?"

"She really wants to see you and she's going to Dartmoor tomorrow, so it might be a good chance for you to say goodbye."

I sighed. "Okay. I'll be there in half an hour."

"See you soon."

He hung up, and I stared at my phone as I felt the walls close in around me. I tried to get some air into my lungs but felt it catch in my throat. I started walking, wanting to get back to my car and the hell away from St Kilda all of a sudden.

"Slow down, Jules," Leo's voice called out from behind me.

I didn't stop and I didn't turn around. I didn't want to hear what he had to say, knowing it was probably words of regret. Fuck that. I kept going, taking short, shallow breaths.

I sensed him behind me the whole way back to his apartment. Fortunately, I had my keys in my handbag, and I bleeped my car as soon as it was in range.

"Don't leave like this," he said when I reached for the door handle. "We need to talk."

I put my hands over my ears and closed my eyes. "Stop talking. Nothing good ever comes after that phrase, so I don't want to hear it." I opened my eyes so he could get a good look at how he was crushing me. "I can't believe you'd even say that to me after last night."

His hands covered mine and gently pried them away from my head. He held them together between us. "I'm sorry, Juliette."

Tears slipped down my cheeks. "You're really breaking up with me." I was going into shock. "I don't understand, Leo. What did I do wrong? You told me you loved me. Why did you lie?" I couldn't look at him.

"I do love you." His thumbs caressed my knuckles, and I saw red.

Air rushed into my lungs, and I pushed him away from me. "I've had enough of people treating me like crap when they're supposed to love me. I thought you were different. I thought you really loved me for me." I clutched my chest. "You obviously don't trust me enough to open up about your past, so I guess this was never going to work anyway. I'm done being a punching bag and I'm done with you." The spiteful words tumbled out of my mouth, and I watched his face drain of blood as if I'd stabbed him through the heart.

I didn't allow any feelings of guilt to stop me getting in my car and driving away without looking back. When I'd turned the first corner and was out of sight, I pulled over and burst into tears, acknowledging the devastating pain of a broken heart.

My phone started ringing, and when I saw Leo's name, I just stared at it. I should've waited for an explanation instead of rushing off. Perhaps after I'd seen my parents, I'd call him back. I knew he had demons, and maybe it was all too much too soon. I had told him I loved him and meant it, yet at the first hurdle, I had run. Perhaps it was too much too soon for me, too.

One thing I knew for sure; I was still a hot mess.

# CHAPTER 40

*Juliette*

"COME ON IN," DAD SAID when he opened the door. "Thanks for coming."

"It's fine." I had an uneasy feeling about it for some reason.

"Let me take your coat." I shrugged out of my black pea coat and scarf and handed them to Dad. While he hung it in the hall cupboard, I wondered where Mum was.

"Hello, darling." My mother appeared at the top of the stairs wearing an impeccable pale pink woollen dress with expensive heels in a matching colour. Her hair was tied back in a tight bun.

"Be nice. Be nice," I reminded myself through clenched teeth as she descended the stairs. "Hello, Mum." I stepped forward when she reached the bottom.

She embraced me warmly. When she stepped back, she looked me up and down. "You scrub up so nicely when you make an effort." I knew I looked terrible, but a backhanded compliment was a step up from outright criticism. I'd spent a lot of time fixing my makeup in the car before I arrived but was unable to hide the signs of my despair.

"Thanks," I replied sarcastically. "I like your dress."

"I'll be in my office if you need me," Dad said. "You mother would like some private time with you."

"Fine." I closed my eyes and took a deep breath. I'd get this over and done with and then I'd go home and hide from the world. I was teetering on the edge of a full-blown freak-out session.

We walked down the hallway towards the back of the house, and I inhaled the smell of Jean's homemade chocolate chip cookies.

Before saying anything, she busied herself getting the tea ready. I was even being honoured with the use of her Versace cups and saucers.

"How are you feeling, Mum?" I asked tentatively.

She looked up at me and smiled. "Wonderful. Thank you."

"Really?" I recoiled. I didn't mean to say that out loud. "I mean. That's great."

When the tea was ready, we moved to the lounge room and sat in the wing chairs facing the fireplace.

"I'm sorry for what happened at Richard's house." She took a sip of her tea, holding the cup's handle delicately between her thumb and pointer finger. "I wasn't myself at all."

"It's okay, Mum." I felt numb to her apology. "I'm just glad you're going to get some help." I stared into my cup and gently moved it around, fixating on the swirling tea and occasional tea leaf popping to the surface.

"You need to know something about Leo before you throw your life away."

"What do you mean?" I looked at her, suddenly wary.

"He's not right for you and he knows it."

I shook my head and sighed. "Mum, I need you to let me make my own mistakes. I need to live my own life."

"I'm really sorry to tell you this, darling, but I wanted to show you what kind of man he was. I offered him a generous monthly allowance to stay away from you."

I almost dropped the expensive gold-plated cup when I jumped up. "You did what?" I snarled, outraged.

"Sit down, Juliette. I've done you a favour."

"By offering money to the man I love to stay away from me? How exactly is that doing me a favour?" I was losing my mind.

Obviously realising I wasn't going to sit back down, she stood up. In heels, she was taller than me. "Have a think about it, Juliette. You're a smart girl." She tapped the side of her head. "I wouldn't be telling you this if he said no."

Everything I knew about Leo told me it wasn't true. "I don't believe you. Leo loves me."

She smiled and nodded, then sashayed from the room, leaving me standing there dumbfounded. She returned moments later holding her phone out to me.

"What is that?"

"It's a text from the man who loves you," she stated sarcastically.

Grimacing, I took the phone and read the message.

*I'll stay away from Juliette.*

I stared at the screen until it faded to black. Once again, loving me had a price tag and once again, the price was right. I calmly returned the phone to my smug mother.

"I hope you get the help you need," I whispered, giving her a kiss on the cheek. "Bye, Mum."

When I was outside, I fumbled for my phone and called Sia.

"You leave for London in two weeks, right?" I asked when she picked up.

"Yep. Why?" she asked slowly.

"I'd like to come with you. I need a break."

"What? Are you serious? What's happened, Jules? What about Leo?"

"Yes or no, Sia."

"Yes. Of course. I'd love you to come with me."

I let out the breath I'd been holding. "Okay."

"Okay."

"So, I'll speak to Heath tomorrow about getting a temp to cover me."

Sia squealed, and I had to hold my phone away from my ear. I tried to share in her excitement, but at that moment I just felt sad.

# CHAPTER 41

## Juliette

IGNORING LEO'S CONSTANT CALLS, MY sadness turned to anger and my anger turned to rage. I told the guys at the front desk not to let him up to my apartment. Years of suppressing my real feelings had taken its toll. I'd become an expert at rationalising others' behaviour and compromising my own. I was a dangerous wreck of swirling hatred, bubbling up from the depths of my stomach. My only saving grace was knowing my debut fight was a matter of days away. If I had any compassion left in me, I might've felt sorry for my opponent, walking around somewhere, ignorant to the fact hell was going to be unleashed on her come Saturday.

"I don't think you're ready, Jules," Zac stated firmly at the end of my Thursday training session.

"What?" My gloved hands dropped to my side, completely deflated. "I've never been more ready for anything in my life." I felt my eyes glaze over and I swallowed hard, refusing to give in to the threatening tears.

"See that," he said, pointing at my eyes. "You're too

emotional. You won't be able to focus properly."

"I'm doing this, Zac," I whispered as he helped me remove my gloves. "With or without you, I'm doing this."

"Well, you have forty-eight hours to get your head in the right place. I know you've been through a lot lately, and you have every right to be a bit fucked up right now, but that will cost you in the ring. Eye of the Tiger, remember?"

"I'll be fine. Trust me."

"Okay, Jules. Rest up and do some of the meditation techniques I showed you."

I rolled my eyes. Despite being a seasoned fighter, dolphin music and crashing waves could be the soundtrack to Zac's life.

Walking back to my apartment, I felt like the weight of the world was back on my shoulders. I missed Leo. I hated that I missed him so much. It was impossible to just switch off my feelings for him when they were so genuine. I'd really fallen hard for him, and he'd discarded me like yesterday's news. It hurt like a bitch. Just when I had summoned the courage to defy my mother and break up with Richard, their affair had been slammed in my face. Leo's love had helped me survive that massive blow. The full weight of that betrayal had not really been given a chance to infiltrate my heart, because I'd been enveloped in Leo's. It had felt like I'd found my soul mate, and being so wrong was a hard pill to swallow.

My phone started ringing, and his face appeared on my screen. It was a photo I'd taken at the farm when he was chopping wood. I'd called out to him and he'd turned around, run his hands through his hair and smiled. I'd captured a candid shot of him looking hotter than he'd ever looked before. My heart ached as I stared at the screen.

"Hello," I whispered. I nearly didn't answer the call, but I'd become too desperate to hear his gravelly voice again. I was too greedy for the way his voice spoke directly to the depths of who I was.

"Juliette," Leo said on an exhale. "Thank God."

"What do you want, Leo?" I closed my eyes, absorbing the way my body shivered.

"I want to talk to you. Fuck. I want so many things, Jules. Why have you ignored all my calls?"

"You don't want me. You made that clear when you accepted money to stay away from me." A wave of nausea hit me, and I had to sit down on the footpath, my back against the brick wall of a shopfront.

"Stop," he demanded. "It's complicated. Please don't give up on us. I just needed time."

"There's nothing complicated here. You said you loved me. I said it back and meant it. You made me feel like you meant it, too. Then the next day, you dumped me. Later, I see a text message you sent my mum, accepting her disgusting offer. Pretty black and white, Leo."

I could hear him groan, and it sounded like something had broken in the background.

"Fuuuck. I didn't take any money. I swear to you."

Taken aback, I paused, trying to process what he'd just said. "But I saw the text."

"Firstly, I thought it was Dick making the threats to your life. He's a money-driven arsehole, so I had to at least consider the threat wasn't idle."

"What do you mean?"

"It's what I wanted to talk to you about at the café and then all week. You've been ignoring my calls and wouldn't see me." He paused, and I tried to reconcile what he was saying. "I was offered money to stay away from you or risk your safety."

A few lonely tears fell from my eyes. What an epic clusterfuck. "It was my mother who made the offer, not Dick."

"I get that now. I just needed time to sort it out and didn't want you endangered in the meantime. I agreed to stay away from you in return for your assured safety. That was the offer I accepted."

I ran my hand through my sweaty hair and closed my eyes. I was a disaster area of colliding emotions, and I couldn't breathe properly. "I'm sorry I jumped to conclusions, Leo, but you should've told me immediately what was going on instead of shutting down the way you did," I whispered. "I'm leaving for Europe with Sia in a week. I just need some space from everything that's happened the last few months. I just need..." I felt the tears threatening and struggled to get any more words out.

"What do you need, Juliette?" Leo's voice sounded as broken as mine.

"I need to forget." I sobbed the words out, allowing the tears to flow freely down my cheeks.

"You need to forget about me." It was a statement rather than a question.

"I don't think I could forget about you even if I wanted to, Leo." I sniffed, wiping my arm across my eyes. "I just need to take a break for a while and just try to forget about my life here. The last few months have been..." I looked to the sky, unable to finish my sentence.

"How long will you be gone?"

"Six weeks."

I could hear him sigh. "You deserve this. You deserve to spread your wings." He paused, and I thought for a second he'd hung up. "This is for the best, but please, can we talk in person when you get home? I love you."

Hearing those words again from him was both confusing and wonderful.

"Okay," I managed to sob out.

"Take care of yourself, Juliette."

His words managed to jolt me from my self-destructive path. I had been a caged bird, held captive by people I loved, was meant to love or who were meant to love me. I was always waiting for the magic moments, but now I had my whole life ahead of me, and the cage door was wide open. My mother wouldn't be telling me what I should or shouldn't do. I had no boyfriend belittling me or using me for his own agenda. Even Leo, the man I loved, had broken my fragile heart even if he didn't mean to.

Friendship had come to have real meaning, and I was slowly finding out who I really was. I wasn't going to be anyone's punching bag, because I was worth more than that.

I still cried myself to sleep that night, like I'd done every night that week, but it felt more therapeutic than the previous nights. I woke up determined and focused.

~~~~~

When I arrived at the Lightning Fight Centre on Saturday evening, I was itching to punch something or someone. I was riddled with nervous energy, and I had no idea if I could channel it properly in the ring. Zac greeted me inside and escorted me to the weigh-in area where I met my opponent, Christina Lee. Her trainer hovered over the scales as my weight was recorded. Zac did the same for Christina to ensure she was a legitimate lightweight. It was all very serious and intimidating, but I kept my shoulders back and my expression neutral.

"You'll be in the red corner," one of the officials stated, as he handed me a red singlet emblazoned with the promoter's logo before turning to Christina and handing one to her. "You're blue."

"Thanks." I walked back to my locker, where Zac was studying his clipboard.

"How are you feeling, Jules?" He looked up when I sat down on the bench next to him.

"I'm nervous but ready. Just want to get it over and done with, really." Butterflies weren't just in my stomach. They had taken over my whole body, and it was hard to sit still. "I'll be back in a sec."

I jumped up and walked to the door that led into the large main room where the crowd was assembling. Poking my head through the door, I gasped. I had already heard the hard rock music from the back room, but once the door was open, it was much louder. The Guns N' Roses song, "Welcome to the Jungle," pulsed out of the speakers. In the middle of the room was the raised boxing ring, surrounded by tables set up for the judges, officials and VIPs. Punters were flooding in through the main entrance to my left, raising the noise level with every passing minute.

I couldn't see them, but Juniper and Sia had insisted on coming when Zac had told them about it, and I wondered if they were there yet. It would be good to have a few friendly faces in the audience for my first fight, and I was grateful for their support. Apparently it's different when you're in the ring, and nothing can prepare you for how you'll react.

Knowing I would be called soon, I made my way back to Zac, who was now standing, and a relieved expression replaced his furrowed brow when he saw me.

"You're on in fifteen minutes. Let's start warming up."

I glanced over at Christina who was busy admiring her reflection in a hand mirror, and I felt some of my butterflies disappear. Vanity has no place in the ring.

"Don't get too complacent, Jules," Zac said when he

saw what I was looking at. "She may look like a show pony, but she has more experience than you in the ring.

"I don't care what experience she's had," I stated. "I'm going to smash her."

After my warm-up, Zac stood in front of me and held both my upper arms, looking me dead in the eye. "Sweat more in peace. Bleed less in war."

I looked at him quizzically, a fine trickle of sweat dripping down the side of my face.

"That's an old boxing mantra." Zac's soothing voice calmed more of my nerves. "You've put in the hard work, Jules, and now it's your time to fight for glory."

"Juliette Salinger. You're up," the official announced. Then he moved over to my opponent, Christina Lee, and I watched her nod as she bounced around, warming up. She'd thrown a few glares my way, but they bounced off me like ping-pongs.

Zac put my red hooded gown over my shoulders and ushered me towards the door. I was glad I'd taken a look earlier so I wasn't so awestruck by the room, even though it was now full and a lot noisier. We made a beeline for the ring as the MC announced us to the sound of loud applause. I climbed into the ring and moved to my corner. I was glad to have Zac with me for last-minute advice based on what he'd seen of Christina's warm-up.

"You've got this, Jules," he stated firmly as he pushed my mouthguard into place. "You've got three rounds of three minutes each. Make every second count."

I nodded and moved away from him, turning to face my opponent. I cast my gaze quickly around the audience, immediately spotting my friends. It was hard to miss Sia jumping up and down like a yo-yo, calling out in an over-excited tone, "That's my friend up there." Sitting down next to her was Juniper, Jason and Aspen.

Wow. I had a lot of support. I scanned the rest of the audience, unable to shake the strange feeling making the hairs on the back of my neck stand on end. I could feel Leo's presence, even though I couldn't see him. It was probably just nervous tension.

I bounced on the spot, my head protector firmly in place and my hands securely covered in black Everlast gloves held up in front of me. My mouthguard was uncomfortable, and I jostled it around in my mouth, trying to get used to its presence.

It was time to focus. It was time to be in the moment and find my magic.

Unlike martial arts, boxing does appear simple, with just the punches, but there's far more to it than that. Unlike kickboxing, where you can kick opponents from a distance and keep them at bay to slow the fight down and get a breather, and Muay Thai, where you can gain a breather by locking your opponent in a grapple, boxing affords you no break. You can't hold, so you can only keep the opponent at arm's length. Effectively, they can always punch you. This will mean the work rate is exceptionally high, as you need to keep exchanging blows to keep ahead on the score cards.

I knew my punches were far from perfect. Zac had done his best to train me, but I had an inner strength and a steely resolve to harness adrenaline rather than be crippled by it. I'd been tapping into it for years, and I was banking on that being my ultimate weapon.

I stared in the eyes of my opponent and, in that moment, I could see all her demons. My eyes were speaking to her, and I knew she understood. "I'm going to win. I'm going to own this fight and I'm going to own you." Her eyes faltered and I thought I had her.

I thought wrong.

The three minutes between the buzzer announcing

the start and finish were a blur. I honestly wouldn't have been able to describe a single thing that happened.

When I stumbled back to my corner, Zac was waiting for me. He took out my mouthguard, wiped my face with a towel and gave me a mouthful of water, holding out a bucket for me to spit in. "You need to slow down, Juliette. You rushed all your punches, and you're not being effective. You're just trying to smash her without thinking."

I nodded my head, barely able to form a single cohesive thought. *What if I can't channel my adrenaline? What if I fail? What if she really hurts me?* A flurry of negative thoughts entered my psyche, and I felt my confidence seeping out of my sweaty pores. When I'd seen all of Christina's demons, I guess she'd seen mine, too.

The second round wasn't much better. If anything, it was worse.

"You totally gassed out on nervous energy, Jules," Zac chided, looking me straight in the eyes. "Fortunately, Christina did, too, so I reckon you're probably about even on points. Tell me what Christina's strongest punch is."

I tried to replay some of the last two rounds in my head. "She has a strong left hook."

"Exactly. Be ready for it and move to your left."

This night was not going to plan. I was supposed to come in and claim victory for myself, annihilating the opposition. Nothing was further from the truth.

I closed my eyes and allowed the noise in the room to disappear. I needed to find something deep inside me and take it into the next round.

The tattoos on Leo's back popped into my head and resonated in me with such force my eyes snapped open. When I'd asked him about them, he was evasive about when and where he'd had them done, but explained with such passion about Buddhist philosophies and finding strength from within.

"What is it, Jules?" Zac asked. "You look like you've just had a breakthrough."

"I think I'm ready now, Zac." I felt an inner calm I realised I'd been lacking to that point.

"You're no quitter, Jules. Go out there and own this. Remember. Cowards never start, the weak never finish and winners never quit. Stay off the ropes and work off the jab."

*Fuck it, I thought to myself. I'm really going to give it a crack. I'm no coward, I'm no quitter and I'm going to use that strength I know is within me.*

# CHAPTER 42

## LEO

SHE WOULDN'T SEE ME. SHE wouldn't know I was there. No one could know I was there. Her life might have depended on it, but it felt like mine depended on seeing her again.

Her first two rounds had been hard to watch. I hoped her trainer was telling her to slow down and stop expending so much nervous energy. I wanted to be in the audience supporting her, then taking her home afterwards, but I had to accept that wasn't going to happen tonight.

A hard slap to my back startled me. "Leo Ashlar? I'll be damned."

Standing next to me was Nick, my childhood boxing coach. I came to this gym three nights a week after school for years until my desire to get into medicine meant devoting every night to studying.

"Nick. Long time, no see. How are things, mate?" I asked, shaking his hand.

"Good. Good. What brings you back out this way? I haven't seen you in a while."

I nodded. "Sorry, mate." I should've stayed in better

touch. I'd approached him at the funeral and asked him to hook me up with a trainer in the city. He gave me a number that I called the very next day. "I've been busy."

"Hey, mate. You weren't in good shape at the funeral. I was real sorry about your parents. Nasty business that."

"Thanks. Appreciate it."

"So word on the street tells me you're making waves in the illegal scene."

It didn't surprise me that he knew. The fighting community was close knit, and everyone knew everyone else's business.

"It helps."

"I get that, mate. I do. Just be careful. I don't want to read about you in a coma in the hospital." His hand slapped my shoulder, and I appreciated his support. "If you ever need anything, you know where I am. Okay?"

I nodded just as the buzzer sounded for Juliette's final round, and both our heads turned towards the ring.

"Blondie up there. She's new. Man, if I was your age. Wow." Nick was laughing and I knew he was joking, but my stomach turned just the same.

"Steady on, old man." I attempted to match his jovial tone.

We half-chatted and half-watched the start of the fight. Something had changed in Juliette and she moved like a lioness, stalking her prey. Our chatting ceased as we both watched, riveted. Her opponent knew she was the gazelle, trying not to stumble, and the scene that played out was poetry in motion. She had the perfect blend of power, grace and a steely resolve, obvious to everyone in the room. Christina had a strong left hook, and finally, Juliette was moving deftly in response.

This was the real Juliette—strong and beautiful, inside and out. This was the Juliette that shone when she allowed her inner self to explode instead of allowing others to push her down.

Juliette dominated every sequence and was declared victorious to the shouts and cheers of the appreciative crowd.

Her whole body glistened with sweat. She'd never looked sexier than she did in that moment, and I couldn't take my eyes off her. I knew she'd seen me when her whole body stiffened and her eyes changed from wide and happy to slits. She was narrowing her vision, clearly unsure if it was actually me. I had to get out of there. I gave her a half-smile, trying to convey my congratulations, and then I turned towards the back door.

"Bye, Nick," I said hurriedly. "I'll come back soon."

"Good luck, mate."

I pushed the fire door open with more strength than needed, keen to make my escape. It burst open, and I exhaled with the cloak of darkness. I pulled my leather jacket on as I made my way over to my bike.

As I pulled my helmet over my head, I glanced back at the door, half-hoping and half-dreading that Juliette would appear. I revved the throttle and counted to three in my head. She wasn't coming. Of course she wasn't coming. I was meant to stay away from her, so it was better that way.

Who the fuck was I kidding? It wasn't better. It was fucking unbearable.

With one more glance back, I sped off, full of rage— an emotion I was very familiar with. I was going to sort this shit out. Then I was going to win her back.

# CHAPTER 43

*Juliette*

**Seven weeks later...**

I'D ONLY FLOWN IN THE night before, so I was exhausted when I pulled into the gravel parking area in front of the Dartmoor Wellness Centre. Despite my jetlag, I was happy. My experience overseas had been incredible, and I felt like a new person. With every day that had passed, my horizons broadened and my instinct to run from situations I feared lessened.

I was so busy staring through the front windshield at the imposing white brick building that I hadn't noticed the black Jeep pull up.

I got out and walked towards the steps leading to the entry, lost in thought. *I can do this.*

The automatic doors opened, and I walked through to a surprisingly welcoming reception area. Perhaps I'd been expecting padded rooms and straitjackets. Pistachio-coloured walls, indoor plants and calming music made it feel more like a health retreat.

A young woman with far too much makeup on greeted

me with indifference at the reception desk. She appeared pained to have to look up from her magazine.

"Welcome to Dartmoor." She spoke in a bored monotone. "How can I help you?"

"I'm here to see my mother. Isabel Fontaine."

"Sign in here." She shoved a form in front of me without looking at me.

"Do you have a pen?"

She huffed out a breath as if I was seriously inconveniencing her. A biro was thrust on top of the form, and she looked at me with a 'there better not be anything else' glare.

"Thank you." I gave her an extra-cheery smile to hopefully annoy her.

When I had signed and dated, she told me to wait while she found out where my mother was.

I made my way over to the cream lounges and took a seat. The coffee table was covered in a variety of brochures and flyers, as well as a few token books on landscapes. There was a distinct lack of trashy magazines. I picked up the book with a collage of lakes and mountains across the front cover.

I closed my eyes and opened the book to a random page. "Queenstown, New Zealand," I said out loud.

"Juliette?"

Leo's gravelly voice startled me, and I snapped my eyes open, dropping the book at the same time. It tumbled to the floor and hit my foot. I scrunched up my face in pain. It was a bloody heavy book.

"Leo." I picked up the book from the floor and replaced it on the coffee table. I closed my eyes and steeled myself against my body's natural attraction to him. When I opened them, I realised it hadn't helped. He was wearing faded, ripped jeans and a white t-shirt, showcasing his incredible body. If anything, he looked like he was more muscular than the last time I'd seen him. A light stubble on his face beckoned for my touch. He looked incredible, and it was physically painful to keep my distance.

"You look really good, Juliette. How are you?"

"What are you doing here?" I croaked, barely able to put words together.

"Your mother called and said she wanted to see me about something important. I thought it might be about you, but I didn't realise you'd be here." A genuine smile lit up his handsome face.

I pulled myself ungracefully to my feet and stood before him, staring into his beautiful, soulful eyes. I had missed this man every second I'd been away, but I'd grown up, too. I was stronger and ready to trust him with my heart again. Gingerly, I reached my hand up and gently cupped his face. I closed my eyes and sighed when he leaned into it slightly.

"Fuck it." Leo grabbed me, and the next thing I knew, I'd been scooped up into his arms and his lips crashed against mine. I threw my arms around his neck and kissed him back in a frenzied daze of pent-up lust and emotion. With our foreheads touching, he whispered against my lips, "I missed you so damn much."

A loud sound of a throat being cleared ended our reunion.

"Sorry to interrupt," the suddenly very friendly receptionist said, directly to Leo.

Leo put me down but kept hold of my hand as we awaited further instructions.

"Mrs Fontaine is in the garden," she continued, a blush rising across her cheeks. "She's been expecting both of you." She ogled Leo like she was starving and he was a juicy steak. "Go through those doors and Jackson will escort you."

"Thank you," I said sarcastically, knowing she had forgotten I was even there.

Jackson led us through multiple sets of doors, some of which required him to use his security pass to gain entry. My eyes darted around trying to take in everything, but I struggled to focus on anything with Leo next to me. I hadn't seen him or my mother in two months, but I'd at least been able to mentally prepare myself to see my mother.

A large, wooden door with a security glass panel opened to a paved courtyard where a few tables and chairs were being used for chess games and reading. Some of the residents looked up and smiled while others just ignored our intrusion. I paused briefly.

"I'm here, Jules." Leo's voice was gentle and reassuring. His physical strength matched the emotional fortitude I wanted but no longer needed.

"I'm fine." I meant it.

"I know." I looked into his eyes and saw only tenderness. "It's really good to see you."

My body yearned for his touch and I squeezed my eyes shut, enjoying the feel of my hand in his—skin against skin.

A gentle slope of beautifully-tended gardens, dotted with fruit trees, led to a lake. In the middle of the lake was an island covered in long grasses and a few small trees. If I were there for any other reason, I would've enjoyed the idyllic scenery.

"She's having some lunch with another resident just beyond the orange grove." Jackson pointed towards an orchard. "I'll be in the courtyard when you're ready to leave."

"Thank you," we both said in unison.

My feet felt heavy, and I couldn't bring myself to

move. I looked to the sky and watched a few clouds drift slowly in the warm, gentle breeze.

"Come on." Leo tugged gently on my hand. "Let's get this over with, and then we have a lot of catching up to do."

I couldn't help inhaling deeply as we walked towards the orchard. The citrus scent was overwhelming.

Beyond the orchard, I could see two women sitting on a pair of Adirondack chairs, facing the lake with their backs to us. They both turned as we approached and stood to greet us.

Leo stopped dead. I didn't recognise the slender brunette woman standing by my mum's side. To me, she seemed friendly, helpful even as she kept a protective hold of my mum's arm. Tension rolled off Leo's body in tidal waves, and my hand felt like it was in a death grip. I glanced at him to see what was wrong and followed his gaze to the stranger. He looked panicked, and a sheen of sweat appeared on his forehead.

"What's wrong?" I murmured from the corner of my mouth. "Who is she?"

"Darling." My mother surged forward. "Thank you for coming."

She hugged me, and I was forced out of Leo's grasp. I returned her embrace half-heartedly, still concerned by the crackling tension in the air.

"Who's your friend, Mum?" I whispered, pulling out of the awkward, lukewarm hug.

Leo's next two words answered my question.

"Hello, Mother."

*All will be revealed in Leo and Juliette's concluding story*
*"Impact (The Fight for Life Series Book 2)"*

*Keep reading for Chapters One and Two.*

*The Fight for Life series, book two*

# IMPACT

## KATE STERRITT

# CHAPTER 1

## LEO

Dartmoor Wellness Centre was no looney bin. I'd envisaged straitjackets and padded cells, but it was more like some sort of fancy health retreat—sprawling gardens, a lake, orange trees. I wanted to see that woman suffer for what she did to Juliette, but this place felt more like a reward. The security was probably to keep people out rather than in.

"Come on." I tugged Juliette's hand gently. "Let's get this over with and then we have a lot of catching up to do." I couldn't wait to get the hell out of there and have her all to myself. I'd spent the past two months missing her with every cell in my body and had hoped she felt the same. Our passionate reunion filled me with hope, but I knew we needed to talk about what had happened before she'd left. She knew her mother had offered me money to stay away from her, and she knew I had rejected it. What she didn't know was why I had pushed her away. I would have to try to find a way to explain it to her, as I was adamant nothing was ever going to come between us again.

Beyond the orchard, two women were sitting on wooden chairs, facing the lake. As we drew nearer, both women stood. When they turned around, my flight instinct gripped my throat as the life I'd spent five years fighting for came crashing down around me. *This can't be fucking happening.*

"What's wrong?" Juliette whispered. "Who is she?"

"Darling." Isabel surged forward. "Thank you for coming."

She wrenched Juliette from me, and we locked eyes. The witch knew what she was doing bringing me here, and smug would be an understatement to describe the look on her face.

Juliette pulled out of the awkward hug. "Who's your friend, Mum?" she asked, sounding extremely uncomfortable.

I knew I had no choice. My hand had been forced, as she was about to find out regardless. Five years hadn't been kind to the virtual stranger standing in front of me. Her dark hair had greyed, and frown lines marred her gaunt face. My next two words were something I never thought I'd utter again, and nausea swirled through me on its ruthless path. I took Juliette's hand and pulled her back to me.

"Hello, Mother."

# CHAPTER 2

*Juliette*

Leo's mother was dead. He'd told me in no uncertain terms on more than one occasion. My heart pounded out of my chest as my mind struggled to process the situation. The fact that Leo didn't sound at all surprised spoke volumes. He'd lied to me. But why? I was face-to-face with his dead mother. His icy tone told me he wasn't at all thrilled about it, and her demeanour was hard to read. She wasn't standoffish, but this definitely wasn't a happy reunion.

"What's going on?" Given the silence, I felt the need to whisper.

Nobody said anything. My eyes darted back and forth from Leo to the woman. They were locked in a standoff.

"Juliette." My mother's cheery tone broke the uncomfortable silence. "This is Gwendolyn." She placed a hand on the woman's shoulder. "Gwendolyn, you have to meet my beautiful daughter, Juliette. Isn't she just gorgeous?"

*Gwendolyn? As in the name of the farmhouse?*

"Lovely to meet you, Juliette," she said, politely extending her hand. "Please call me Gwen. Your mother has told me so much about you."

"I... um... don't know what to say." When I touched her hand, my eyes flitted to Leo. It was the same look I saw on his face the first time I laid eyes on him at fight club. The icy stare was back and my whole body shuddered, but I refused to jump to any false conclusions again. I shook her hand briefly, then took a step closer to Leo.

"Juliette." Leo took hold of my hand and pulled me closer to him. His voice was grave but demanding. "We're leaving."

"Juliette isn't going anywhere." My mother grabbed my hand and roughly pulled me away from Leo. "You just got here, and we have so much catching up to do." She looked at Leo, her expression smug. "Leave if you must." Clearly she'd set this up, and Leo's presence was no longer required. My heart dropped. After all we'd been through, she was still interfering in my life.

He glanced at me with questioning eyes. I was blindsided and confused on top of being horribly jetlagged. Why had he lied to me about his mother when he clearly knew she was alive? Misjudging my hesitation, pain flashed through his eyes. "I have to go." His voice was strained and laced with anger.

Horrified, I watched him stride purposefully away while I stood there, unable to get my head around the situation.

"I was worried that would happen," Gwendolyn whispered, snapping me from my paralysed state. I saw what I believed to be genuine sadness flash across her eyes, and my curiosity hit fever pitch.

"I'll be back in two minutes," I said, holding up two fingers.

I ran up the hill after Leo before my mother could protest.

"Wait!" I called out. He was beyond the orchard when I caught up to him. He stopped but didn't turn around. "Look at me, Leo."

I stopped a few feet behind him and waited for him to turn. His shoulders stiffened, and he glanced upwards at the darkening clouds. His whole body was so expressive, and I realised in that moment just how much I missed him. I missed how his body felt against mine and how he made me feel. Perhaps we'd just taken a giant step back, but I wasn't going to be the one to run. I was no longer the girl who ran. I would stay and fight because he was worth fighting for.

The look of pain on his face as he turned back was crushing.

"I need to get out of here, Juliette." His gravelly voice was strained and tortured. His hands were clenching and unclenching. "I'd like to force you to come with me. I'd like to get you the hell away from that woman, but I'm about to lose my shit completely and you don't need to be around that."

I took another step forward and waited until he looked me in the eye. "Why did you lie to me about your mother?"

He blew out a long breath. "I'm sorry you had to find out like that. I'm more sorry you had to find out at all, but I told you *my* truth." He flattened the palm of his hand against his chest. "The only truth I can live with."

I shook my head, completely confused. "What does that mean?"

"That woman over there is dead to me." He pierced me with his gaze. "Do you get that? Dead. To. Me." Despite the determination in his voice, his shoulders slumped.

"Why?" I croaked. "What happened in that goddamned house?"

"I don't talk about that." He pushed his shoulders back and stood up straighter. "I *can't* talk about it, and I don't have to justify myself to you or anyone else. No one could possibly understand, and I don't feel like explaining it. I've managed to avoid her for five years, and your mum, the Queen of Manipulation, managed to set me up. Again. But compared to my mother, yours is Mother Teresa."

I felt like he'd stabbed me in the chest. Our reunion in the reception had been so full of passion and our magnetic attraction was still irrefutable, but now I could feel him slipping through my fingers. "This is all so messed up, Leo."

"You've obviously found a way to forgive your mother for what she did." He couldn't even look me in the eye when he practically spat the words at me. "You have a forgiving heart, Jules, but you and I are not the same."

"She's your mother, Leo." I knew what my own mother had done was reprehensible, but she was still my mother. "It can't be that bad."

He just nodded, his hands firmly planted in the pockets of his shorts. "Go back to your mum. She obviously wanted us both to come but only one of us to stay." He spoke with zero emotion. "I'm leaving."

Unsure if my touch would be welcomed, I tentatively placed my hand on his arm. "Don't shut me out, Leo. Before I left to go overseas six weeks ago, you said you wanted to talk to me when I got back." I gave his arm a gentle squeeze. "Well, I'm back now."

He stared down at my hand on his arm, his brow furrowed. I had no idea what he was thinking. When he finally met my eyes, he appeared tortured. "I want to, Jules. I do. I have so much to tell you, and I wanted to hear all about your trip, but I can't right now. I can't talk about her, and I know you want to. You have to trust me when I tell you to stay away from that woman."

A sob escaped me, but I managed to win the war against the threatening tears. "I don't know if I trust you, but I know that I want to."

I had gutted him with my words, but I had opened my heart to him and he'd pushed me away at the first hurdle. I'd come home ready to fight, but he had to meet me halfway.

"I know. I fucked up with you and I thought we could get past it, but this is different, Jules." He pushed my hair behind my ears and held my face. "I have my life under control, and it hasn't always been that way." I covered his hands with mine while he continued. "It's a chapter of my life that's best left closed and in the past. No good can come from talking about it." His hands dropped from my face. "I made a choice almost five years ago to block her out of my life, and that was taken away from me today."

I swallowed the lump in my throat as the realisation hit. Leo was far more damaged than I'd ever suspected. As much as I couldn't deny I loved him deeply, I knew our happily ever after was now nowhere in sight. I closed my eyes briefly, trying not to appear defeated.

"You're asking me to trust you, but you're giving me nothing," I mumbled.

"Can you just promise me one thing?" he asked.

I met his eyes, and the desperation in them floored me. I nodded, knowing I would do just about anything to take away some of his pain.

"Don't believe anything she says. She's manipulative and she's a liar. I can't force you to come with me now, but I need this to be the end of it. Regardless of whether you want anything to do with me after this, I don't want you having anything to do with her once you leave here today."

I stared at my feet, kicking divots in the grass. "I thought this was going to be our new start."

"I'll call you in a few days. Okay?" He closed his

darkened eyes briefly. My heart ached for the sadness they conveyed. "I need some time to sort things through in my head again. I'm sorry, Jules."

"Leo." His name fell from my lips. I didn't want him to leave, but I could see he couldn't stay. "Whatever happened to you, I'm sorry."

"Don't be sorry." He grazed the back of his hand across my cheekbones. "Just don't ever mention it again."

I glanced back before I made it to the first orange tree because I couldn't resist. I wished I hadn't. The crazy part of me hoped he'd still be there. Instead, I saw him jogging up the hill, clearly in a hurry to get away. What the hell had happened to make him react like this to his own mother?

A lone tear slipped down my cheek, and I brushed it away angrily. He didn't need my tears. He needed my strength, and I would give it to him because he still held every part of my heart.

# ALSO BY
## KATE STERRITT

**The Fight for Life Duet** *(Romantic Suspense)*

Collision (Book 1)
Impact (Book 2)

### Standalone Novels

The Holly Project *(Contemporary romance)*
Love My Way *(Contemporary Romance/ Women's Fiction)*
*Releasing in 2019*—In My Own Time *(Contemporary Romance/ Women's Fiction)*

# ABOUT THE AUTHOR

Kate Sterritt lives in Sydney, Australia with her husband, three young sons and highly energetic German Shorthaired Pointer puppy.

When she's not madly juggling the logistics of soccer trainings, play dates and volunteering at the school, she can be found at her laptop, writing the types of novels she loves to read. Her characters are inspired by her own experiences, blended with her imagination and a healthy dose of wishful thinking.

Thank you so much for your support. I hope you enjoyed the story as much as I enjoyed writing it and will consider leaving a review. If you'd like to get in touch with me, there are plenty of ways and I'd love to hear from you!

Facebook.com/authorkatesterritt

Twitter.com/KASterritt

Instagram.com/katesterritt

www.katesterritt.com

Email me at kate@katesterritt.com

You can also chat to me in my Facebook readers group
*Kate Sterritt's Hummingbirds*

If you'd like to subscribe to my email newsletter, here is the signup form www.eepurl.com/bxylHH

# ACKNOWLEDGEMENTS

Adriana Leiker, Beth Flynn, Brittainy McCane, Eli Peters, Gill Melling, Jess Milliken, Lynette Kelly, Lyndsey Aaron, Nicole Sands, Pam Lilley, Sunshine Lykos and Tesrin Afzal. I love you ladies!! Thank you so much for believing in me and for being incredible friends and loyal supporters, not only to me, but to so many of my fellow authors with your promoting and blogging. I really hope I do you proud and want you to know how much I appreciate all you do.

Adriana. What can I say to my book bestie and all round beautiful friend? You made me believe in myself when I was crippled by self-doubt and you make me laugh. I love our quick chats that last for hours! Thank you. Seriously.

Pam, Gill, Lynette, Brittainy and Jess. I loved you before I met you in London, but now you're stuck with me forever. Thank you, Pam for setting up a readers group for me knowing I would never do it for myself. Thank you, Brittainy not only for your friendship, but for bringing lovely Lyndsey into my readers group and for being such a generous author supporter on Sisterhood of the Travelling Book Blog.

Eli and Tesrin. Thank you both for being phenomenal beta readers. I haven't known you very long, but very quickly knew we'd be friends for life. Collision benefitted immensely from your constructive critique and ongoing support. Eli, you're the greatest wing woman a girl could hope for and I wish your blog, Page Turning Addiction, the greatest success. Tesrin, your teasers are incredible and I'm humbled by the time you take creating them on top of your busy life and the work you do on Wicked Women Book Blog.

Beth. You rocked my world with your incredible books and again with your immediate kindness and love. It's yet another reason I'm grateful to Adriana for insisting I read Nine Minutes. I admire you as an author and love you as a friend. It was because of you that Nicole Sands and many other Niner friends including Eli and Tesrin came into my life and for that I feel blessed.

Sunshine. You are one of the kindest, most open-hearted and generous people I've met in the book community and I'm honoured to call you my friend. Thank you for all you do for me and for authors in general with the gorgeous Charity Pearce at Saucy Books.

Tara Hanrahan. Thank you for once again proof reading for me. You have eagle eyes and caught a few things that would've driven me crazy. See you at Opera Bar!

Gemma. Here is my something true. I love your books because they are brilliant, but even more so because they led me to you. We'll be friends for life and beyond. It's true. You know it and I know it. Thank you for your continued support of my writing and for the friendship I treasure.

ES Carter, my northern hemisphere twin, and to all the indie girls—we're in this together! I'm so grateful to be part of such a wonderful support network.

My writing buddy and long-time friend, Lucy Fenton, acknowledged me in her latest book saying *There's no one I'd rather spend the day not talking to*. It made me laugh and I agree wholeheartedly.

To all the blogs who help promote my books and to the readers who take a chance on me. Thank you from the bottom of my heart.

Murphy Rae at Indie Solutions. I love that you designed my cover and edited my story. I can't speak highly enough of your talent and professionalism and look forward to continuing this journey with you. When I meet you one day, I'll bring Tim Tams!

Thank you to my family and friends. I write about love and friendship because I know about love and friendship. I have a blessed life with an amazing husband and children I love and adore. I am grateful for supportive parents and beautiful sisters, Zoë and Susie. Jen, you are my third sister and best friend of twenty-five years. We are lucky.

Last, but certainly not least, I want to thank my new friend, Nick Lundh, founder of the Lightning Fight Centres in Victoria. This is one of the great joys of writing. When else would I have had reason to gain such an insight into a whole other world and befriend a Former World Professional Middle Weight Kickboxing Champion, Professional Boxer and Muay Thai Fighter? Nick, you went above and beyond helping me give the Collision fight scenes an authentic edge beyond the limits of my imagination. nicklundh.com.au/